I0531454

Corvino

LM Foster

This is a work of fiction. Names, characters, places and incidents are products of the author's imagination. Any resemblance to actual events, locales, organizations, or persons, either living or dead, is entirely coincidental.

ISBN-10: 0615971377
ISBN-13: 978-0615971377

Cover Design by
Ravenna Young
www.ravennayoung.blogspot.ca

9th Street Press
www.9thstreetpress.com

In loving memory of Rick Zieffler
.

ONE

"Hey," he said and I looked up. His name was Troy, and he was just as adorable as ever. "Are you going to this retirement thing tonight?"

"Are you talking about the happy hour thing? For Walter? At the *Y Not?*"

He nodded. "What kind of a name is that for a bar?"

"I understand it's a hole in the wall out on Arlington. Holds some significance for Walter. I'm not sure what – something to do with where they used to drink when he first started working here, I think."

"Are you going?"

"Are you?" Because if he was, then I was. Because if he was, then I wouldn't miss it for the world. Because if he was, then wild horses couldn't keep me away.

He smiled his adorable smile, dimples aplenty. "I asked you first."

Throwing caution to the wind, I replied, "I'll go if you will."

Troy's smile took on a little edge, and that was what made him so damn sexy; he was no innocent, no boy; no matter how boyish he looked. He knew exactly how much I liked him, what kind of an effect he never failed to have upon me. He said, "That sounds a lot like *I won't tell if you won't.*"

Even though I was old enough to be his mother's not much younger sister, I blushed like a schoolgirl. "You're gonna get me fired," I said.

Satisfied with my reaction, he said, "Don't let me down now. I don't know many of these old farts. I'm counting on you to entertain me if things get boring." That devious grin again.

Long-suffering, I overcame an involuntary shiver. "You're gonna get me fired," I repeated. "I'll see you there."

He nodded, still smiling, and walked out of my cubicle, all six-foot-four good-looking inches of him, just as fine as he wanted to be. I sighed. Cathy, my friend in the next cubicle, peeked out at me and grinned. She knew about the crush I had on Troy. "One of these days," I said, "he's going to get me fired. One of these days, he's going to make one of those cute remarks, and I'm going to say something back that makes *him* blush. And then I'll get fired for sexual harassment."

Young, twenty-eightish, his age, she giggled. "It might almost be worth it."

I nodded. It would most definitely be worth it, because he was what my mamma used to call a *doll baby*. And once upon a time, I would have risked anything for such a one as he, any such a one that caught my eye and tickled my fancy as he did. But these days, I wouldn't dare. I was not really afraid of a sexual harassment suit: if anyone was being harassed, or at least made to feel hot and bothered, it was me.

Troy was married to an adorable little woman, and once upon a time such a hurdle would not have much stayed my course, either. But nowadays, I had become a bit more aware of the feelings of others. I acknowledged that there indeed existed right and wrong. Besides, I was seventeen years older than him. He'd never be interested in me. If I did mount some kind of a pass at him, he would politely decline.

Or worse still, he might accept, and I'd learned my lesson on those May-December romances. My own had been done for about a year. I was damn near sure of it, as, day by day, my flown young bird did not return home to roost again.

His departure was all for the best; for me, for him, for the world at large. It would never have worked in the long run. There was not now nor had there ever been any future in it.

I met him at my niece's graduation party. For clarification, that would be graduation from high school. He was one of her boyfriend's buddies. I was in the kitchen with my sister Corrine, being one of the grownups on hand, chaperone-like, if you will, when my then almost nineteen-year-old niece Darlene dragged them in for introduction, all unwilling, her boyfriend and his buddy. The boyfriend's name escapes me, as my own name escaped me upon beholding this Adonis that was his friend. I finally stammered it out, limply shook his hand. He smiled at me and I stared at him, open-mouthed. Then mercifully, all the young people left the kitchen.

He was simply stunning. Never had I been so affected by anyone. I looked at my sister. She hadn't noticed my reaction, and I couldn't commiserate with her. She wouldn't get it. This was her daughter's peer. His name was Devin. He was twenty-two. I was forty-two.

I am afraid that I quite frankly stared at Devin throughout my sister's little celebratory dinner party. Every time he caught me looking at him, he would smile, however, and even made his way across the joyous crowd of kids a couple times to make small talk with me.

I'd been divorced for about five years at the time, without any prospects. I wasn't even out looking for any. We'd married at thirty, produced no offspring, drifted apart. Still the process of the ending of it had left me feeling like a rung out beach towel, and I still had felt no desire to leap back into the water. But when I saw this kid, I felt life and hope flow back into me. He was just that breathtaking, at least to me. I watched him interact with my niece and the other girls his age, and none of them seemed at all impressed with him. But he was just the cutest thing I'd ever seen.

The night wore on and the youngsters left in twos and threes. There were other parties to attend, and there would be no underage drinking at my sister's house. When Devin left with my niece and her boyfriend, he turned and waved good bye to me. I waved back, probably with entirely too much enthusiasm. I sighed and considered that thinking about this one would keep me occupied for months.

I helped my sister clean up a little bit and then retired to her guest room. Since I'd been drinking at the festivities, she thought it prudent that I didn't drive home that evening. It didn't bother me that Corrine thought I was drunk, because I was, a little bit. She'd always made it a point to pass judgment on me, and unfortunately, she was usually correct in her assessment. So I climbed between the crisp sheets in her guest room and thought about the young man.

I'd always been a big romantic thinker, a big planner, a concocter of intricate fantasies, if you will. It all started in high school, when I had a crush on an adorable green-eyed kid named Bob. I wrote many a sonnet to Bob's green eyes, and thank God for readers of poetry everywhere, I tore them all up almost before the ink was dry.

Come to think of it, Devin looked a little like ol' Bob had looked, going on thirty years ago. Same green eyes, same curly, sandy-brown hair. When I was fifteen, I'd go to bed early, just so I could think about how things would go down, how somehow Bob and I would find ourselves all alone at the normally crowded bus stop some morning, how one thing would lead to another and we would wind up in the bushes behind the bus stop, how we would just not make it to school at all that day. And I would rehearse what I would say, and what he would say, and so on, until the entire event was planned out, beginning to end. With those first fantasies about Bob, I wasn't really sure exactly how it would end, but by the time I got around to the culmination of the plan in my mind, I'd usually drifted off to sleep, anyway.

This is not to say that any of these plans were ever going to happen, especially since I didn't have the nerve to even look Bob in the eye, nonetheless speak to him, or traipse off into the bushes with him. It was the planning, the imagining that was the fun part.

And so it went throughout my life. Outrageous scenarios with attractive people. Outrageous, yes, but not necessarily impossible, if certain facts were ignored, like that they were married or that I was married, or that they were famous or that they were on other continents, or dead, from generations long past. No fact of reality was ever too great to be ignored, not time, space, history. After all, they were only fantasies. They only happened inside my head. I never told anyone and I certainly never planned for even any of the plausible ones to come to fruition. The thinking was all the fun, a private little amusement that always helped me go to sleep. Maybe everyone does it.

So I figured that Devin, exceptional, impossibly young, would make for much fodder for many fantasies. Imagine my delight, therefore, *just imagine my delight*, when at about 3 am, I heard a soft knock at my door. I whispered, "Yes?" and he peeked his head into the room.

He didn't speak, hesitated. I wondered if I was dreaming, and if I was, then there was absolutely no harm in going with the flow. It was a split second decision on my part; I motioned for him to come in, just to see what he would do next. He crossed the room quickly and sat on the corner of the bed, just looking at me. I admired his courage, even if I could smell that it was the liquid kind. After a pause, he slowly leaned over and kissed me.

Never one to pass up a fantasy come to life, I kissed him back.

At first light, he looked every second of his age; he didn't even need a shave. When the alarm went off, he jumped up and dressed quickly. I could tell that the ramifications of what had happened weighed heavily on him, and he most surely didn't want to get caught here, with me. But he was charming, and he paused to kiss me good-bye. For something to do, I reached into my purse and handed him my business card, just in case he'd missed my last name, as I had missed his.

He looked at it for a long time, then said, "I don't know if we can do this again."

I didn't know either, as it was all a little too much for me in the brutal light of day. I was sure I looked unlike any woman he had ever been with at the moment, and I was very self-conscious of the fact. Dumbstruck at the implications, all around, I just shrugged. "Hurry," I said at last, indicating the door.

He kissed me again and silently padded out of the room. I flopped back onto the bed and stared at the ceiling, thinking, *What have I done? Corrine will have puppies*. But I smiled.

I didn't really think about Devin like a real person, like what we had done was a real event. What had happened was simply a delicious fantasy to me for about two weeks, until he called my office phone, and asked if I wanted to have dinner. I said that would be great. Or better yet, he suggested, "Could I come over and cook dinner for you? I don't get much chance to try new things at home."

How delightful! He liked to cook, to try new things. All this was certainly a new thing for me. I agreed. Home, I would find out, was Mom, Dad, and younger brother.

He didn't stay the night, although he did do a lot more than just cook dinner, and once again, he said, "I don't know if we can do this again."

Again, I was noncommittal. But it was very nice, and I found myself hoping that he would change his mind and come back. And it went on like that for about a year, him coming to visit me every so often, and saying it would be the last time, every time, until the next time. And every time I liked it a little bit more, and wished he would stay a little bit longer.

And eventually his parents threw him out, or so he said, because they wanted him to get a job or go to school or do something with his life. I didn't care what he did or didn't do with his life, not at first. I was just glad that he was there when I got home from work.

For the first couple of months, everything was nice. I figured that he was just a slow starter, that he would eventually get a job or go back to school or something. But after six months, even I couldn't help but notice that mostly what he did was drink and smoke pot with his dwindling pool of friends (they were all growing up, all of them but him). Resentment began to creep in, as day after day I got up and went to work, while he slept until two.

So we fought. He drank too much and I couldn't stand it, and I said mean, hateful things to him when he was drunk, and he said mean, hateful, drunken things right back.

He used the door three or four times in the last six months we were together, staying with friends, going back to Mom and Dad. And each time he did, I was numb for a few days, and I cried, and I missed him, but I muddled through, telling myself that it was all for the best, that we had no future, that he was better off with his peers. And then he would call and say he was sorry and that he would do better, and ask to come back and I'd let him come back and I'd be so glad that he was there again, and all would be wonderful, but then he'd slide back into his old ways, and I'd slide back into resentment, and soon we'd be fighting again, and soon he'd get mad and pack his shit and leave. Then after a few days or a week, he'd ask to come back, and I'd let him come back, and the whole cycle would start over.

Except he had not come back this time. He'd been gone for almost a year now. At first, he called and said hi once or twice a week, no hard feelings, and he even came over and stayed for the weekend after about six weeks. I even waited for him to say, "I don't know if we can do this again," which he didn't say, because I think he knew I'd have laughed at him.

But I hadn't heard a peep from him at all for six months now, and I suspected that he'd no doubt met a young woman. I was beginning to function again, almost as I had for the forty-two years before I'd met him. I kept telling myself that it was all for the best, etc., and might've even been starting to believe it. In the two years I'd known him, I'd allowed myself to become entirely too attached. So even after a year of no longer living with him, after six months of not having spoken to him, I still felt numb, encompassed by a sort of dumb, wondering disbelief.

It really looked like he wasn't coming back this time, and I struggled daily with it, even if I knew it was for the best. Even if I reminded myself of how miserable I'd really been, ninety percent of the time. It was just that the ten percent that was good was great, even if the miserable was miserable, and it was the good that I missed.

When Devin first left, I attempted to get on with my life. My sister was feeling restless, so I took a public speaking class at the community college with her. We were assigned to give a speech about who we were, and what out motivations for the future might be. Corrine talked about her pride in her daughter's achievements more than about herself; I talked about looking forward to retirement in a short decade or so. This wowed the young people – I might as well have said that I was looking forward to the grave for as much as they could relate.

But then little Rolando Rodriguez got up and regaled us with the story of his life. He was just a bantam fellow, all of nineteen, maybe five foot seven or so. I was enrapt by his sad tale. He'd had a baseball scholarship, he told us, but had to give it up and remain in town and go to lowly community college with all of us, because he'd been so devastated by his parents' sudden divorce that he couldn't function for six months. His story ended on a high note, however, as he told us that his love of the game had finally pulled him through and that he knew that his determination to succeed would bring him out on top in the end.

I applauded the loudest, and my sister looked at me in alarm. The dark thought dawned on me that with a little sympathy and a conveniently placed shoulder to cry on, with a few kind words and maybe a few hugs, I could have little Rolando in my hip pocket. It would be so easy; I knew just what to say. Then the even darker thought occurred to me: the only reason I didn't proceed to do so was

6

that young Rolando was just too young, and more importantly (and darker still), the boy was just not attractive to me in the least. I wondered what my actions might have been had he been a big strapping football player instead of a little bitty baseball player.

I realized then that I'd become a roué, in thought if not in deed. I was like any louche old man, trolling for teenaged girls: I knew what to say; I knew what young Rolando needed to hear. It would be a piece of cake.

This sudden self-awareness troubled me, however. I found it unsettling to think that I had it in my power to take advantage of young men. I didn't have to be thin or beautiful or even rich or as young as they were. I certainly didn't want another young man; Devin had put me through the ringer. I might be persuaded to take him back again, if he came back again (which seemed less likely with each silent, passing day). And I told myself that I was willing to make this concession only because he was a known quantity, we had a history. But I surely didn't want another one.

Corrine kept looking at me after class until finally I just said, "What?"

"You're not thinking about taking up with that kid are you?"

She always knew me so well, or always thought she did. "No," I replied.

"Oh, thank God."

"I'm so glad you're pleased."

"I guess, since it's over now, I can tell you. Finally say it to your face. Do you have any idea what a disgrace you've been?" The floodgates burst. "Imagine, taking up with someone half your age. Thank God Mom and Dad weren't alive to see it."

"I don't think it would've bothered Mom too much," I pointed out.

"Mom always did approve of whatever you did."

Now I looked at her. "Where is all this coming from?"

"Never mind, it's not important. You were just freaking me out a little bit. I thought it was going to be a replay of the last time."

"You know, I didn't like Devin just because he was young." *Did I?*

Corrine would not relent. "It apparently didn't hurt, though, did it?"

I couldn't argue with that, not even to defend myself. I hated it when my sister was right, and coupled with the revelation of how easily Rolando and his gullible young brethren could be had, I came to a decision on the spot. "I'll make you a promise," I told Mrs. High and

Mighty. "The next person I associate with will be age-appropriate. I promise. What d'ya think?"

"We'll see."

But that didn't preclude me from going to Walter's retirement Happy Hour at the *Y Not* with adorable Troy. Troy was not in the realm of possibility, being too young and too cute, too married and too well-adjusted. Corrine would frown at my going anyway, but about this I couldn't possibly care less. Troy had started working at my office about six months previously, at just about the time that Devin seemed to have fallen off the world, and he had had a starring role in my fantasies ever since.

TWO

The *Y Not* was a little bar on a large lot surrounded by plenty of parking; the old-timey word *honky-tonk* might apply. On one side was a newly built, brightly lit gas station; on the other was the remains of some place that had burned down decades before. I'd driven by the abandoned hulk of the building for as long as I could remember. I could never remember it as a viable business.

It was the day after Halloween, a Friday, and by the time I arrived at six o'clock, the burned-out building beside the bar was sheathed in darkness, beyond the reach of the lights of either the *Y Not's* parking lot or the gas station next door. I drove behind the bar, looking for Troy's big blue Toyota Tundra. There it was, and I smiled and parked next to it.

My colleagues were grouped around two tables toward the back. Troy was standing at the bar with his back to me, just as tall and fine as he wanted to be. I envied his adorable little wife. I dared to touch him on the shoulder so he would turn and look at me.

He smiled genuinely, showing all his dimples. "What are you drinking?" he asked.

"Just a ginger ale for me," I said and smiled back at him. "I'm driving." *Besides,* I thought, *you are way too cute to be drinking with.*

He ordered me a ginger ale, and chose a table that was close enough to the ten or twelve men toasting Walter to seem like we were part of the festivities, but far enough away that we didn't have to actually participate.

We made small talk for a few minutes. It was pleasant to just look at him and his dimples and his sparkling brown eyes. In the middle of laughing at a comment he made about one of our co-workers, I looked up to see Devin standing beside our table. It was a good thing I was not drinking at the moment, or I would've choked on my drink.

"Hi," he said simply.

I tried to say hi, could not, tried again. I finally got it out, then said, "Devin, this is my friend, Troy, from work. Troy, this is . . ." What? My friend Devin who I haven't spoken to in six months? My friend Devin who is four years younger than you? My friend Devin, who was once my entirely inappropriately good friend, but who is not my friend anymore?

"Devin," he said.

They looked at each other for a minute. Devin could see that Troy was wearing a wedding ring, so he knew that Troy wasn't my date, even if he cared about such things. Troy wasn't my date, so he couldn't care less who Devin was, although he might've been a little curious. So all the awkwardness was on my part.

"I brought you something," Devin said to me.

"How did you know where to find me?" I asked. It was good to see Devin, because in seeing him, I realized that all the bad that had existed, all the grinding disillusionment, was the truest thing about whatever we'd once had together. He was still cute, and one part of me was thrilled to be in the company of not one but two attractive young men. But the realist in me, just by seeing him again, saw everything for exactly what it was: it would be nothing but heartache to let Devin come back again, and it was nothing but a waste of time to be missing him.

"I called your office and they said something about a party here." He looked around for the party.

"Over there." Troy nodded at the other table.

"Won't you join us?" I said, feeling like someone else was speaking. What kind of ridiculous thing was that? Do people ever really say that in real life? But I didn't know what else to say. He was making me nervous just standing there.

"I can only stay a second. I brought this for you." He set a tall, thin, fat-bottomed bottle on the table. It was wrapped in a plastic grocery sack. "It's absinthe."

"Really?" Troy exclaimed. "Real absinthe?"

Devin nodded. "Imported. Some might say smuggled." He smiled at me.

Absinthe. The green fairy. Toulouse-Lautrec. Van Gogh. Hemmingway. Oscar Wilde. Said to cause hallucinations, favored by French artistes. Special spoons and sugar cubes.

Troy took the bottle out of the bag. It was a thin fiasco, label-less, with a cork. He looked at the bottom. There was a sticker that said *Mohini's House of Dreams*, with an address in downtown Riverside.

"Did you try it?" I asked Devin.

"No. The seal's unbroken." He indicated a thin white strip pasted over the cork. "I don't drink anymore, Rae."

Well, isn't that just wonderful, I thought. *If anyone should not drink anymore, it's you.* Again, a feeling of so-glad-to-be-rid-of-him washed over me. What a nightmare it would be to be stuck with a recovering alcoholic, twenty years my junior.

10

"My . . ." he hesitated, then just went right ahead and said it. "My girlfriend had it at her place, and when we started going to meetings . . . I thought of you." He glanced toward the door and I saw a woman standing by it smile at him. She was very young with very red hair, and was wearing a very nice calf length black coat. She was very pretty. Devin's girlfriend. *He's your problem now, Red,* I thought, and smiled to myself.

Hi, my name is Devin, and I'm an alcoholic.

Hi, Devin.

I used to go with a woman that was old enough to be my mother, and that's one of the reasons I'm an alcoholic, I think. Not that I wasn't already an alcoholic when we met. But I've got a new girlfriend now, another alcoholic just like myself, and as a pledge to our new sobriety, I gave her bottle of smuggled, label-less absinthe to the old gal. Thought she could hallucinate and reminisce about the old days.

"You've had absinthe?" Troy asked in amazement.

"No," I said. "I've always wanted to, though." I looked at Devin. "I used to talk about it a lot." He smiled at me, and I told him thanks.

"Enjoy," he said, and walked away. No *goodbye,* or *see ya,* and I was grateful for that. I watched him put his arm around the young woman. She kissed him lightly and they swept out of the door.

Goodbye, Devin, I thought. *It was nice seein' ya, only because it made me realize that I never want to see you again. I might think about you sometime, or at least parts of you, but only after I'm done thinking about Troy, here.*

I looked at him. He was grinning. "Let's drink it," he suggested.

"Here?" A million answers popped into my head, all denials, not all of which I could say aloud to him. Drinking anything with him would not be a good idea, what with the loosening of inhibitions that alcohol caused. But especially not the utterly unknown quantity of the green fairy.

"Sure. Why not? If we get too drunk, I'll call Elaine to come pick us up." Elaine was his wife.

"Troy, you're not allowed to drink liquor that you brought in. Kinda defeats the purpose of running a bar, don't you think? I think it might even be against the law."

He continued to grin, with all those adorable dimples. "Nobody will notice. Just slam that ginger ale and I'll pour some of it in there. I'll do the same thing with mine. If it's any good, and you're still nervous, we'll go out and sit in the truck and drink it. Come on, Rae! It's absinthe!"

All I heard was *any good, nervous, we'll sit in the truck.* Alone. With gorgeous Troy. Maybe . . . nah, I couldn't be thinking that. He wasn't flirting with me, not propositioning me. He was married, he was too young, and Daddy always said, *Don't play in your plate.* He wasn't coming on to me. That was ridiculous. He was just curious about the legendary, infamous absinthe, as I had been for years.

What could it hurt? I didn't have to ride home with him and his wife. I could always call a cab.

"Okay," I whispered. "Just be careful."

"Careful is my middle name, Rae."

He glanced around. Walter and the crew were talking shop. The lone server was busy at the other end of the bar; the bartender was invisible behind a wall of customers. Troy gingerly tore the white strip off the cork. *Ah, this isn't gonna happen after all,* I thought. What was he gonna do, request a corkscrew from the busy bartender?

But Troy, every resourceful, was as much of a Boy Scout as he looked. He took a Swiss Army knife out of his pocket, showed me the corkscrew on it. He stabbed the cork with it, then held the bottle out of view beneath the table. There was a very quiet pop.

I downed the rest of my ginger ale quickly, and Troy also slammed the rest of whatever it was he was drinking. Under the table, he poured some of the absinthe into his glass. He set it on the table, then did the same with mine. He put the cork back in the bottle, put the bottle back in the plastic grocery bag, then set the bag on the floor by our feet.

We looked at the milky green liquid.

"There's supposed to be sugar," I said.

Fortunately, the *Y Not* must've also served food, or at least coffee, because there was a little plastic box with sugar envelopes right there on the table. "How many?" Troy asked.

"Let's try two," I suggested. He nodded, and we tore opened and dumped two sugars each into our contraband drinks, stirred them.

"Here goes nothing," he said and we clinked glasses, took a tentative taste.

The absinthe was cloyingly sweet, and I thought maybe we'd put too much sugar into it. Troy's glass was smaller than mine, so I imagined that his must be sweet indeed. Just like he was. The liquor had a thick texture, almost syrupy, and I remembered that I'd read that you were supposed to cut it a little bit, pour something over the sugar cube to dilute it. Oh, well. I wasn't going to call the waitress over for a glass of water so I could step on my absinthe with it.

"It's good," Troy said, taking another sip. "Sweet."

Just like you, I thought again.

THREE

By the second time Troy filled my glass, I was beginning to feel warm and tingly, but not really drunk. It was more of a clear-headed, attentive kind of thing, mentally, but a warm and fuzzy, physically. Troy seemed a little more animated than he was at the office – the absinthe was leading him to cut loose a little bit. We made small talk some more, told jokes, laughed and giggled.

Then Troy got up to use the men's. When he came back, he said, "Hey." I loved it when he said *hey*. "They're having a masquerade party next door." He pointed toward the back of the bar, down a hall – there was an open door at the end. A riot of lights shown from the parking lot next door. I blinked. They must've built a new club next door. Funny that I hadn't noticed it when I drove in; but the parking lot had been in darkness then.

Alone with Troy in a club full of strangers – no co-workers looking over their shoulders at us, wondering why the new, young, married guy was hanging out with the old, single secretary. Alone at a masquerade party with Troy, the day after Halloween, at a brand new club, with a bottle of absinthe.

Oh, hell, yeah.

We left out the back door, and went over to the place next door through a breach in the chain-link fence. It was better than going all the way around to the street.

There was a pagoda-shaped side door, flanked with red Chinese lanterns. The small neon sign said *Wong's*. It was a Chinese restaurant. A banner beneath that said, "Welcome, Race Fans!" And another one proclaimed, "Halloween Masquerade Ball!" Noise and light and laughter from inside lured us.

A woman dressed in a short, red Cheongsam stood just inside the door. She was wearing a matching mask of red feathers. Troy offered her a twenty, thinking there might be a cover, but the woman just laughed and handed us each a plain black mask. Troy put his on, then immediately pushed it up on his forehead. It made him even more adorable.

There was a loud live band, costumed as skeletons. The place was packed, but we managed to find a little booth in the back. A waitress wearing a peacock-feather mask and the same red Cheongsam as the girl at the door – it must be the uniform – asked us what we were drinking.

"Bring us something green," Troy said and winked at me.

The masked waitress smiled. "Grasshoppers?"

"Sure," Troy said. "Whatever." He had never heard of a Grasshopper. I hadn't heard of one since I was a kid; my Uncle Gary used to drink them.

The waitress left. Troy and I looked around at the masked revelers. The dance floor jumped and flashed; the band was covering some old disco tune. There were costumes from the Roaring Twenties: flappers and men in evening dress. Zoot suits. Vampires and ghosts and skeletons, even a werewolf. I saw an Egyptian princess and an opera-style Viking woman, complete with horned hat. No plugs and sockets, no zombies, no cardboard Facebook placards – but nearly everyone was wearing a mask. It was weird and strange and awesome. *Wong's* was a kickin' club.

I noticed a man smoking a cigar at the table next to me; his companion was smoking a cigarette in a long onyx holder. The waitress brought our Grasshoppers; when she set them down, I looked at her incredulously. "You're allowed to smoke in here?"

She giggled. "The boss always calls this place a firetrap. Why shouldn't you be allowed to smoke in here? We always say, if you don't like the smoke, go somewhere else."

Troy and I both looked at the people breaking California law in the booth next to us. When we looked back, the waitress was gone.

Troy shrugged. "She must be running us a tab." He knocked back half of his Grasshopper, than refilled it from the absinthe bottle under the table. I did the same. I was beginning to feel a little bit blurry: things were fading in and out. Shadowy, then into sharp focus; darker, then brighter.

Troy asked me if I wanted to dance, and the next thing I knew, I snapped awake, not aware that I'd been asleep. I was looking at the inside of a truck door. I blinked, confused, afraid to move, not knowing where I was. Then Troy stirred, and I realized that we were in his truck, in the parking lot of the *Y Not,* and I'd been sleeping with my head in his lap. I sat up slowly – I expected to have a pounding, top drawer caliber headache – but I just felt a little fuzzy. There was no pain. We looked at each other, amazed, appalled, guilty. It was daytime.

Finally he said, "What happened, Rae?"

I thought back, tried to recall how we had spent, obviously, the entire night. I remembered the light and darkness thumping in and out with the driving disco beat. I remembered Troy dancing close to me, spinning me around and catching me a few times. I remembered beginning to feel hot and sweaty and incredibly excited, just like I had

14

at the teen disco as a kid. The music got louder and louder, the beat faster and faster; the crowd pressed closer and closer, flappers and Chicago-style gangsters.

My eyes widened: I clearly remembered kissing Troy, long and hard, right there in the middle of the dance floor – his mouth tasted like cherries. I didn't remember going into a stall in the men's room with him, and I only could remember flashes of the glorious, forbidden things we did in that small, cramped, black-painted space. Overwhelmingly, I remembered the music and the crowd and the pulsing of the light and darkness.

Something had happened last night, something that shouldn't have happened. Thankfully, mercifully, I could tell that Troy couldn't remember it any clearer than I could.

I shook my head. "I'm not sure, Troy. Maybe it was the absinthe." The bottle was on the floor of the truck. I picked it up and looked at it. It was corked, still about half full. The plastic grocery bag was gone.

Troy dragged his hands across his pretty face, worried, embarrassed. "I gotta go, Rae," he said. "I'm not sure how I'm going to explain all this. You won't–"

"No," I assured him. "I won't." Who was I gonna tell? "I don't remember anything, anyway." I looked at the bottle. "Maybe that's why this stuff used to be banned."

"I gotta go, Rae," he said again. He was looking at his phone with huge, round eyes.

"Just say you had too much to drink, Troy. Say you passed out in your truck."

"Yeah. That happens all the time." I could tell from his expression that it never happened. "And that's why I missed all twelve calls." He looked helplessly at me.

I truly felt sorry for him. I was going home with no hangover, to try to sort out and giddily remember what may or may not have happened between tall, good-looking, young, married Troy and me. He was going home to his angry, frightened, beloved wife, to no doubt try and *forget* what may or may not have happened. Poor baby. I hadn't even hoped for any of this; it was wrong. I pitied him.

"I'll see you at work," I said as I opened the door to the truck. "It's okay, Troy. Nothing happened. She'll believe you. Don't even tell her I was there." He nodded, and I climbed out of the truck. I watched him drive quickly out of the parking lot. He didn't wave goodbye.

I put the key into my car door, then turned and looked behind me, across the parking lot to *Wong's.*

Wong's was a burned-out hulk. There was nothing left but a blackened skeleton of only the heartiest timbers; one door. No walls, no roof. I thought that it would only take a few good hard shoves from a bulldozer to make it disappear entirely. There was a fence around it to keep out curious kids, but it had been breached along the side of the lot closest to the *Y Not*.

I blinked, then looked to the other side of the *Y Not's* parking lot. Nope. No club over there. Just a gas station. I looked back at the burned-out restaurant again. I opened the car and set the absinthe bottle on the floor in the backseat. I slammed the door and crossed the parking lot.

I stepped through the hole in the chain link fence, glanced back at the side door to the *Y Not,* now closed. Yeah. This was the way we'd walked last night, out that door, across that driveway, through this fence, into . . . I looked at the pagoda door. It was still there, but there was nothing on the other side except for the blackened skeleton of the club. The faded, ragged banner still read, "Welcome, Race Fans!" The one beneath it had come loose on one side; I pulled it up and read it again. "Halloween Masquerade Ball – 1980," it said.

1980.

I dropped the banner. It ripped free from the door and dropped to the ground. A plastic grocery bag blew across my feet, caught a larger gust of wind and flew over the fence.

I went back to the car, sat in it. I Googled *Wong's Fire.* Then I added *1980.* At the top of the search was a *Wikipedia* entry. I skimmed it.

The Wong's fire claimed the lives of forty-three patrons and employees on October 31, 1980, in Riverside, California. The bar was hosting a Halloween Masquerade Ball that evening. At approximately 10:15, a grease fire erupted in the kitchen, then quickly spread to the bar and dance floor area. The fire blocked the front entrance, and most loss of life occurred when patrons panicked and attempted to exit through the side door.

There was a picture of the front of *Wong's,* which was long gone now. There was a smiling Asian man, flanked by a gaggle of smiling Asian girls, each wearing a short, red Cheongsam.

The boss always calls this place a firetrap. If you don't like the smoke, go somewhere else.

Troy and I had drank and danced and done God-only-knew-what in the bathroom of a club that had burned to the ground in 1980, taking forty-three people with it. I accepted this, without question, because I knew it had occurred. Why, how – these were other questions. But I was sure it had happened.

16

I reached behind the seat and recovered the absinthe. Maybe it *was* hallucinogenic, like the legends said. But how could it reach across time, space, planes of existence? I looked at the label on the bottom of the fiasco again: *Mohini's House of Dreams*. Maybe they would have some insight there.

FOUR

I stopped on the sidewalk in front of *Mohini's House of Dreams* and peered in the storefront window. I wasn't sure exactly what I was expecting – an imaginatively named liquor store, perhaps? Who else would carry absinthe? It was not a liquor store, however. It was an occult bookstore.

The door opened, the bell tinkled. Three people stepped out onto the sidewalk: a lovely blonde girl, a tall young man with brown hair and a Van Dyke style beard, and a striking, black-haired young man.

"How long have they been open?" the black-haired kid said.

"About a month," the bearded one replied.

"It's the same place, the same inventory," the girl said.

"I told you," the one with the beard said. "It's too prime of a location to just close up shop after all these years." He indicated the sign in the window. *"Under new management.* I told you."

"Do you think the lady in there knows . . . ?" the black-haired kid asked. I noticed that he had blue eyes.

The taller one said, "I don't think she'd tell us if she did."

The three of them walked away down the sidewalk.

I entered *Mohini's House of Dreams,* wondering what had happened to cause the place to change management. But these thoughts left my mind when I saw the woman behind the counter. She was the most unusually gorgeous woman I'd ever seen. She wasn't young – she was my age, at least. She was statuesque, with yellow hair worn in a thick braid down her back. She had large, violet-blue eyes; she was a Valkyrie.

I just stood there staring at her in silence. At last she asked me how she could help me. I stammered out that I had a question about something from the store. I took the bottle out of another plastic grocery bag and set it on the counter.

"Ah!" A smile bloomed on the Nordic features. "Wherever did you get this, if you don't my asking?"

"An old boyfriend gave it to me," I replied.

"Really?" The violet eyes flickered up from the bottle and met mine. "Did he say where he got it?"

I frowned. "He said it was his . . . his new girlfriend's, that they'd quit drinking, so he gave it to me."

"Would this be a young, red-haired women? About this tall?" She held a hand out at shoulder height. I nodded. "Her name is Christi. She worked here the first weekend I opened, and then she quit. I wouldn't have kept her anyway – she smelled of alcohol. Apparently, she's a thief." She regarded me curiously – as if she wondered why I was keeping company with thieves.

"I don't know her," I said. "I don't even know *him,* anymore. I understand that they're recovering alcoholics, now." I smiled; the blonde woman behind the counter smiled back. "I wouldn't think that a place like this would have a liquor license."

The violet eyes blinked. "A liquor license?"

"Well, yeah . . . you sell this here, right?"

The blonde woman lowered her lashes. "Well, it's a somewhat special order item. This is actually my personal property."

"You still need a liquor license to sell absinthe, don't you?"

She looked up and smiled in amusement. "Is that what you think this is? Absinthe?"

"That's what they said it was. There were some odd–"

"I'm Iris, by the way," she interrupted. It was an apt name for someone with such beautiful eyes. I introduced myself. Then she said, "This isn't absinthe, Rae. Absinthe doesn't come in a fiasco." She smiled in amusement again. "This doesn't even contain alcohol. It's used in certain . . . magical rituals, shall we say? Rituals of a . . . solitary nature. Consuming this in public, with another, could result in all manner of mayhem." Again, that curiosity. "Did you drink this with someone, Rae? Was there mayhem?"

I nodded. "Involving a twenty-eight-year-old, married co-worker, Iris. The kid'll probably never look me in the eye again."

Iris lowered her lashes in sympathetic embarrassment, then looked up at me again. "Was there anything else?"

I glanced around. The store was empty. "Are you familiar with Riverside history at all?"

She shook her head. "I'm not from . . . around here."

"In 1980, a bar called *Wong's* burned to the ground. Forty-three people died."

Iris waited.

"Last night, this young man and I attended a rather boring retirement party at a bar called the *Y Not.* We had a few shots of what we believed was absinthe, then we noticed lights shining in through the side door. The club next door seemed more jumpin' – they were having a masquerade ball. So we went over there.

"It was an odd place. Didn't have to pay to get in. The waitresses wore uniforms, Cheongsams. They still served Grasshoppers, but the waitress walked away before Troy could pay her. They played disco music, let people smoke inside." Iris still looked at me silently. "Troy

19

and I drank absinthe," I gestured at the bottle. "We danced. One thing led to another, and while I'm sure something happened, I can't quite remember–"

"Would you like to remember?" Iris asked with a sly smile.

I held up my finger. "Let's come back to that. I woke up this morning with this guy, in his truck, which we'd left parked at the *Y Not*. He was ashamed, upset, worried about what he was going to tell his wife. I got out of the truck and he drove away quickly. I'm sure he didn't look over at the bar next door, didn't notice that it wasn't a bar at all anymore, just a burned-out ruin, like it's been every day, year in and year out, rain or shine, since 1980.

"But I noticed. So I came over here to see if maybe someone could tell me a little about this absinthe, and how it might allow such a thing to occur."

"And what will you do if you find out?"

A good question. "I imagine that I'll be enlightened," I replied, and she smiled at me again, showing all her small, pearly teeth. "This happened, Iris. I didn't dream it, didn't make it up in my head. Something went on with Troy and me – I could tell by the look on his face that he knew it. And yes, I'd like to remember that more clearly." I grinned at her, and she grinned right back. "But I'm also sure that he didn't notice that there was no bar, and I'm sure he wants to forget about it all as quickly as possible, anyway. But there *was no bar*, Iris. And I'd like to know a little bit more about that. There was no party, no band, no crowd. Just . . . ghosts."

Iris asked the next most obvious question. "Do you believe in ghosts?"

"In this case, I believe in what I saw."

"What do you do, Rae?"

I didn't see how that was any of her business, didn't see how that could relate to whatever supernatural thing I'd just experienced. But like a great shrink or a good bartender, Iris just radiated a type of interest that put a person in a confessional mood. Maybe it was her big purple eyes. "I'm a secretary."

Iris shook her head. "No, I didn't mean *what do you do for a living.*" She gestured around us. "I'm in retail, for God's sake. That's what I do for a living. But it's not what I *do.*" Her eyes glowed. "I mean, what do you do, do you think, that would make you amenable to what you experienced last night? If you don't mind me asking, what were you doing in a bar with a young, married man?"

"There was a retirement party for a co-worker. The young, married man is another co-worker, and he asked me if I was going to it. So I went."

Iris grinned. "No ulterior motives?"

I grinned back. It was rather a forward question, but not an unreasonable one. She was my age, and it's not unknown that old women sometimes have ulterior motives toward young men. I had not long ago realized with what ease such motives could be put into action.

"No. I just thought it would be enjoyable to look at him for a little while. He's a doll baby." Iris's grin widened at the appellation. I sensed that we were simpatico. She understood perfectly what a *doll baby* was. "I might've thought about all the stuff that happened—"

"You've thought about it before." Not a question, but a statement.

"Yes."

"Frequently, perhaps." Still, not a question.

"Yes. But I never would've done such a thing, if it wasn't for the . . ." I gestured at the bottle. It sounded like a lame excuse, blaming an indiscretion on the liquor, so I felt compelled to explain further. "The whole idea is just not viable in the real world, Iris. I never would've made a pass at Troy. He's young and sweet and cute. He's very much in love with his adorable wife. In my mind, there were two thoughts about the whole idea of having a drink with him – I wouldn't have made a pass at him – I felt safe that he wouldn't go for it, anyway. I'm old enough to be his mother. And secondly, if he did go for it – such a thing would be wrong – what am I, a geriatric homewrecker? So, once again, I wouldn't have made a pass at him. So, no. Despite what happened, I had no ulterior motives."

"You have no man of your own?"

There was a bald statement. Stark. True. Not pretty. Maybe even sad, at my age, even though I didn't feel sad about it. Not often, anyway. I shook my head, wondering what conclusions Iris was going to draw from it, how she would judge me. Into what light would that put my stated intentions toward Troy?

"I can see that you believe in the life of the mind," she said. "It's satisfactory for you to simply think of some things, more than to actually attempt to bring them about."

How perceptive of her. "I've been that way all my life," I admitted.

Iris smiled. "You are therefore more sensitive to the effects of this . . . for lack of a better word, this *potion*. Would you like to know more about it?"

21

Retaining a healthy skepticism, I nodded. Iris gracefully walked around the counter, went to the door and turned the *Open* sign over to *Closed.* She turned the lock on the door. "Step into my office," she said with a smile.

She picked up the bottle from the counter and showed me into an office behind a blue velvet curtain. It was empty – blank bookshelves stood behind a desk with nothing on it but an *In* box containing a few unopened letters. Iris plucked a chair from where it stood against the wall and set it in front of the desk, then went around and sat behind it. She set the bottle off to one side.

I gestured at the emptiness of the room, said, "The sign says you're under new management."

"Yes. The previous regime was involved in a rather unfortunate . . . I'm not sure how much of a believer you are, Rae."

"After last night, I'm prepared to believe damn near anything."

Iris smiled slyly again. "Let me just say that the young woman that ran the store previously attempted to cast a spell that rather backfired on her. No one was hurt, or anything so *CSI* as all that. She was just embarrassed that things didn't turn out the way she'd intended, and she thought that it would be best for all involved if she just left town. The owner of the store and I go way back – *way back* – and she asked if I'd like to try my hand at the retail game for a change. So here I am."

"Do these . . . spells go awry often?" I asked, ignoring the fact that I didn't believe in spells.

Iris laughed; it was a soft, melodic sound. "Did your evening go awry last night?"

"It certainly did for Troy, I'll have to admit." I grinned. "You're expecting me to believe that all that was the result of some kind of a magical spell?"

"In a manner of speaking. I can tell that you're not usually of a mystical bent, Rae. You experienced something last night that you don't understand. But you're not afraid of it; you're just curious as to how such a thing could happen. I was raised in the mystical tradition. The idea that there are other worlds, and doorways to them, all around us, is second nature to me. Just because I cannot see something before my eyes, doesn't mean I believe it doesn't exist."

"I can't see gravity," I opined. "Yet I know it's real."

"Precisely. And you can't see your bones, yet you know they're there. And with the aid of an x-ray – why, there they are. You can see them. Spells and potions – they can be like an x-ray, revealing to us those things that exist right outside the periphery of the things that we can actually see and touch."

"I'm listening."

Iris laughed again. "I feel like Morpheus explaining the Matrix. But since you've already experimented with the green pill . . ." She nodded at the bottle. "I guess I owe you an explanation."

"You don't owe me anything, Iris. But if you have an explanation for me, I'm down to hear it. The whole thing was . . . the whole thing was something else."

Again, Iris smiled; her dark eyes glowed. "I don't know why that little alcoholic thief would imagine that this was absinthe. Perhaps we were talking about the green fairy in some context, and she, not bright enough to be a believer, just naturally assumed that a green liquid, stashed away in my desk drawer, must be something so commonplace. But like I said, there's no alcohol in it."

"I noticed that I didn't have a hangover."

"Maybe just a warm feeling, eh?" I nodded. "What this does, when taken within the confines of a sacred circle, with the aid of a few words, is open the doors of your mind. In a somewhat specific way."

"What kind of specific way?" Although I thought I knew.

Iris ignored my question. "You draw a protected circle on the floor. Don't make it a little thing that you have to sit in with your knees up around your ears."

Okay, I thought. *I'll play her silly game.* "Not like the devil worshippers in the movies?"

Iris dismissed devil worshippers with a wave of her hand. "Satanism is about raising the physical above the spiritual. Even those that only call themselves witches, not Satanists, around here . . . it's mostly about anonymous romps in the woods of a weekend. They use the rituals for something else besides . . . enlightenment."

"Is that what this provides?" I nodded at the bottle. "Enlightenment?"

Again that sly smile. "Let's just say that this particular mixture provides a level of . . . purity, not found out in the woods."

"I'm listening," I said again.

Iris sighed, but smiled. "Here's how it works, Rae. You draw a circle on the floor, say a few words. You drink some of the potion. Then . . . then you can imagine anything you want, with anyone you want. This young man you spoke of. Anyone. And it'll be as real to you as what happened last night. More real, actually."

"You don't say," I said, mostly because some response was required.

"Personally, I like to indulge and watch *Fight Club.*"

"With Brad Pitt?" I asked in surprise.

23

Iris nodded, grinned. I opened my mouth to say, *You don't say* again, but thought better of it.

"Who's your favorite movie star?" Iris asked. I considered. Brad was not really my type; he was a mite skinny for me, especially in *Fight Club*. "Say the first person that pops into your mind," Iris insisted.

"Richard Dean Anderson. From *MacGyver.*"

Iris blinked. She was not familiar with *MacGyver*. "Well, it can be anyone," she said. "As long as they're not dead."

What a ridiculous stipulation. That cut down my list of favorite movie stars considerably. I thought briefly of poor Paul Walker. I said to Iris, "In other words, *Gone With the Wind* is out."

She ignored my sarcasm. "This is how it works, Rae. You can think of whatever man you like. If you like movies, the ritual will allow you to actually feel like you're in the movie with your leading man. You can make your own rules, so to speak. What happens is only limited by your imagination."

Wasn't this the plot to *The Purple Rose of Cairo?* Movie character steps into real life? Or bored, lonely, old woman steps into the movie? Or more ominously, wasn't this a key element to *The Ring?* Things coming out of your television? *Seven days . . .* It was just silly.

"How long does it last?" I asked.

Iris smiled. "It's like a dream. It lasts till the morning, generally."

Just like all my fantasies, leading off to dreamland. But I'd never needed any kind of pharmacological/supernatural help before. I'd always done just fine with my imagination alone, no sacred circle required. Yet what had happened with Troy had seemed very real, more real than I could hope to just imagine in my head, even if I couldn't quite remember all the details. "So what is this, Iris? A drug? Some kind of hallucinogen? You said there's no alcohol in it."

Iris smiled dimmed a little; she might've been becoming annoyed with my skepticism. "Could a simple drug bring about what you experienced last night?"

"So what are you saying? That it's magic?"

"Why don't you try it again, Rae? Under the proper, controlled conditions?" There was a challenge in the purple eyes. "Humor me. I think you'll love it."

"If I draw the circle. Follow the rules."

Iris stopped smiling entirely. "The rules are there for your safety."

I didn't want to offend her. She had closed up shop, cut into her profits, just to tell me about all this. So I said, "Tell me about the rules, then."

"There is energy in the universe," Iris began. "If you choose to dream of someone like your young friend, there's no danger, although again, I stress that you must stay within the protected circle until the potion wears off. The energy of the ritual flows through you and out into the world, seeking that living person. He may even receive a warm feeling from it, although most people never notice." She smiled, then frowned. "But if the person you choose is dead . . . they're now on another plane of energy, another plane of existence, if you will. Those people that you saw last night . . . they haven't crossed over. They were attracted to your energy, the energy of the potion."

"And this was dangerous somehow?"

Iris laughed. "You don't find it dangerous partying with the dead?"

I shrugged. "It turned out all right. For me, anyway."

"Would I be too theatrical if I told you that you blaspheme, Rae?" Iris said evenly. "Dancing with the dead is not something to be taken lightly. You emerged unscathed, but you were lucky . . . they could've dragged you over into their plane. Where that Halloween party is going on and on. Forever."

I considered her words. There was no denying that we'd been there at a reconstituted *Wong's*, from that night in 1980, before the fire, before everyone died. It was fun, but I wouldn't want to be there for eternity.

"If you want to commune with the dead, those that have not yet gone on, and do it safely, that's a different potion. A different ritual. Those that have passed on are beyond our reach."

I shook my head. "Tell me more about this other thing. The movie stars."

"If you cast this spell, and someone in the film is dead, then your energy collects within the room. It doesn't dissipate as quickly, because there's no living object for it to seek. And there are demons . . ."

I barked laughter. "Demons? Like with horns and wings?"

"We're nothing if not products of our culture, are we not?" Iris smiled a trifle tightly. I could tell that she was becoming unsure as to whether or not she was wasting her time revealing the secrets of the universe to me. But she continued. "You have a picture in your mind of what a demon is like. It's a product of Hollywood – the demons are waiting just outside the sacred circle to devour you, to drag you off to Hell. Slavering, toothy monsters with wings and horns.

"There are those, of course, although I've never seen any. Why would anyone want to commune with them? They are agents of death, of revenge. But there are all kinds of other creatures, Rae, right outside that invisible door, that door that you open through ritual and magic. Creatures that are not inherently malevolent. There are angels and incubi, ghosts, lost souls. Not all of them are dangerous to your immortal soul, not all of them are out to get you. None of them are entirely safe, either, however, and sometimes it's difficult to ascertain exactly what their motivations are. But that's true of any strangers that we meet, isn't it? Corporeal humanity or astral beings?" I nodded. Couldn't argue with that.

"There is a give and take in any exchange between beings. You want something; they want something. So we have the sacred circle. It allows us to commune with invisible beings, or take part in pleasurable rituals, without danger of these creatures gaining the upper hand when we're not paying attention. And the demons I'm referring to in connection with this aren't soul-sucking demons, nor possessing demons, nor death-dealing demons. They're simply annoying demons. They knock things over, cause you to knock things over. They incite the cat to tear up your favorite pillow. They engage in activities that you've been told a poltergeist might do.

"These demons sense the energy generated by you and the potion and the ritual. They seek the energy; that which is meant for those still alive draws them, but they can't catch it. So they feed on the built up energy that results if those you think about are dead; they come to absorb it, to feed on it. If you summon one of these demons, accidentally or carelessly, they will plague you for a few weeks, then fade away."

It was all so fantastic. I'd never been a believer in ghosts and demons and poltergeists, in an afterlife. I'd always thought it was all just the product of a species aware of its own mortality – this life we live can't be all, it can't just end so suddenly, so irrevocably – there must be something else. I'd always felt that a belief in supernatural beings was all just wishful thinking.

But I couldn't deny that I'd seen ghosts the night before, had seen evidence that perhaps there might be some glimmer of truth to all these things Iris was telling me. How nice if it was true – how nice that we all didn't just wind up as worm chow. I was becoming intrigued.

"Tell me what to do, Iris. I'll obey the rules."

FIVE

That night I found myself with the bottle of not-absinthe and a shot glass. I had candles and colored chalk and a manual on how to draw out the protective magic circle.

To keep out the demons. Right.

While I'd listened to Iris talk, I'd been on the brink of becoming a believer. Just like a great shrink or a good bartender, just like a persuasive infomercial pitchman, Iris had been convincing, her tale compelling. But once again out in the cold light of day, on the quite solid sidewalk, with the knowledge of the real dangers of the world all around me – weren't there enough diseases and faulty wiring, bad people and runaway cars in the world to fear, without bringing in demons and ghosts from another dimension? – my native skepticism began to reassert itself. I believed that the potion was some kind of drug, that the ritual and the charmed, chalk circle were just window-dressing. Maybe Troy and I had just had some kind of shared hallucination. That and the fact that Iris had charged me $216.50 for all the stuff she said I would need – she said she was throwing in the potion for free – grounded me firmly in the real world again.

But still the thought kept creeping in that there had to be something to it. If it had been a hallucination, it had been incredibly real. I would testify in court that I'd been inside *Wong's*, there had been a party, it had been 1980. And hallucinations or not, I couldn't ignore the fact that young Troy had behaved in a manner that he wouldn't have dreamt of, had he not been dosed with something.

"Just draw the diagram around your bed," Iris instructed with her sly little grin. "Make sure you have everything you're going to need; include a night table of some kind within the circle. Don't forget that remote." She grinned. "Once you drift off to sleep, the energy from the ritual will dissipate, and it will be safe to emerge from the circle in the morning."

I had a girlfriend that used to say, "Try anything once, twice if you like it, three times if it feels good, four times it's a habit." What the hell, why not? I felt ridiculous, but no one would ever know about my engaging in a magical ritual in order to make a commonplace sex fantasy more realistic. No one but Iris and me. She claimed that she did it all the time. *Fight Club*, indeed.

So I drew the circle on the floor, copied down all the little squiggly lines as best as I could. I removed the dust ruffle from my bed and lit the candles – some of them were quite close and I didn't want to journey off into cinematic wonderland and burn the house down. I'd had quite enough experience with fires and their astral aftermath. I recited the invocation, begged the Great Mother to send me the vision I sought. I downed a generous shot of the sweet, syrupy potion. ("Absinthe isn't sweet," Iris had told me. "That's why you have to add the sugar.")

I plopped down on my bed and turned on the television, dialed in the *Netflix*.

Even though I hadn't thought of it in years, since Richard Dean Anderson and *MacGyver* were the first things that popped into my head when I was talking to Iris, I thought I'd give it a try. *MacGyver* was on for seven seasons, starting in 1985, in those primitive days of television when it was a big deal for the network to flash *In Stereo – Where Available* on the bottom of the screen.

For the first couple of seasons, they had what they called the *opening gambit* on *MacGyver*. It showed him on some cool adventure, allowed him to do some neat trick, make an atomic bomb out of toothpaste or something, before the first round of commercials. The opening gambit didn't have one thing to do with the rest of the episode, and in the later seasons, they dropped the concept all together.

My very favorite episode was the fourth one from Season One. The description from *Netflix: The Gauntlet. It's up to MacGyver to get a photographer out of harm's way after she snaps photos of a Latin American dictator with an international arms dealer.* The opening gambit shows our hero climbing over roofs in a stereotypical Middle-Eastern village, right out of *Aladdin,* something so clichéd – with camels and keffiyehs – that it would never play today. It was still Season One – MacGyver wasn't as cute as they would make him later, and he was still reciting homey Minnesota aphorisms in the voiceover, like *Be prepared,* and *The best company you can have in a strange place is a map.* He is there to steal just such a troublemakin' map. He does so, slips the map under a locked door, pushes the key through on the other side, slides the map out, recovers the key. Cool.

By this time, the enemy, dressed in French Foreign Legion looking uniforms, is after him. He flees across the desert, uses the map as a toboggan to slide down a dune out of range of the enemy's automatic weapons, escapes in a convenient hot air balloon. He uses his ever present, ever wonderful duct tape and the purloined map to patch up a few bullet holes in the balloon. Roll opening credits.

I kid you not. This was on for seven seasons.

Next, MacGyver finds himself in another clichéd village, this time in Central America, complete with mission-style buildings, burros, serapes. He recites further aphorisms. He's there to rescue the pretty American photographer. She's wearing the standard od-green tank top that indicates she's a tough, no-nonsense kind of gal. She's got masses of all that wonderfully curly 80's hair.

I don't remember the whole plot to the thing – something about damning photographs she took of some American arms dealer, played by John Vernon – Dean Wormer of *Animal House* fame – in collusion with the local dictator. She's gotta take more pictures. She begs for MacGyver's help, and of course he can't refuse. I fast-forwarded through most of it. The plot wasn't important. It was basically the same plot every week.

This was my favorite episode of *MacGyver* because it was one of the few in which he has any kind of interaction with a woman. He was such a goody-two-shoes, ninety-nine percent of the time. But in this one, there is a little tension between him and the photographer – we see him checking her out before he tells the local good-guy that he doesn't have any use for firearms. He comforts her, touches her shoulder frequently, stuff like that. She takes his picture, listens to his life story, tells him he's a romantic. There is a chemistry between them, something that was not usually a staple of the series.

MacGyver was tall and lean and rocked the best mullet in the history of the 1980s. But he was no ladies' man. If you wanted a ladies' man kind of show, you went over a few channels and tuned into the incomparable Don Johnson on *Miami Vice,* or even *Moonlighting,* with Bruce Willis. And if Iris's potion indeed engendered some kind of magical *cinéma vérité,* then I would definitely be checking out those other 80's staples, too.

But there was a scene in this particular episode of *MacGyver...*

The bad guys chase MacGyver and Pretty Photographer, until they wind up camped out in the wilderness. He's on one side of the fire, she on the other. Lots of smiles and lengthy looks pass between them; there is piano music. She tells him she thinks she likes him, then says, "Wanna share?" indicating her pillow.

He looks at her, unsmiling. He is a goody-two-shoes after all, not one to be just *sharing* with every endangered woman he's there to rescue. But then he smiles, looks sheepish, says, "That's quite an offer."

She says, "Is that a yes or no?"

And we expect MacGyver to demure, but he just hops right over there next to Pretty Photographer. He goes to kiss her but then he pauses, just long enough to let her think that maybe he's not going to kiss her. Maybe he's gonna wait until she kisses him. But then he does kiss her. It's awesome.

All of Richard Dean Anderson's acting chops were displayed in that one kiss – all the cuteness and sexiness of the whole *MacGyver* phenomenon. Anyone that ever called themselves a fan dreamt of him kissing us *just like that*.

Fade to black.

And under the influence of the potion, suddenly it was me kissing MacGyver instead of Pretty Photographer. Fade to black indeed.

SIX

I awoke the next morning feeling refreshed and rested. Again, there was nothing even vaguely resembling a hangover. I had a memory of something that could be described as a rather lengthy, entirely satisfying sex dream. Nothing earthshattering – there are few enough sex dreams like that. But it was exceedingly nice. Maybe it was the goody-two-shoes aspect that prevented it from being entirely spectacular. It was better than I could have consciously imagined, but not as awesome as my mind had produced on its own once or twice in my life, in those brief, infrequent, utterly stupendous sex dreams. But one didn't get to pick one's partners for those – seldom anyone as cute as MacGyver. In fact, sometimes the partners were not anyone one would ever choose.

I always considered sex dreams as something that were a more physical thing than a subconscious one, anyway. It wasn't the mailman or your middle-aged math teacher that was somehow making you hot in your sleep. You were already hot in your sleep – something that occurred entirely too seldom as far as I was concerned – and your subconscious mind just supplied the dear old mailman or your frumpy next door neighbor for a partner. Perhaps the physical thing came on too quickly for your mind to supply a better one.

And there was a difference between dreaming about sex and a sex dream, in my experience. Dreaming about sex was where you would find yourself in what could be construed as a sexy situation with that one desirable person, and there might be sexy words or glances or maybe even a little kissing. But seldom was there any fruition. Other dream elements usually intruded – you couldn't do this with this person right now because you were late for some meeting at work that you just couldn't seem to get to, or something like that. These dreams were more of a wish fulfillment kind of thing to me, although, like I say, the wishes are seldom fulfilled.

Not like in a sex dream. Those were usually quick and intense, the physical sensations real and alive – you only realize in the middle of it that there is someone else with you – and damned if it isn't usually someone odd. But it's an orgasm in your sleep – a physical thing – so who cares who it's with? That's just your mind picking someone at random, to go along with the physical sensations, not any kind of wish fulfillment. At least that's how I've always thought of it.

But Iris's potion seemed to have the effect of combining the two. I'd experienced the wish fulfillment of taking the place of the Pretty Photographer from that episode of *MacGyver*, and had also felt the physical manifestations of a mildly satisfying sex dream.

Well, hot damn. That was okey-dokey.

I sat up in bed and looked around. The candles had all gone out on their own. Even the fire hazard was gone. My room was bright and cheerful, as it always was first thing in the morning. There was not one single demon lurking in the well-lit corners.

I still didn't believe in magic; I believed that Iris's potion was some kind of drug. Some kind of preparation of herbs, *eye of newt and toe of frog, wool of bat and tongue of dog*, perhaps. But there was nothing magical about it, no more than aspirin curing a headache was magical. It was the ingredients working in my blood, in the receptors of my brain, no more enchanted than the vaunted serotonin reuptake inhibitors. The words and the magic circle hadn't contributed to the awesome dream. It was caused by the ingredients alone, like some kind of soporific Spanish Fly.

SEVEN

I got dressed, had a cup of coffee, decided that I needed to go to the supermarket. As I went out onto the front porch, I glanced over at my car in the driveway, and was startled to see a man standing beside it. Or at least, he was dressed like a man, in a white short-sleeved shirt, a black tie, black slacks. But instead of a head, instead of a *face*, he looked like a cartoon, like the logo from Spitfire skateboards: a one dimensional, U-shaped face topped with flaming hair, triangular, evilly grinning teeth, blank eyes, no nose. He turned this countenance upon me and cackled, then with a taloned fingernail, he keyed the entire driver's side of my car. He cackled again, then ran off down the driveway, knocking over my garbage cans and the neighbor's, too, as he fled. There was a teenaged kid coming down the sidewalk on a skateboard – I don't know if it was a Spitfire or not – and the thing gracelessly shoved him off of it onto the grassy parkway, then turned around and grinned at me again. I took a step forward and the thing capered away down the sidewalk, knocking over a few more garbage cans as it went.

I hurried down the porch steps and approached the teenager, still sprawled on the grass. He sat up and shook his head. I asked him if he was okay.

"Yeah," he said and stood up. He recovered his board from where it had come to rest against a tree, dusted a few grass clippings off himself. "Thanks. I'd like to know what I hit though," he said and looked at the sidewalk.

"You didn't see the man, the . . ." The flaming-headed *thing*?

The kid kicked at a small twig on the sidewalk, then his eyes flickered up to mine. "I didn't see anybody, lady." He kicked at the stick again. "This is probably what did it, right here." He regarded me suspiciously, cautiously. "What did you see?"

"I saw you fall. You're right. It must've been that stick." He hadn't seen the creature, and I wasn't going to bring it up again. "I'm glad you're okay."

"Thanks," he said again. He skated away down the sidewalk, looking over his shoulder once with a little curious glance.

This creature that I'd seen but the kid hadn't must've been one of the demons that Iris had warned me about. And just like she'd said, it had been neither fanged, nor scaly, nor winged. Just malevolent in a cartoonish kind of way.

"Without a doubt," Iris said.

After witnessing the flaming-headed thing cavort down my street, I'd forgotten all about the grocery shopping. Instead I went to *Mohini's House of Dreams*.

Iris paused and rang up a young girl dressed all in black. She was buying three black candles, shaped like women. After the girl left, Iris said, "That was a demon." She pursed her lips and looked at me in annoyance. "Did you just ignore everything I said? Now that thing is loosed in the world, knocking kids off skateboards for a week or so. It might even come back to key the other side of your car."

"MacGyver – Richard Dean Anderson – isn't dead," I protested. "I said the words, drew the circle, lit the candles."

"Well, you apparently did that part right. Or you might've woke up with that thing in bed next to you." Iris frowned.

"Would it have . . . hurt me?" I asked. I began to think that maybe she hadn't explained the full ramifications of all these magical sojourns to me. Perhaps there had been major details that she'd glossed over, or left out entirely. Perhaps this new chapter in my *life of the mind* was not such a good idea, after all.

Iris shook her head. "It might've scratched you. Maybe bit you. Said really not nice things in a hoarse demonic voice, perhaps. But it couldn't hurt you. It couldn't . . . it's not equipped for . . . that's another kind of demon entirely. I told you they weren't out for your immortal soul, Rae. They're just destructive."

"But I followed the rules!" I insisted. "MacGyver's not dead!"

Iris shook her head. She was still unaware of the clever, mullet-wearing, 1980's icon that was MacGyver. "How do you know?"

"It would've made the news," I told her.

"Who else was in this show? That's the danger of the cinematic thing, Rae. I thought I made that clear to you. It's not just the main character. If anyone else in the scene is deceased . . ." She looked at her phone. "How do you spell it?"

After several minutes looking around the interwebs, it was determined that while Richard Dean Anderson was indeed still alive and kicking, the actor who had played the arms dealer – John Vernon – had passed in 2005.

"But I wasn't thinking about–"

Again Iris shook her head. "You watched the whole episode, right? After you'd done the ritual?" I nodded. "The main portion of your energy is of course dedicated to the main character, but there's still some generated just by acknowledging the other actors. That's where the demon came from, from the energy that couldn't dissipate because the peripheral character is no longer on this plane."

"I misunderstood, Iris. I thought it was only the main person that had to be still alive, not everybody." She continued to frown. "How long did you say that this . . ."

"Demon, Rae. Go ahead and say it. You said you believe what you can see, and you said you saw the thing manifest, saw it key your car and knock over trash cans. So you have to believe in it, right?"

I certainly couldn't argue with that. I *had* seen it, even if the kid on the skateboard – "No one can see it but me?"

"Sensitives can see it. People who know where to look."

"But I'm not a—"

"This is *your* demon, Rae. You summoned it. That's why you can see it. That's why it was grinning at you, why it keyed your car, and not someone else's. Although it might have gone on to do that, too. Whatever you do, don't talk to it, don't even tell it your name. That'll only make it stronger, make it stick around longer."

"How long will I see it?"

"It might not come back. But if it . . . liked you, if it liked tormenting you . . . it might stick around for as long as a week, ten days. Then its energy will fade and it'll be gone." She continued to frown at me. "Maybe you should try something a little . . . newer. A lot of 80's actors are dead now, Rae. If you insist on using these old TV shows . . ." She gestured with her phone. "You're going to have to do a little research, first."

Research? But most of my television and movie star crushes were from when I was young, when they were still young, too. From the 80s or even earlier. And most of them were still alive, but some of the supporting character actors . . . I guessed that Captain Kirk was definitely out. Although there was a new Captain Kirk, and a new Mr. Spock, and he wouldn't be gay with the aid of Iris's potion.

"I'll try to be more careful, Iris."

"I hope so," she replied with a frown. "You don't want a whole cohort of those demons surrounding you, wrecking stuff."

"No more dead guys," I promised. "Not even supporting ones."

Now the smile blossomed again on her pretty face. "There's always your young friend from work. Or someone, anyone, you actually know."

Devin, I thought fleetingly. But no. No Devin, and no Troy, either. The overall feeling that I had come away with was that Devin and all his personality problems had caused me to age prematurely, to become old before my time. I would never want to take up with Devin again. Not even in the dreamworld.

And Troy . . . ah, I didn't really need to be thinking about him either, didn't really need to be generating warm energy feelings that he may or may not feel, that he may or may not know were coming from me. I was amazed and appalled that I was beginning to accept all of the stuff that Iris was telling me about energy transference, but that thing that I'd seen running down my street this morning certainly hadn't been human.

I'd feel a little guilty summoning up Troy to do my bidding, anyway – he was a Boy Scout after all, steadfast and true and loyal to his little wife. Actors were okay . . . my desires were just extensions attached to the characters they portrayed, after all. The characters weren't real, any more than my fantasies were. But Troy was real, and somehow . . . I just didn't think I would feel right thinking about Troy in conjunction with the potion . . . like I was using him, somehow. It would be disrespectful.

"I'll be more careful," I repeated to Iris. A group of girls came into the store and I told her goodbye. The grocery shopping wasn't going to do itself.

EIGHT

I saw the demon again in the parking lot, when I was coming out with my groceries. It was waiting for me, and when it was sure I'd noticed it, it sent a shopping cart careening into the front of my car. I heard the tinkle of glass. A woman turned around at the sound, but she didn't run screaming into the store, so I knew that she couldn't see the demon, any more than the boy on the skateboard could. The demon threw its head back, grabbed its stomach and enjoyed a hearty belly-laugh, a parody of Santa Claus. Ho, ho, ho. Hardy, har, har.

I glared at it, and it glared menacingly back at me. But if I was going to trust in the secrets Iris had imparted to me, then it had to be all the way. I couldn't allow myself to be afraid of the destructive thing. Supernatural or not, invisible to everyone but me or not, Iris had said it couldn't hurt me, so I advanced across the parking lot toward it. Perhaps I could scare it away or something. The demon stood its ground – another woman crossing the parking lot looked behind her, no doubt wondering what I was glaring so fiercely at – but of course, she saw nothing.

I noticed that the demon seemed more insubstantial than it had when I'd first seen it: faded, almost milky. Maybe soon it would be transparent, then gone altogether, like Iris had indicated. I wondered if it would be hot to the touch, because I intended on shoving it, just like it had shoved the kid off the skateboard, shoved the grocery cart into my car. Iris had said the most it could do was scratch me or bite me – and I thought maybe if I threatened it, it would go away.

But the demon had other ideas. Before I was anywhere near close enough to engage it physically, it raised its arm above its head and waved at me. I was reminded of the white-eyes and the grin of the Underwood Deviled Ham logo – would all my demons look like the devil-themed shills from popular products? Would the next one (if there was a next one) sport horns and a mustache and carry a trident like the Arizona State Sun Devils' mascot? The thing scampered away across the parking lot before I could close with it.

I stopped at the *AutoZone* to purchase a new headlight, and while I was waiting to pay for it, my sister Corrine called. She asked me where I was, asked me if I'd like to come over for lunch. I told her that a shopping cart had rolled into my car, busted out the headlight.

"All the more reason to come over for a visit," she said. "I'll ask Warren to fix it for you. I'm sure he wouldn't mind."

"That's very nice of you, Corrine," I told her. "I'll be right there."

Whether Warren would mind or not was really a moot point. Warren was my brother-in-law, and his wife had trained him well. He did as he was told. Don't get me wrong, Corrine was not an overbearing monster to her husband, to her child. Not too much. But she definitely wore the pants in the family. Warren was a nice guy, but if he'd ever had any fire to him, my sister had extinguished it long ago.

It would be nice to see my sister and her family. It would certainly take my mind off of demons, and the vast eddying pool of the supernatural into which I'd seemed to have fallen. I wouldn't ponder potion-driven sex fantasies, wouldn't think about facing Troy at work tomorrow, if I had a nice little lunch with Corrine.

I especially looked forward to seeing my niece, Darlene. It had been at Darlene's high-school graduation party that I'd met Devin – he'd been friends with her boyfriend. Darlene and I had been close her whole life – she certainly didn't have a cool mom, so she was glad to have a cool aunt. She and her various boyfriends and girlfriends had hung out at my house on occasion since she'd been old enough to drive, and in my mind, I'd always taken a little credit for the fact that Darlene was a fairly level-headed girl. Anytime that she'd felt like rebelling against her mother's sometimes suffocating strictures, Darlene had come over to my house, instead of blowing off steam on the boulevard. I'd always felt that she'd stayed out of trouble at least partially because she'd always felt safe and unjudged at my house. If she wanted a beer or two, I'd let her drink them there. She no doubt felt that she was getting back a little at her mom when she did so, but at least there was no one at my house to take advantage of her rebellion. I think that a lot of times I was able to defuse her anger with her mother, and that kept her from running out and doing things she might've regretted latter.

Darlene confided in me, told me things about her boyfriends that she could never discuss with Corrine, bitched about her girlfriends on a level that her mother wouldn't have understood, or would've dismissed as childish or immature.

Darlene had also been non-judgmental about the Devin thing, and I appreciated that. I certainly got enough disapprobation about it from her mother. Being young herself, she couldn't see what her mother was so upset about; she just didn't realize that such things were generally frowned upon. As an individual, she thought Devin was somewhat of an ass, and as it would turn out, she was right – but she never thought there was anything wrong with the age difference.

Darlene had just turned twenty-two. She didn't come and visit me as much as she used to – she didn't need a secret place to go if she wanted a beer anymore – but we texted nearly every day. She was the one who had insisted that I get a cellphone, had taught me how to use it, brought me up to speed in the modern world. She considered herself grown now, even though she still lived at home with Mom and Dad while she went to school. She considered us friends now, more than aunt and niece. I enjoyed our friendship – hearing about all her boyfriend escapades and her tempests-in-a-teapot with her girlfriends made me feel almost as young as she was.

Darlene gave me a hug when I came in the house – she was tall and willowy, with strawberry blonde hair and dark brown eyes – she reminded me more of myself at her age than of her mother. Corrine had set out a nice lunch of roast beef sandwiches, salad and lemonade. Warren said hi around a mouthful of roast beef, then immediately went outside to fix my headlight. Corrine had indeed trained him well.

We made small talk, and during a lull, Corrine peered at me minutely and said, "Are you feeling all right, Rae? You look a little tired."

Oh, it might just be that my dance card's been a little full, this weekend, I thought. *On Friday night, I may or may not have committed adultery in a bathroom stall in a club that no longer exists, with a man young enough to be dating your daughter, if it wasn't for the fact that he is quite happily married. And then last night, I invoked the Mother Goddess and imbibed a magical potion, all to better help me enjoy an old episode of* MacGyver. *You remember* MacGyver, *don't cha, Corrine? You used to always tell me how ridiculous it was. But this episode, thanks to the magic, was a little more personal, and not ridiculous at all. But Dean Wormer is dead, and this morning I was confronted twice with a flame-headed demon of my own summoning . . .*

"I don't feel tired," I said.

"You look great, Aunt Rae," Darlene said, offering her mother a little glare. She only used the honorific *aunt* around Corrine. When she wasn't around, I was just Rae, her friend. "You don't look tired at all."

"Thanks, Darlene," I said.

"Maybe you're just looking lonely," said my sister, ever complimentary. "Have you been out searching for that age-appropriate Mr. Right?" She smiled a little smugly at me, and I thought about Warren, her own Mr. Right, the same one she'd had for twenty-five odd years. She could go right on ahead and be smug. I'd rather be alone than shackled to a lap-dog like my brother-in-law.

"Haven't really been looking, no," I said.

"Have you ever thought about one of those online dating services? I was just reading the other day that in today's world, the stigma of all that has more or less been removed, and–"

"You don't want to do that, Aunt Rae," Darlene assured me. "Those things are full of weirdos."

"How would you know?" her mother asked. Her tone indicated not that she suspected Darlene of visiting dating sites. It was more just motherly condescension, as if she still thought of Darlene as a little kid, unaware of what a weirdo was, nor where they lurked.

"A friend of mine tried it for a little while. She answered a bunch of questions, said she liked to take windy walks and all that on her profile. She thought it would be a scientific way to meet guys. Apparently that's what they want you to believe. All she got was guys looking for the quick hook-up."

"I'm sure that just had to do with how young she is," Corrine said, again condescendingly. "Whereas men your aunt's age would be a little more respectful."

Yeah, just want I want, Corrine, I thought. *A respectful old guy. Just like your husband. Pass.*

"I've got a better plan, Aunt Rae," Darlene said, more or less dismissing her mother's entire train of thought. "Why don't you come out to the show with us on Friday? There are plenty of men your age there, and I'm sure that–"

"What kind of shows are you going to where there are men your aunt's age?" Corrine demanded.

Darlene ignored her mother. "There's this band called Rolling Blackout. They play at this place called *The Beachcomber* on Fridays and sometimes Saturdays."

"You've been going to the beach every weekend?" Corrine's voice rose an octave. "That's too far for you to be driving at night, Darlene. I don't want you to be going all the way to the–"

"It's not at the beach, Mom. It's right here in town." Darlene rolled her eyes, and I smiled. "They're really great, Aunt Rae, and the singer is just . . ." Darlene shook her head. "The singer is just *awesome*. Yum, yum, gimme *some!*" She ignored her mother's annoyed expression. "You should come out with us this Friday."

My sister glanced at me – *I'm sorry that our little girl thinks that you still want to play her childish games* – her look said. But I wouldn't blow off Darlene's kind invite, just because her mother might be right, that I was a little old to be going to bars to see *awesome* bands. "Let me think about it," I told her. "If I don't make it this Friday, be sure to ask me again."

"Okay," my niece said. "But I guarantee you'll love it."

40

NINE

I utilized Iris's potion a great deal for about a month. I had to re-up on candles twice in that short period of time. I spent a great deal of time masquerading as Cybill Shepherd and keeping company with Bruce Willis (from when he still had hair), a la *Moonlighting*. It was another oldie, having run from 1985 to 1989, and I obliging took Iris's advice and looked up the supporting characters before indulging. There were quite a few that had passed out of this plane of existence, including the incomparable Orson Welles.

Miami Vice, another 1980's hit, became a veritable staple. I found myself retiring almost immediately after arriving home from work, just so I could spend some quality time with Don Johnson. On more than one occasion, I might have been found at my desk at work doing the research, just so I wouldn't have to waste any time on it once I got home. There was even an episode where Don was not the main attraction. I wanted to see instead a thirty-something, very blue-eyed Jeff Fahey in the part of scuzzy arms' dealer Eddie Kaye. *Yum, yum, gimme some*, indeed.

But when the new month began, I looked back over the past thirty days and began to feel decidedly distressed. I discovered that I'd stayed in every single night, like a hermit. It wasn't that I was a social butterfly, but I hadn't even seen my sister, or Darlene, once. Hell, I'd only seen Iris twice, when I'd gone in to *Mohini's* to buy more candles for the ritual. I'd skipped dinner frequently, in a hurry as I was to meet Don or Jeff or Bruce in dreamland. I discovered I'd lost ten pounds.

Wait a minute. That wasn't bad at all.

But still . . . I was a healthy and youthful forty-five, now ten pounds lighter, and there was a whole world out there that was passing me by, that I'd shunned for the past thirty days in favor of incredible sex dreams. And they were incredible. But while I always woke up glowing and refreshed, as if they had been real, they were not real. I always woke up alone.

The thought struck me that I would be alone forever, if I didn't rein in these activities. I reflected that Iris had said that all things involving the magical spheres were a give and take. I knew what I was taking, but what was I giving? This thing had become almost an addiction to me. I needed to get out, interact with some real people for a change. Perhaps before it was too late. Before I gave up on a real, often trying and disappointing world in favor of a false, colorful and never dull one, where there was always a happy ending.

Where did one meet eligible men, though? Work was out. I knew them all, and they were all too young, too old, too married, or too just-not-for-me. I'd never even considered the bar scene. That was also just not the thing for me. I'd read *Looking for Mr. Goodbar* way too young, in middle school, before I even understood Theresa's motivations – and the idea that the charmer you meet at the local bar just might kill you never left me. If it hadn't been for Devin, I would've been completely without companionship, lo, these many years.

Wait. A few months after my divorce became final, there *had* been one other guy. I'd almost forgotten about him.

His name was Chet. I met him at *Morry's*, the local dinosaur of a used bookstore. The place consisted of shelf after over-burdened shelf of the world's cast off reading material: old textbooks, mismatched encyclopedias that still listed nine planets and the currencies of all the countries in the European Union. Thousands of paperbacks written by the famous, the infamous, the utterly unknown. They didn't have a lot to offer that was to my tastes, excepting of course for the new owner. He was tall and dark-haired and just as friendly and charming as he wanted to be. We even had dinner once, but the meal was interrupted not far from its conclusion, when a young woman with purple hair stomped into the restaurant and stood sullenly by our table. He apologized, told me that she was his daughter. She stared at me silently until her dad gave her all the cash in his wallet. Then she snatched up the doggie bag that the waiter had just brought to the table, and with a snarky look at me, she departed.

She was just out of rehab, he explained – for what, he didn't specify – and he didn't think that it had taken all that well. He complained that she was crashing at his small apartment above the bookstore, and that he didn't really care too much for her friends, young men and women that showed up at all hours of the night, calling up to her from the street like Stanley Kowalski.

Needless to say, there wasn't a second date. He was certainly attractive enough, but our conversation had stumbled during dinner, and we didn't seem to have too much in common. And I was not anxious to get involved with someone with so much baggage. I was on the rebound from my divorce, and just didn't want to become immersed in any more drama.

But I still went in to *Morry's* every now and then to say hi to the bookstore owner, and ask after his daughter. He would always shake his head and say that she was still having problems, and I thanked my lucky stars that all her problems were his problems and not mine. It was on one of these occasions that I met Chet.

I was standing in front of a shelf full of old hardbacks, not really interested in reading material, but actually just contemplating the proprietor out of the corner of my eye. I glanced in the other direction, so as not to make it obvious that I was watching him, and that was when I noticed that there was a man beside me, also perusing the tall shelf. We were of an age, and he had milk chocolate-colored hair, the exact same shade as his eyes. He smiled at me, then said, "There's a Keats up there. Keats and Shelley." When I looked up at the dusty books, he added, "If you're into poetry." When I didn't speak, he said, "I've always thought of myself more like Byron," and grinned.

"Mad, bad, and dangerous to know?" I knew nothing of Keats and only knew that Shelley had been married to the woman that wrote *Frankenstein*. I'd gleaned that epigram about Byron from some Ken Russell film about the writing of the famous novel. Gabriel Byrne had played Byron. But I was completely ignorant of his poetry, also.

Chet introduced himself, again asked me what kind of literature I was looking for. *I was just looking at the owner of the store,* I thought. *Wishing his daughter would go back to rehab.* But this one was just as attractive, if not as tall. "Just looking," I said.

He considered me for a moment and then asked if I'd like to have a drink.

I would soon discover that Chet was charming, well-read and well-travelled. He had an awesome intellect – I was frequently challenged to keep up with him in conversation. He also liked to drink, which was okay with me then, because I was at a time in my life when I liked to have a few myself.

We went out to dinner a few times, got drunk together. He liked to talk, which was a welcome change from my saturnine ex-husband. And his words were always witty and thought-provoking, at least until the alcohol took hold, at which point he began to ruminate darkly, in exhaustingly, annoyingly repetitive circles. But I didn't notice too much, because I was usually half in the bag myself by then.

And Chet was confident – one could say that he was full of himself. Before he would devolve into inane circular babbling, when he was just drunk enough to be free of all inhibitions, he would lean closer to me across the table and whisper that he could guess what I liked, and he was sure that he could provide me with quite the run for my money. He had studied the arts of the East, he'd tell me with a sly smile. Such activities were his chief avocation.

He was attractive, and he was so charming. I began to feel fortunate that I'd so quickly met someone so different from my ex, and yet so entirely suitable. After several dates of listening to Chet brag on himself, I decided to take him up on his offer. With much anticipation, I took him home from the bar. I liked him very much – he was bright and fun and said he was great in bed. What was there not to like?

To say I was disappointed would be an exponential understatement. He was not well-endowed, which sometimes makes a man hone his skills in other areas, like they say blind people develop exceptional hearing. But not Chet. He wasn't any good at that either.

His meagerness was further compounded by his drinking. But the very worst part was that he acknowledged nothing amiss whatsoever: he seemed to believe it perfectly normal for there to be long, talk-filled pauses throughout the thing, while we waited for his forces to marshal, so to speak.

I went back two or three times, hoping, dreaming, that it might get better. I liked his wit and his intelligence. And his line was arousing, all those promises of how good he was. Perhaps it was just not a good idea to incite my imagination – few things in real life can hold a candle to the things which I can imagine.

But never has my imagination spoiled a decent real-life encounter. Chet was just grievously mistaken. Not only wasn't he any good – he wasn't even on the same continent as good. He was, in locker room parlance, *a dead lay*. After a month of dates I began to become quite frustrated. He could've been so perfect – we were so well-matched outside of the bedroom. Still he bragged of his expertise, and still he failed to deliver and didn't even realize how terrible he was. I began to actively dislike him. After a while, I wanted to tell him, to let him know that he couldn't be more wrong in his bravado. It wasn't a front to cover his inadequacies: he actually believed he was a modern-day Casanova. I wanted to be cruel and laugh in his face when he asked me to tell him how much I'd enjoyed myself.

But I wasn't cruel. Let some other woman show him his delusion. He was a nice enough guy, would no doubt make a great friend if I was a lesbian. But if we kept going out, and he kept telling me about his way with the ladies, something that I'd unfortunately found out for myself was all in his head, then sooner or later I was going to hurt his feelings. Perhaps if he'd been a little more humble, if he'd acknowledged his awesome array of shortcomings . . . but all the wit and erudition in the world weren't going to make up for someone whose high opinion of himself was so completely without merit. So I broke it off.

There hadn't been any others until Devin had snuck into my room, about five years after my divorce. Perhaps it had been the sustained lack of male companionship for all that time that had led me to glom onto him so completely. I think that's what a shrink might've told me if I'd ever asked a shrink why I'd missed him so keenly when he finally left. The good doctor would've explained that I'd been lonely, looking to fill a void in my life, and that was why I'd missed the worthless waste of breath so much after he finally stayed gone.

But I don't think that was entirely the reason. I hadn't being feeling lonely or confronted with a void at first, all those times he was making the fantasy a reality. What I missed about Devin was what Chet was missing before I ever met him: Devin was an alcoholic, as much as Chet was, but his alcohol intake affected his performance not in the slightest. He was tall and young and healthy and very, very good. When Devin bragged, which was seldom, he backed it up. Call it selfish, but that was what I'd missed the most about him, not his charm and wit, or lack of it. I missed what we'd had physically. And that was nothing that one should base a relationship on, now was it?

TEN

I thought about Corrine's suggestion regarding online dating. Despite what Darlene said about it being all about men looking only for the easy hook-up, maybe there could be something to it. I had to try something.

So on the first Sunday afternoon of the month, I went to visit Iris at *Mohini's House of Dreams*. She looked up and smiled in greeting when the bell over the door tinkled. I waited until she was done waiting on a few customers, then got right to the point. "Have you ever thought about one of those dating sites? I mean, maybe meet a real, flesh and blood man for a change?"

Iris blinked her enormous blue-purple eyes, nonplussed. "You haven't enjoyed . . . ?"

"That's just the point," I said. "I've been thinking that perhaps I've been enjoying it a little too much." I looked down at my hands, splayed flat on the counter. "Don't you ever wish that you had someone real and alive to come home to at night?"

Iris blinked again. "I'm old, Rae, as old as . . . you. I've had my share of real men. I've been completely happy with just myself for a long time now. I'm set in my ways, as the old chestnut goes. I think I might find a real man to be . . . annoying. A real man wouldn't begin to live up to all the things I've experienced with men made accessible through our potion. Would a real man live up to what you dreamed with Mac-What's-His-Name?"

"No." A real man wouldn't even live up to what I may or may not have done with Troy. "But that's just the point, Iris. It wasn't real. I just sometimes worry that my time is running out. I figure maybe I only have a few more years to . . . find someone. So I don't wind up all alone."

"So you don't die alone?"

Now it was my turn to blink. "Yeah. Maybe that's it. I don't want to die alone."

Iris smiled. "Orson Welles said, *We're born alone, we live alone, we die alone. Only through our love and friendship can we create the illusion for the moment that we're not alone.* But I don't need real men for the love part of my illusion. That part of my illusion is just a little more real than most people's, at least to me. Aren't your illusions real to you?"

"Maybe I want something more than just an illusion." I found it a little disconcerting that Iris would be quoting the late Orson Welles, when I'd only recently skipped an episode of *Moonlighting* as potion fodder because he'd had a small part in it. It really did seem like Iris could read my mind sometimes.

"You're also part of my illusion, Rae – the reality, the friendship part. We're friends, right? You don't think that I tell just everybody about these things?"

"Yes, we're friends, Iris."

Iris paused and considered me. She smiled. "If you think you need a real, flesh and blood man – maybe you're right. Maybe I could use one, too. It's been a very long time. You've thought this out." A statement. Seldom did Iris ask questions, I'd noticed. She grinned broadly, showing all her little pearly teeth. "But I remember my youth vividly, my hunting days, if you will, so I'm prepared to be enthusiastic in this little experiment. Real men you want, and real men you shall have. I imagine it's a lot easier for a woman nowadays, what with our vaunted liberation and all the modern methods of communication. But I have absolutely no idea what the rules to the current game are, Rae. Like I said, it's been many years since I've felt the need for a real man."

"I feel the need all the time, Iris," I admitted. I didn't need them for the physical things that the potion so wondrously provided. But there was more to a real relationship than sex. A real relationship involved camaraderie and travel and . . . and love, maybe.

"Allow me to amend – I feel the need all the time, too. But it's been an extremely long time since I've had the desire to satisfy the need for a real man with an actual real man." Again she grinned. She was thinking about neither camaraderie nor love. "I've not studied the invisible worlds all around us for naught, my friend. They've served to keep me healthy, wealthy and wise. And I thought it was working for you, as well."

"It's working, but–"

"Maybe you should try entertainment from this decade. From this century." I opened my mouth to object, but Iris held up her hand. "I'm just kidding, Rae. I'll give this online dating thing a try. For you."

ELEVEN

Iris and I signed up for a dating site called OkCupid. It was free – neither of us were serious enough about the whole idea to spend any money on it just yet. We took pictures of each other, wrote brief profiles. Thinking of Darlene's friend, I didn't say anything about windy walks.

Before she had even posted her picture, Iris got a message from an eighteen-year-old boy. *I think you're cute,* it said.

"Maybe it's just a test," I said. "Because, of course, you are cute." I nudged her. "But there's no way he could know it, yet."

"A test," she said, and erased the message from the boy.

There was a lull for perhaps a minute. Iris and I waited. Then we both received a message. Mine was from another young man, all of twenty-two. His picture showed him to be a little on the chubby side, unfortunately, not at all attractive to me. I've always preferred them long and lean, no matter their age. I thought that perhaps this one hadn't finished growing yet.

Hello, cutie, his message said.

Right, I thought. I said hello back, and considering my vow to find an age-appropriate swain, I added, *I think I'm a little old for you.*

I like older women.

What kind of psychopathology was it, I wondered, that would make a twenty-two year old *boy* think he was interested in someone twenty-three years older than him? I mean, the whole Devin thing had been situational – Devin hadn't been out trolling for old women, any more than I'd been looking for someone twenty years younger than me. It had just . . . happened. Someone twenty years younger than me, as had been amply demonstrated, was a boy. Been there, done that, what's next?

That's very flattering, honey, I wrote. And it was flattering, but still . . . *I'm afraid you're just too young for me.*

Aw, come on. What are you afraid of?

Was I afraid? Damn right I was. I was still emotionally wrung out from Devin and all the ups and downs of that May-December relationship. I'd learned my lesson. I didn't think it was wrong – this kid was of age, after all, and he'd solicited me first – but it wasn't for me. Not ever again, not in the real world. If I wanted someone twenty-two, I could use Iris's potion and pick me out a young movie star.

In deciding that it might be almost past time to settle down again and find someone that was real, I guess I had a picture in my mind of a trim, well-preserved man my own age, someone that maybe had a little fire left. I certainly had a little fire left. Such an appropriate suitor did I believe I could meet on OkCupid. Not any more boys.

So I told him, *My last relationship was with a man much younger than me. It was a train wreck. So, thanks, honey, but no thanks.*

Aw, come on, he said again. *I know I could make you feel good.*

How presumptuous of you, Chubby, I thought. *I doubt it sincerely.* I was amazed and slightly disconcerted with the kid's nerve. But kids were nervy, were they not? Wasn't that part of their charm? One part of me thought fleetingly that it was a shame that the kid was so homely, but . . . no. I'd had my fill of braggarts, and I was looking for a companion, not just someone to make me *feel good.* I had all that, did I not? In the sacred circle.

Iris asked me, "What does *NSA* mean?" She handed me her phone.

The profile picture showed a white man's slender torso from just below the chin to just below the navel. His message told Iris that he would send her a picture of his face if she provided him with an email address. His profile said he was looking for an *NSA sex partner.*

I'd never heard the acronym before, but it didn't take a genius to figure it out. "It means *no strings attached,* Iris." She looked at me expectantly. "That isn't what we're looking for, is it?"

She blinked. "Sure. Right. Not what we're looking for." She paused. "What are we looking for again?"

"A relationship. A relationship, with a real, age-appropriate man."

"This guy is forty-nine," she protested. "That's close enough."

I shook my head. "He's just out for a hook-up. And we've already got that kind of thing, do we not?" I tapped the side of my head.

"Right. No random hook-ups. A relationship." She nodded firmly. "With a real man. Because . . ." she looked uncertainly at me.

"Because we don't want to die alone. We're looking for a companion in our dotage."

"If you say so, Rae." Iris deleted the message from the NSA man, and I told the kid *Thanks, but no thanks* again, and deleted his messages.

Iris and I stood across the counter from each other at *Mohini's,* and paged through the pictures and profiles on our phones. "I must say, some of them are quite . . . fetching," Iris said. She looked up at me and grinned. "I feel a little like a kid in a candy store."

Iris waited on a few customers and I continued to look at pictures. There was one attractive sandy-haired guy, the appropriate age, but when he started quoting the Bible on his profile, I passed. I looked around at the occult bookstore, thought about my recent run-ins with demons and sacred circles. I considered beautiful Iris, who said she'd been raised in the mystical tradition, who, for lack of a more descriptive word, termed herself a witch. No. A Bible-thumper would definitely understand neither me nor my friend.

I paged through pictures; Iris waited on a few more customers. I looked up to make a comment once, but she was on her phone. So I looked at a few more pictures. When next I glanced up, Iris was smiling at me. She held up her phone. "What do you think?" The picture was of a cute, round-faced guy with brown hair and green eyes. A killer smile. He was wearing a white dress shirt and a black tie.

"How old is he?" I asked.

"He says he's thirty-nine." Iris smiled fondly at the picture. "It's a little young, maybe, but he sounds very sweet. His name is Gerry."

"You talked to him?" I asked incredulously. *"Already?"*

Iris looked at me mildly. "Why not? Is there a time limit? Do banns need to be read first? He says he's looking for . . ." She consulted his profile. *"Companionship with that special someone.* Isn't that what you said we were looking for?"

Well, yes, but, came to my mind. I didn't say it. In theory, there was nothing wrong with Iris talking to the guy already. What was I afraid of? I finally said, "Don't you think you should've gotten to know him a little better first?"

"On this?" Iris gestured with her phone. "The eyes are the windows of the soul, Rae. How can I tell if this guy will make a suitable . . . *companion,* if I don't look him in the eye?"

"Tell me you haven't already said you'd meet him." But I knew the answer.

"Why not?" Iris's long fingernails were painted the same violet-blue color as her eyes, and she tapped them on the counter in annoyance. "You're the one that wanted to play this game, Rae. Am I not playing it right?"

I realized that it *was* all just a game to Iris. She was happy with her solitary life, and had only agreed to look for a flesh and blood man because I wanted to find one, and she was my friend. That was kindness, a show of solidarity.

I leaned a little closer to her over the counter. "Aren't you afraid, Iris? To meet some strange guy so soon?"

Iris grinned, again showing all her teeth. "Is this a dangerous game, Rae? You didn't tell me that." She paged through a few more OkCupid pictures on her phone. "Are these men dangerous?"

50

I realized that she was making fun of me, and that was all right, but I didn't share her flippancy. "You don't think it could be dangerous to meet some strange man immediately?"

Iris threw back her blonde head and laughed, and the sound reminded me of delicate wind chimes tinkling furiously in a hurricane. "If he has ulterior motives, do you think he's going to explain them to me in a text?" She laughed again. "I'm not afraid of men, Rae, strange or familiar. I'm protected by forces most men couldn't even understand."

She reached into her blouse and brought out a small Eye of Horus pendant on a delicate chain. She held it in her palm, ran her thumb thoughtfully over it. Then she took in off and gave it to me, saying, "Here. This will protect you from dangerous men."

I put the lovely thing around my neck and told her thanks. She offered no explanation for how the charm was supposed to work, and I asked for none. If she said it would protect me, then I believed her. I had seen demons.

"And if you'd like protection against werewolves, I think I might have some wolfbane in the back," she told me. "Or if your dangerous man isn't a werewolf, but he bothers you overly, you can just drop some of the wolfbane in his drink. It's poisonous." Iris winked at me. "I'm not afraid of dangerous men, Rae. I'm more than just a little dangerous myself."

Of this, I had little doubt. I thought Iris was a little naïve in her eagerness to play this game, but on the other hand, she was no babe in the woods. She was a middle-aged woman, just like myself.

"In fact," she said, "I belonged to a very dangerous man once, and he belonged to me. It was in my long ago youth, in the idyllic paradise of the Florida Keys. He was a sailor, after a fashion, a smuggler. Some might even say a pirate." Iris grinned. "We had a cottage on the beach and were very much in love." She sighed. "But then one morning, he failed to return. After a storm, his ship went down with all hands on a coral reef. They were all seasoned sailors, and it was thought that they foundered due to wreckers."

"Wreckers?"

"Once upon a time, people used to set false signal fires to lure ships aground on the reefs. Then they would plunder the wrecked vessels."

"But didn't they have instruments? Compasses and radar and–"

"It was a long time ago, Rae. I was very young. All I know for sure is that my man never returned." Iris sighed again, then she brightened. "But you've talked me into looking for a new man." She glanced at the black and white Kit-Kat Klock on the wall behind her. "And a new man is going to be here very soon. Do you want to meet him? Having a witness on hand might curtail any nefarious intentions he has toward me."

"I wouldn't miss it for the world," I told her.

Gerry showed up at *Mohini's House of Dreams* at six o'clock. He was even better looking in person than in his picture. He was about six feet tall, with dark, sparkling green eyes, and wavy brown hair. He had a large, sensuous mouth, and the very boyishness of it led me to believe that he was younger than thirty-nine. He brought Iris a dozen roses and a heart-shaped box of candy, like something out of *I Love Lucy*. It was a delightful gesture, however, and Iris was clearly delighted by it.

She thanked him and introduced us, and said she would go find a vase for the roses. She took them and the candy behind the curtain into the office, telling us that she would enjoy it later.

Gerry had a friendly, open smile, and he asked me what I thought about the nice weather we'd been having lately. The weather was always nice, pretty much all of the time. That's why I live in Southern California. But I didn't say any of these things to Gerry; I thought they'd make me come off as stiff and sarcastic. What were we supposed to talk about, foreign policy? He wasn't there to see me. I was even more of a stranger to him than his date, whom he'd talked to only once.

Iris returned with the bouquet, skillfully arranged in an antique, cut-glass vase. She set it on the counter and admired it, and thanked Gerry again for his thoughtfulness. There was a moment of awkward silence while we all looked at each other, but it was only a moment. Gerry said, "Well, Iris, would you like to go to dinner now? I have reservations for six-thirty." He looked at me nervously for a split-second, no doubt wondering if I was coming along, and what was he going to do, his reservations were for only two, and what kind of woman in her forties needs a chaperone, anyway?

Iris retrieved her purse from under the counter, extracted her keys. "Just let me lock up, Gerry," she told him. "I'll be right there."

Gerry nodded, said that it was nice meeting me, and went out the door. Iris paused until the door closed, then looked at me expectantly.

"Good job," I said. "Don't do anything I wouldn't do."

"What wouldn't you do?" she replied and winked.

Iris turned out the lights, and turned the *Open* sign over to *Closed*. She locked the door and I bid them good evening.

TWELVE

I went home and settled in with my laptop to see if I had any more OkCupid messages. The pictures were clearer on the computer than on my phone.

I had one note from someone called CC745. CC's profile said he was forty-two, and that he was a photographer. His pictures showed an attractive Asian man, the tiniest bit heavy, but which of us past forty are not? One photo was a dramatic shot of just his delightful tan eyes.

His message was of a somewhat advisory tone. *You should post more pictures, it said. You have a lovely smile, but you should put up some full body shots. Guys like to see the whole package.* ☺

I told him thanks for the compliment, and the advice. I told him that the arty shot of just his eyes was very attractive.

He wrote back and said he'd never received a compliment from anyone on the site before. He said thanks and told me that I should have no trouble finding a suitable man here.

I thought he seemed genuine, willing to make small talk, just as a person would when talking face to face. He seemed very nice so far: he hadn't mentioned *NSA* or told me I was *a cutie*, or that he could *make me feel good*. When he asked what kind of man I was looking for, I said someone with a sense of humor, who didn't take himself too seriously. I thought, but didn't write: *someone who believed life was for the living, unlike my ex-husband. Someone who wasn't a doormat, like my brother-in-law. Someone who wasn't delusional about his abilities, like Chet. Someone who wasn't an alcoholic boy, like Devin.*

A smart-ass, perhaps? CC wrote back.

How delightfully perceptive, Pretty Eyes, I thought.

I like big girls, he wrote next. *Let's just say that I like a woman who, if she bumps into a wall, she leaves a dent. A woman who makes the floor shake when she walks into the room.*

He should have no trouble in today's world, I thought. Even though his description didn't fit me, I thought his honesty was amusing. My sister had always posited that little guys inordinately liked big women, so curiously, I asked, *How tall are you?*

He said he was five foot eight, the same height as me, which was a little shorter than I liked. *That's right,* he wrote, *a girl your size likes a man with a little heft.*

Was he saying I was fat? I looked at my profile picture – I'd always considered myself average, and I didn't look fat in my picture. Coming from him, it might be considered a compliment, but I didn't consider myself to be the kind of woman he was looking for. I decided to take the high road and believe he was talking about my height, the same as his own, and not my weight. I wrote, *Let's just say that maybe you're not as tall as I might like and maybe I'm not as fat as you might like.* There was some honesty for him.

Maybe I'm not as tall as I said and maybe you weigh more than you said ☺, he replied.

Here was a perfect stranger, admitting to lying, accusing me of lying. And I wasn't lying. What was the point of lying about my weight? If and when I met someone, he'd be able to see how much I weigh, so why would I even consider lying about it?

Maybe I was looking for a smart-ass, but this somewhat accusatory remark was a little jarring, so early in our correspondence. It turned me off immediately. *Sorry pal,* I thought. *I'm not looking for any shrimpy chubby chasers.*

I replied, *Maybe,* and deleted his messages.

Discouraged for the evening, I thought of Iris and younger-than-thirty-nine Gerry, hopefully not doing anything I wouldn't do, at least not on the first date. But Iris was a grown woman, a dangerous woman, by her own estimation. I thought with a grin that maybe I should be fearing for Gerry's safety. Iris had stated several times that it had been a very long time.

I curled up in bed, lit no candles, said no words, took no potion. It was a Sunday night, after all. I would save Iris's magic for Friday and Saturday nights from now on, just like I'd limit my real dates, if I ever got any.

THIRTEEN

Young, adorable Troy had been working out of our desert office, since the Monday after our little party with the dead. Some of our personnel routinely went to the desert; it was just his turn. If I hadn't known that there was nothing whatsoever suspicious about it, I might've worried that he was avoiding me. That would be unfortunate. Seeing Troy's smiling, dimpled face every now and then was the highlight of my work week.

And he came in that day and said hi, as if nothing had happened between us. Maybe he'd convinced himself that nothing had, since his recall was no doubt as sketchy as mine. All must've gone well at home; whatever story he'd told his darling wife about why he'd stayed out all night must've been believed. I was relieved. I would never want Troy to come to any kind of grief whatsoever because of me.

I stopped by *Mohini's* after work, almost consumed by my curiosity. I wanted to hear all about Iris's date.

She seemed a little judicious in her observations. But perhaps she hadn't taken the guy home and ravished him, after all; perhaps she'd behaved like the lady she appeared to be. No one else knew about Iris's journeys with imaginary men within the magic circle, any more than anyone else knew about mine. Only she and I knew that one did not have to be a lady there. Gerry certainly didn't know, couldn't even guess.

Iris told me that he'd taken her to *Paul's*, the most expensive restaurant in town, and they'd enjoyed pleasant small talk while dining upon excellent, pan-roasted Australian lamb chops. She mentioned further charming conversation over some expensive Austrian wine. Then he brought her back to the door to her apartment – she lived over *Mohini's*. He didn't even ask to come up, but instead asked if he could see her again the following Friday. "A whole week to think about him," Iris said, a trifle wistfully, I observed. "He was every inch the gentleman."

"How lucky you are," I observed.

"That remains to be seen," she replied and winked at me, not wistfully at all.

FOURTEEN

Buoyed by Iris's tale of her lovely first date with her perfect gentleman, when I arrived home, I immediately and eagerly opened my computer to check my latest batch of OkCupid messages.

The first one was from a nice looking fellow, aged 50, with a lot of very blonde hair and two very blue eyes. He wrote, *Hi, I'm Greg, From Chicago. What did you want in a man and how did you want your man to treat you?*

Surprised, I looked at my profile again. Yes, I'd listed that I wanted someone local.

I wrote back, *Mostly, I was looking for a man that lives a little bit closer* ☺.

He answered immediately, and I glanced at the clock. It was getting late in his time zone. He wrote, *I'm very happy to hear from you. I hope you don't mind us getting to know more about each other. I believe in good communication. With that we can get to know each other better and see what happens.*

I said, *It's very nice to talk to you, Greg. However, I don't think there's much chance of anything happening between us, because you live 2400 miles away.*

Yes, I know, my dear. But I don't have a problem with the distance between us because I'm willing to relocate for the right person. One's soul mate can be anywhere in the world. It's just a matter of time to find the right person. Communication is the key.

Oh, no thanks, pal, I thought. *I don't want anybody moving across the country for me.* Just like Iris said, you have to look a person in the eye. Communication might be the key, but it had to be interpersonal communication eventually, not OkCupid messages, not emails, or texts, or phone calls. If this guy thought we could get to know each other well enough through these means alone, well enough that he would consider relocating, I thought he was nuts. Besides, I wasn't ready for that kind of commitment yet. I sought something more than a fantasy, something more than a boy, but definitely not a husband. I just wanted a boyfriend. On Sunday evening, I wanted to be able to say, "I had a great time, honey, see you next weekend." This guy was making me feel trapped already, from Chi-town. Pass. I deleted his messages.

My phone rang. It was Darlene. She was asking again if I wanted to accompany her and her friends to some bar on Friday night to see her favorite band. "Wait to you see the singer, Rae," she told me again. "He's awesome."

Ah, Darlene! She was so sweet! She saw not one single thing wrong with her aging aunt tagging along with her and her friends to see some teeny-bopper band. It was because she didn't see me as her aging aunt at all, but just another one of her girlfriends. I felt proud that she thought of me that way. She certainly wouldn't invite her mother along.

Things surely weren't progressing as I'd anticipated with the online dating, and Iris no doubt would have the weekend all sewn up with her new beau. I showed no reluctance to Darlene when I told her it sounded like fun, even though I was a little reluctant. I wasn't really hep to what the kids were listening to these days, but I was pretty sure I wouldn't like it. But Darlene had been thoughtful enough to ask, so it would just be churlish of me to refuse. Besides, it might be fun to hang out with a bunch of careless, carefree young women for a change.

"Do you want me to pick you up or do you want to just meet us there?"

"Won't I be a third wheel for you and Darryl?" Darryl was Darlene's latest boyfriend. He was also very blonde, like my recent back-East suitor. But he wasn't fifty. I hadn't met him personally, but Darlene had shared pictures of the two of them together, along with glowing commentary. They went to school together. She seemed to like him very much.

"Darryl isn't coming this week," she said. "He says he's bored with the band, and he'd rather study." Darlene paused. "Whatever."

"Maybe you're getting bored with him?" I suggested.

Darlene giggled. "Oh, he's all right, I guess. He's no Wes Thomerville, but he'll do for now."

"Who's—"

"He's the singer for this band – Rolling Blackout. *He is not to be believed,*" Darlene added emphatically. "I can't wait for you to see him."

"I'll meet you there," I told her. "What time?"

"Their set usually starts about nine, but we like to get there early."

I sighed, thinking that nine o'clock was damn late to be just starting an evening, but I figured that it was only my age talking.

"We like to get there about eight, eight-fifteen," Darlene continued. "Especially if Darryl isn't coming along." She giggled again. "Sometimes he talks to us."

"Darryl?"

"*Wes,* silly. Just wait till you see him!"

I'd never known Darlene to be so smitten, to show such enthusiasm for a young man. I imagined this Wes Thomerville to be another cute blondie, probably not too different from bored Darryl himself. But I found her zeal to be contagious. It would be fun to go see a band with a cute singer. It had been years since I'd done such a thing; not since Darlene had been in diapers, probably.

"I can't wait," I told her. "And Darlene? Thanks so much for the invite."

"It is absolutely no problem at all, Rae. You're the coolest person I know!"

I thought that might be a little bit of an exaggeration for my benefit, but I thanked her nonetheless, and told her again that I would see her on Friday. We hung up, and I went back to perusing my hopefuls on OkCupid.

It seemed like it was going to be the night for long distance poets, Mr. Rights separated from me by vast geographical distances.

From John in Alabama: *From your profile, you sound like all I want, you are my perfect match. I am serious about wanting to establish a quality friendship that will lead to something strong with you.*

You got all that from just my profile. All the way from Alabama. Right. Deleted.

From Marshall in Montreal: *The reason I came on to the internet is to find the special person who deserves all the love and passion that makes up my heart and soul. I feel you can learn so much about someone through messages, as a person has to take their time and think about the words they want to express, so it allows you to gain a better understanding of someone than you would probably otherwise.*

But if we would want to have dinner I would need airfare and a passport, so . . . pass. Deleted.

From Calvin in Tennessee: *To get a better understanding of me, picture a waterfall, and instead of all the water overflowing it, is all the love and passion I have in my heart to give to you, as the love and passion has an endless flow coming out of my heart. The good thing is that I found you already.*

You just stay there in the Volunteer State and flow, nutball, I thought.

CC745, the guy that liked big women, messaged me. Again, he said nothing about wanting to meet me. He just said hi, and asked me how my day had been.

It was a pleasant break from the odd, long-distance declarations of my perfection from men I had never met, men I was never going to meet. I asked CC745 if he had any idea why these guys from across the country were talking me up. He sent a smiley face and said it was the old lonely hearts scam.

They've got lots of romantic old gals on the hook, he told me. *Ones that dig that longing from afar bullshit. Pretty soon, they'll be asking you for money.*

Really? I wrote back, appalled.

I guarantee it. By the way, can I borrow $50? ☺

I'll write you a check.

I prefer cash.
Don't we all. ☺

Men asking me for money was almost as hilarious as the boys offering to *make me feel good*. I had no doubt that there would've been a price attached to that, too. But I'd already paid, and more or less gladly, all the time that chronically unemployed Devin had been with me. I wasn't going to pay again. Were there really women dumb enough to send money? What did they suppose they were buying?

CC745 told me that he was off to cruise the local *Wai-Mart*. I told him goodnight and happy hunting.

I sighed and closed my computer. This online dating thing was not at all turning out to be what I thought it was. But I still had hope. In life, ya gotta kiss a lot of frogs, and all that. It had only been a couple of days, after all.

FIFTEEN

The Beachcomber was a modest-sized hole in the wall sitting in the middle of a large parking lot, not unlike the *Y Not*. It was the same kind of place: no windows, a little seedy, smelling of the ghosts of a million cigarettes of yesteryear, a smell no barely decades-old California laws against smoking in bars could completely exorcise. Not in a place as old as *The Beachcomber*. Not without a fresh paint job.

I was fashionably late. It was eight-forty already when I walked in. I didn't have to look far for Darlene. She and her five friends were standing in a semi-circle just inside the door, giggling and whispering, eyes glued to the stage where the unfortunately named Rolling Blackout was setting up.

The stage was small, perhaps only twelve feet on a side. I counted three completely average-looking men there, all in their mid to late-thirties: a very tall, very large one wearing a cowboy hat was tuning his bass; an average-sized guitarist with a very large nose was looking down and adjusting his pedals on the stage, the shadow from that schnoz blacking out the entire bottom half of his face. The drummer was a shaggy long-hair. I looked at Darlene in annoyance.

She read my expression faultlessly. "Oh, he's not here yet. Let me introduce you to the girls. We like to call ourselves *The Every Friday Night Wes Thomerville Fan Club*. Except for Amy, here. She's not impressed."

Amy shrugged. "He's not all that." She smiled and told me it was nice to meet me.

Then Darlene introduced me to the rest of the faithful: Celine, Dani, Gwen, and Paige. All pretty young things, all bubbling with excited anticipation, like teenagers, waiting for this singer to make his appearance.

There was a large round table behind where they were standing, and I put my purse down on it and sat. I wasn't twenty-two. I wasn't going to stand up all night. As if it was some kind of sign, the young women grouped themselves around the table, also, and Darlene said, "Rae hasn't seen him yet."

"I'm telling you, you're not missing anything," Amy said and smiled at me again, as if, being older than her friends, I might share her level head. Just because I was her mother's age, so far, I did share her disdain. I smiled back.

"He's just . . . *so sexy!*" Celine, sitting on my right, whispered. "I just want to *squeeze* him."

"I love his voice," Paige said. "It's just incredible."

And they went around the table, each describing what they found so fascinating about this local singer: his blue eyes, his curly black hair, his smile. The way he held his guitar. His broad shoulders, his nice ass. Except for Amy, who only shrugged, sipped her beer and watched the rest of the band as they set up, they were quite graphic, quite emphatic in their descriptions. I ordered a drink from the lone waitress, and listened while the girls went around the table again with more detailed descriptions. They pretended that these were all for my benefit, because I had somehow successfully reached the ripe old age of forty-five without ever beholding the walking, talking, guitar-playing awesomeness that was Wes Thomerville, but I think they really did it for each other. I think listening to each other's appreciative remarks only served to heighten the excitement for all of them.

I asked questions and they gleefully answered. Wes wasn't a rock star full time, but had a day job for some construction company. The fan club had been coming to see Rolling Blackout every Friday night and sometimes Saturdays for about six months. There used to be more diehard fans, probably another five or six girls, but Dani termed them poseurs, because they'd stopped coming after a while.

"They're only out to see who they can screw," Gwen told me. "Wes doesn't mess around with groupies."

"We're not groupies," Paige said. "We wouldn't sleep with some guy just because he was a musician."

"Unless it was *him,*" Celine whispered.

I wondered what kind of a musician it was that wouldn't be down to take advantage of the obvious affections of any one of these lovely young women – it wasn't like they were underage. Again, Darlene read my expression. "Wes is married," she said. She waited while the waitress set down my drink, and thanked me for the tip. The girls didn't want anything else to drink right then, because the band was about to start, and the waitress walked away. "That's his wife, right there." Darlene said when she was gone. She nodded at the bar.

Curious to see what the bride of Riverside's answer to Justin Bieber looked like, I was surprised that she was just a normal looking young woman, perhaps six or seven years older than the masses of estrogen grouped around the table with me. Not overly made up, not dressed in leather. Just a tiny, cute little blonde knocking hard on the door to thirty. Darlene frowned at Mrs. Thomerville, stared at her while she shared a laugh with the middle-aged bartender.

"Your claws are showing, Kitty," Amy told her conversationally, and sipped her beer.

"If anybody's *not all that*, it's her," Darlene observed.

"But he's going home with her, is he not?" Amy said. "None of you stand the chance of the oft-mentioned snowball."

Darlene stuck her tongue out at her friend, then turned back to me. "Just you wait, Rae," she said, brown eyes all a'sparkle. *"Just you fucking wait*. He's awesome."

The young women's anticipation was tangible, and I found that I was becoming a little impatient to see this young man that had them so wound up. At last the drummer counted off and the set began. The crowd of perhaps thirty or thirty-five people cheered, and Darlene and her friends rushed up to stand in front of the stage, to be as close as they could get to their idol. Darlene looked over her shoulder at me, and I gestured with my drink, letting her know that I could see fine from where I was.

And then Wes Thomerville took the stage, and I was rather sorry that I'd stayed behind. Rolling Blackout began some poppy, fairly juvenile tune, a paean to the joys of staying up late on a Saturday night. An utterly unmemorable drinking song. Wes Thomerville was not blonde, he was not Darlene's age; he resembled frat-boy Darryl not at all. He was not even remotely a boy like Justin Bieber.

He was thirty-something, perhaps as old as thirty-five, but certainly no older than that, and all their gushing descriptions had failed to capture just how attractive he was. He had big, dark blue eyes and not-quite-shoulder-length, curly, impossibly inky-black hair, just as the girls had described. He was about six feet tall, broad-shouldered, and I suspected that he did indeed have a nice ass, even though I couldn't see it, because he was wearing a long, blue flannel shirt. He had a nice voice, as Paige had noted, deep, punctuated by little melodic yelps. A devious, killer smile. Taken individually, all these aspects would've made for a pleasant, mildly attractive guy. Someone whose smile you would return, but probably not someone whom you'd think about twice.

But on Wes Thomerville, they combined to make a striking, *stunningly* attractive man, the kind you would turn around and look at again as he passed you, the kind you would think about *all the time*, just like Darlene and her friends did. *Hot damn*, I thought, *they're right*. Wes Thomerville was *awesome*.

The totally forgettable drinking song ended and the crowd whooped its appreciation. Darlene turned around and looked at me. She opened her mouth, then pushed it closed again, her fingers on her chin. I realized that she was mimicking me, that I was gaping, and I snapped my mouth shut. I smiled and gave her a thumbs up. She smiled back, returned the gesture. My niece and I were simpatico in our appreciation of the blue-eyed singer.

SIXTEEN

I accompanied Darlene and her friends to see Rolling Blackout ever Friday night for a month. Iris was busy with Gerry, so I didn't have anyone else to hang out with, anyway. I always sat at the table by the door – there was absolutely no reason for me to join them in front of the stage, nor to participate when they managed to corral the singer after his sets to sign autographs. He wasn't going to be interested in me any more than he was interested in them, and I felt a little self-conscious about the fact that I shared their unsaddled, unbridled appreciation for him. No point in letting him see it on my face.

Tonight, he'd left the bar immediately after their set – no time for autographs. The girls sat around the big table with me, silent, a little let down, I thought. To make conversation, I said, "Do they have a CD?" Although it wasn't Rolling Blackout's amalgam of forgettable, rock-country peppiness that was the main draw. At least not for me, and I didn't think for them, either. Except maybe Paige.

"No, but there is a movie," she said. Five delicate hands ventured into five purses. Each brought out a slim DVD jewel case. Paige handed me hers. On the front was a picture of a high-rise office building, and the legend *Rolling Blackout's Hometown Debut* across the middle. The back showed a picture of some bar called *Mickey's* and a brief description of the band's start there. The last sentence caught my eye – *featuring the video to My Disgrace.*

I opened the CD case. The disk showed a picture of a sunny blue sky and again the title, *Rolling Blackout's Hometown Debut.* I thought the director was perhaps being clever, juxtaposing the band's ponderous name with the cheery background – he was telling us that though their name was metal, their sound most assuredly was not. *My Disgrace* was apparently the band's hit – the lyrics were printed on the inside of the front cover.

> *Met you in a parking lot*
> *It would become our garden*
> *You caused my sin and my disgrace*
> *And I still beg your pardon*

Watch out for that railing, baby
There's not one thing to see
The drop makes people look like ants
Too far down for me

You corrupted what I've been
But I can't forget your touch
I'm not sure but if this is love
I must thank you very much

Don't go out on the deck right now
It's not a place to dance
One slip and you'd be gone for good
Not one single chance

You're the witch that stole my will
Always miss my will the most
I have become your spineless slave
Your private transparent ghost

Sorry these old stairs are so dark
The bulb blew out today
Just go on down ahead of me
You can lead the way

My sky's always black like night
Yet you remain my sun
Your light is the demonic kind
You are my only one

The jumpers really like this bridge
Once here they seldom fail
Only one step into the air
Past this fateful rail

Hope they catch you when you fall
It will be from my shove
How can I endure all this pain
And believe that you're my love?

I couldn't place the song in the band's set, even after listening to it every weekend for a month. But then, like I say, it wasn't their music that kept me coming back. "There's a video?" I said and closed the case. I looked up to find them all staring at me.

"You haven't seen the video?" Paige asked, snatching her DVD back.

"Is it any good?" I asked, and was answered immediately by five grins.

Amy rolled her eyes. "No. It isn't any good. It's awful. Puerile."

I looked at my niece. "It's awesome," she said, just like I knew she would. "In fact, I think we should go over to your house and watch it right now." She glanced around the bar. "There's nothing to keep us here anymore." Her friends nodded. "What do you say, Rae?"

Since none of them had a date tonight, I thought that it would be cheaper and probably safer for them to have a nightcap or three at my place, anyway. I nodded.

"Rae's got a big screen," Darlene said to her friends. "It's gonna be great."

SEVENTEEN

So there I was with six little girls, not one of them a minute over twenty-two years old. Darlene was the ringleader, seating me in the middle of the couch, next to Dani. Celine perched on the arm of the couch. Gwen and Paige sat on the loveseat to our right. Amy sat in a chair to our left. Darlene put *Rolling Blackout's Hometown Debut* in the DVD player, dimmed the lights, took a seat beside me on the couch and pressed play.

The video to *My Disgrace* captured every single thing that was sexy about Wes Thomerville and distilled it, projected it out into the room like a palpable mist. It certainly wasn't because of the production values: the stock footage of high places intercut with the band performing were ho-hum; the lighting was good, but the arty, maddeningly unfocused aspect of most of it was enough to make you scream. He was so damned cute – "Why didn't they shoot him in focus?" I asked.

"It would've been too much," Darlene said with a sage grin. "We wouldn't have been able to stand it."

Whomever had dressed up the band would go far in the music video business, I thought. *Wardrobe by Carmen* was all it had said on the back of the case. Well, Carmen certainly knew what she was doing. She'd clothed Wes in tight black denim and a black leather jacket, snakeskin boots, and a dark blue, V-necked t-shirt that brought out the cobalt color of his eyes until they seemed to glow. He played a shiny black guitar that seemed to be a natural extension of all the rest of that dark sexiness.

"I want to bite him *right there*," Dani whispered breathlessly, indicating the place where Wes's exquisite neck joined his shoulder.

The way Carmen had got him up was textbook, every woman's dream of the quintessential bad boy. Nobody looked that good in real life, not even Wes himself. When he performed live, he wore flannel shirts and regular jeans, faded Converse. He played a plain, off-white colored guitar. He was awesome enough in person, but the costumer and the director had captured every nuance of his native charisma and amplified it in this video. The easy, friendly, completely amused smile he shared with the big-nosed guitar player when they harmonized made you want to be his friend, but the way he rocked back on his heels and threw his head back limned the exquisiteness of sexual abandon in a manner that made you yearn to be *so much more* than just his friend. The way he put that flawless mouth close to the mike and made eye contact with the camera, whispering the lyrics for the briefest heartbeat, was as if he was sharing the most intimate of secrets with you; the snarl on his face when he sang *It will be from my shove* put you inescapably in mind of an ultimate, mind-blowing release.

I wouldn't say it was pornographic, but watching Rolling Blackout's video to *My Disgrace* made me want a cigarette, and I'd quit smoking when I turned thirty.

Darlene hit the pause button when the brief credits rolled. "I think we should watch it again," she said, and smiled slyly at me. "I think we should let Amy deconstruct it for us. Explain to us why it's not nearly as good as we think it is."

Aside from Thomerville's mesmerizing magnetism, the video wasn't very good. And since she was unaffected by the one good thing about it, Amy was more than happy to oblige. "Okay," she said. "Play it again. I'll do just that."

Darlene shared a conspiratorial smile with her other friends and hit the button on the remote. It took three and a half more viewings of *My Disgrace* before Amy realized that she had been had. Her friends ignored her quite insightful dissertation on the myriad flaws and poorly hidden Freudian symbolism in the video. They simply sat, entranced, enmeshed to the height and depth and breadth their young souls could reach, mesmerized by Wes Thomerville's sexiness.

"Don't you think?" Amy said after reaching some salient point, which I, too, had failed to hear. When she realized that no one was paying attention to her, she said, "Oh, for God's sake!" and snatched the remote from Darlene. She killed the power to the television and when her friends still stared at its blankness, each lost in her own reverie, she clapped her hands together, making them all jump. "You people are insane!"

Darlene grinned at her and said, "Indubitably."

Amy frowned, vexed. Not only was she not in the least bit impressed with Wes Thomerville, she couldn't begin to ken why the rest of us were. Darlene had dragged her along to all the Rolling Blackout worshipfests, insisting that she would get it eventually. But Amy had been bored to tears. I think she just tagged along because she didn't have anything else to do. She couldn't see what we saw in the singer, and she wasn't a fan of Rolling Blackout's sound, either.

"Their music is just too poppy," she'd complained to Darlene on the second Friday I'd gone with them. "No substance. And that one you like so much? *My Disgrace?* Seriously. Do we need another revenge song?"

On that night, Darlene had talked herself into the idea that it was Thomerville's lyrics instead of his looks that had touched her soul. "It's more than just about revenge. It's such a sad song," she'd insisted to Amy. "He loves her, he hates her. It's just so sad."

It was a dumb song – all their songs were dumb, but he looked so damn good singing them. I knew that Darlene was kidding herself. It wasn't her soul that she wanted Wes Thomerville to touch.

Maybe Amy wasn't as bored as she let on. Sure, she didn't care for the band, but she was amazed with this hometown phenomenon's effect on her friends. She'd watched them watch the band, endured their lengthy sets, waited while her friends asked for autographs. And Amy didn't get any of it, the fascination with the corny video least of all.

"I want to understand this," she said to us. "Hell, maybe if I could understand it, I *could* enjoy it as much as you guys do." In my head, I heard all the demons of Hollywood say *Join us*, and smiled.

It was a nice thing to say. Amy wasn't making fun of us. She just wanted to understand exactly what it was that made her friends and a middle-aged aunt so nuts for Wes Thomerville, and especially for the cheesy video of his dark, deceptively poppy song.

"So I wrote down some questions," she said and smiled at each of us. "I have a theory, and I want to test it out on you."

Darlene was not amused. "What are we, fucking guinea pigs?" She went past non-amusement, actually, more into offense. "What's there to understand? He's absolutely beyond compare, the best looking guy I've ever seen," she stated, "and that video is the sexiest 3:35 ever recorded."

Amy considered her friend's displeasure, smiled. "I'm just trying to understand," she repeated.

I nudged Darlene. "What have we got to lose? I know I'd sure like to understand."

Darlene glared at me. "What's there to understand?" she repeated. "He's awesome."

"But why?" Amy said. "Why do you all think so? He's so . . . average. You don't even know him. Maybe he beats his wife. Maybe he's a drunk."

"I'll buy him a drink," Gwen said.

"He certainly doesn't cheat on his wife," Darlene observed. She shrugged. "I don't need to know him. I can *see* him. I just . . . I just know he's awesome."

"But there's no way you can really know," Amy insisted. "Here's what I think. I think that somehow, Wes Thomerville must remind you guys of someone you've known, someone you used to date. Someone who was special to you – very special. I'm sure of it, and I'm gonna prove it to you.

"Because, please-don't-hate-me-Darlene, there's just not much that's all that special about him. He's not ugly, but there isn't one single thing about him that should make you guys so gaga over him." She looked pointedly at me, like I should know better, and I felt a whiff of Darlene's offense. Who was Amy to try to psychoanalyze us, just because she had poor taste in men, just because she didn't recognize awesomeness when she saw it?

But I was curious enough to want to hear her out. Because it was ridiculous, just like she said. Rolling Blackout was only nominally talented. I was ten or more years older than the singer, and I didn't know him, either – yet I couldn't disagree with Darlene – the video to *My Disgrace* was the sexiest 3:35 ever, and Wes Thomerville was indeed the best looking man I'd ever seen.

"I realize that there's something about him to you guys," Amy said, "but I'm here to show ya that it isn't him, *it's you*. It's you projecting things you already know from other boyfriends onto him."

Darlene snorted. "When did I ever have a boyfriend that looked like him?"

Amy reached into her purse on the floor beside the couch and pulled several sheets of folded notebook paper out of it. Darlene and I exchanged a glance. Apparently Amy had put some thought into this.

"I'm gonna ask you guys a series of questions about your perceptions of Wes Thomerville, for comparison purposes. Okay?" I and four of the guinea pigs nodded; Darlene just rolled her eyes. "Okay," Amy repeated. "Who does he sing like? If you had to compare him to someone else, who would it be?"

We all looked at each other silently, then Darlene gave us a voice. "He sings like *him*," she said simply. "That little hitch in his voice – it's like nobody else."

"It goes right through me," Celine agreed. "Like some kind of molten . . . something. I dunno. But the way he sings is . . . not like anybody else."

Amy looked at all of us and we all nodded. The way Wes sang was all his own. "Okay," she said yet again. "His singing voice is his own. Has any of you heard him talk?"

"Of course we've heard him talk," Darlene snapped in annoyance. "He talks to us every weekend."

I considered that. He said, "Thanks for your support," a lot, and he signed autographs. But mostly he did these things quickly – he always seemed to be in a hurry to take the hand of his adorable little blonde wife and leave with her as soon as possible after the band's set was over. So, I thought, you really couldn't say that Wes conversated with his fans; they'd heard him say a few words, but you really couldn't call it a dialogue.

"He talks in the movie," Paige said.

"There ya go," Darlene agreed.

"I want you to think about the way he talks," Amy said, and immediately five pairs of eyes closed. Tell them to think about any part of Wes Thomerville and they would instantly comply. Amy looked at me as if I was supposed to be the calmer head in the group, due to my years, no doubt. She was dreaming. I just didn't have to close my eyes to think about him.

"Who does he talk like? Think about his accent, his inflection . . . who do you know that talks like him?"

"Nobody," Paige said immediately, her eyes still closed.

Wes had a nice, deep, very masculine voice. He was so pretty that I'd expected his voice to be a little effeminate, for there to be a little lilt to it, maybe. But there wasn't – when he spoke you could tell there was not one thing effeminate about him – he couldn't help being somewhere in the middle of his thirties and still being pretty.

"I could listen to him read the phone book," Paige added. "I love his voice. He doesn't sound like anybody else . . . but him."

Darlene opened her eyes, and glanced dubiously, smugly at Amy. "So far, you ain't proved shit."

Amy frowned. "Okay. I'll give you the way he sings–"

"And the way he talks," Paige added, her eyes still closed.

"And the way he talks – his voice, let's say. I'll give you that they are unique to him. I say there is nothing awesome about them, but I'll give you that they are individual to him." Amy looked at all of us. Gwen nudged Paige so she opened her eyes. "You guys have heard him sing, heard him talk. But that's all you know about him," Amy reiterated.

Dani said, "I shook hands with him once. His hands are rough."

"That's because he works in construction," Gwen said.

"For some place called *BF Walker,*" Paige provided. "I drove by there a couple times, looking for him . . ."

Amy held up her hand. "I don't even want to know how you found out where he works, but I know that you guys know all kinds of biographical details." She looked at Paige. "*Stalker details.* But I'm telling you – you don't know him, and the only reason that you like him so much is that he reminds you, either consciously or unconsciously, of someone you *do* know. Help me prove it to you, my friends. Knowledge is power, and self-knowledge is empowering." She grinned at us, then consulted her notes. "Who does he smell like?"

"I think he wears *Polo*," Darlene said.

Paige shook her head. "No, it's *Obsession*," she disagreed.

And Dani agreed with Paige and Celine agreed with Darlene, and Gwen said she hadn't noticed what scent he wore, that she hadn't been that close to him to notice it. I, too, had only gazed at the local phenom from across the room. I'd never been close enough to even look him in the eye, nonetheless smell him. But I realized what Amy was trying to establish, and all this talk of cologne brands was running right past her point. So I spoke up.

"That's not what you asked, though, is it, Amy? You didn't say, *'What* does he smell like?' You said, *'Who* does he smell like?' You want us to imagine, right? If Wes Thomerville is perfect, we should be able to imagine what he smells like, close-up." I winked at Darlene, and she leered back at me. "You want us to tell you, if we had to imagine it, *who* he'd smell like."

Amy smiled gratefully. "That's exactly it. Precisely. If you had to imagine how he smells, who would he smell like?"

And just like that, Amy had me convinced. She had my number. Because Wes Thomerville might sing like himself, and talk like himself, but I knew, I *just knew* in all those parts that noticed Wes Thomerville, and so thoroughly – I just knew that he would smell like Devin.

Devin had other redeeming qualities, not the least of which was the resilience of youth, and he had many bad qualities – but if asked to examine it, the most striking thing about him was not his scent, *but how much I liked his scent*. He wore a nice-smelling cologne, but it was the smell of *him* – his skin, his hair – that had been intoxicating to me. I'd tell him all the time how much I loved the way he smelled, and he'd just look at me like I was crazy.

Amy was onto something here. To me, Wes Thomerville would smell just like Devin.

Darlene shrugged. "He would smell like someone who wears *Polo*," she said.

"Or *Obsession*," Paige said.

Amy had their attention, but it was only because she had so far proved nothing, and they were feeling a little triumphant in their obsession. It had continued to defy Amy's attempt at scientific explanation, so far – Wes Thomerville was still just awesome. If she didn't make a relevant point soon, one of them would dismiss her entirely and turn the video on again.

Amy shook her head. "Okay, forget who he smells like. Next question." She looked at her notes. "Since you don't know personally – but if I was asking you to describe it, who would you imagine he kisses like?"

Now Amy's peers blinked at her, grinned. They liked this kind of exercise.

"He'd kiss like Eddie – hard, fast, rough," Celine said.

"Eddie Dawson?" Dani said.

Celine nodded, grinned. "You've kissed Eddie Dawson?" she asked, with no trace of jealousy.

"Back in high school," Dani said.

Celine said, "He's an awesome kisser. If you like it a little bit rough, that is." She asked Dani, "Don't you think Wes would kiss like him?"

Dani thought it over, smiled. Nodded. "Just like him."

Gwen shook her head. "Wes wouldn't be a rough kisser. He'd be slow and sweet and sexy, like my first boyfriend, Gilbert."

Amy looked at me, because she could see that I was getting her point, even if her friends were not. We were indeed projecting aspects of our favorite men unto Wes Thomerville's broad shoulders – because while I just knew he'd smell like Devin, he wouldn't kiss like him. My favorite kisser was my ex-husband Jay. Jay and Rae, weren't we cute? But just like Devin, too many problems had eventually amassed for that relationship to remain viable, but hot damn, had Jay been a helluva kisser. Slow and soft and sexy like Gwen's Gilbert, Jay would turn rough and demanding at just the precise moment, like Celine and Dani's Eddie.

Oh, yeah. I was becoming Amy's staunchest supporter. There wasn't anything special about Wes Thomerville at all – it was only what we projected onto him.

In an earlier era, even before mine, Amy might've next asked us who we thought Wes might dance like. But men and women didn't dance anymore; not as couples, like my parents did. Disco had put the kibosh on all that. I'd been too young to experience the disco era as a grown-up, but I went to a few high school dances and the teen disco, and learned a few steps to *The Hustle* there. Dancing was a lot of fun, and you didn't really need a partner, even then. But if you had a partner . . . there is nothing sexier than a man who can dance. I wondered if these young women had been far enough around the block to know that a man that is comfortable and confident enough with himself to get out on a dance floor, is always just as comfortable and confident in bed. I wondered if they knew that.

73

But Amy wasn't going to inquire about something as mundane as dancing. She was prepared to get right to the point. "Ok, ladies. You're familiar with word association? When someone says a word, you're supposed to say the very first thing that pops into your mind. This next exercise is something like that.

"I'll even play his video again." She queued the start of the song. "You guys watch him, and think all the nasty little thoughts that you think. And here's my question. When you're watching Wes Thomerville sing this tiresome little song, and you're thinking about what it would be like to be with him, who are you really thinking about?" She grinned at her friends and hit play. All eyes were glued to the screen. "When you picture fucking Wes, who would he fuck just like?"

I didn't have time to be shocked at the earthiness of Amy's phrasing, because she immediately said, "Celine? Quickly, now! First guy that pops into your mind!"

"Jordan!" Celine said gleefully.

"Paige?"

"Willie," Paige whispered. "Oh, *yeah!* He'd be just like Willie."

"Oh, Eddie!" Dani crooned, and we all laughed.

"Rae?"

I smiled at her. "It was long ago and far away, Amy, but I get your point."

"Gwen?"

Gwen nodded also. "Yes, I see what you're saying. To me, he'd be just like Keith, because Keith was the best, ever. You're just saying that we think he's so attractive because we're imagining that he would be just like the best we've ever had."

"Darlene?" Amy turned to her most skeptical friend.

My niece shook her head. She wasn't copping to anything. "You're missing a fundamental thing here, Amy. Really, the chunk missing out of your premise amazes me."

She arose, took the remote from Amy and turned the television off again. "It should've been your first question, but you've failed to ask it. To prove the fallacious nature of your logic, to prove that there is no dismissible, deep-seated psychological reason for why we all find Wes Thomerville to be irresistible – he simply *is* irresistible, to paraphrase the old song." Darlene grinned. She could be just as analytical as her not-impressed-at-all-with-Wes-Thomerville friend could be. Darlene could present an argument, too.

"*He is fine;* he's unequaled, and it doesn't have anything to do with anybody but him," she said. "To prove this, may I now ask your guinea pigs a question, the very first question that you should've asked?"

"You may."

"Okay," Darlene said. "Celine thinks he'd kiss like Eddie Dawson, but fuck like Jordan. Dani is rather a one trick pony, thinks he'd kiss and fuck like Eddie. Aunt Rae harkens back to some caveman she remembers from back in the day." She winked at me. "Paige thinks he'd be just like Willie, who've none of us has even met. And Gwen says Keith, and I say, you have got to be kidding." She grinned at Gwen, who grinned back, shrugged.

My how the little girls get around, I thought.

"But here is my question, ladies – no matter who we imagine he might smell like or kiss like or fuck like – *who does he look like?* Does he remind any of you of one single old boyfriend from yesteryear?"

I thought that their yesteryears couldn't go back very far. I had regrets older than they were and I had stuff in the back of my refrigerator that had probably been in there for longer than they'd been having boyfriends.

"Apparently, we must all be kinda partial to dark-haired, blue-eyed, white boys," Darlene continued. "I'll give Amy that much. And there are plenty of those, are there not? Keith, for example?" Darlene grinned at Gwen again. "But Keith is not even remotely like Wes, not in this lifetime, and Wes is not like anyone else that might be of a similar coloring. You might say he is the original, what all of them *should* look like. I ask you, does he remind you of anybody, of one other black-haired, blue-eyed guy you've ever seen?"

One by one, we each shook their heads.

"No!" Darlene cried in triumph. "There's the flaw in your argument, Amy, and it sinks it like a torpedo. Sure, we don't know him – so maybe we do project how he might smell or kiss or fuck – but why would we do that? Why would we project anything? Why would we not just think of these other guys individually, and leave Wes out of it entirely? Why ladies? Who does Wes Thomerville remind you of? Who does he *look* like?"

"Just him," Paige said. "He doesn't remind me of anybody."

One by one, we all nodded.

"He's just the best looking-man we've ever seen, Amy. There isn't anything deeper or more complicated to it than that."

"He's just not your type, maybe?" Gwen suggested.

Amy smiled. "He's not my type because of that fact that I don't know him. He's good-looking enough, but he's married. He's not interested in me." She looked at her friends. "Maybe that's why I can't understand you people and your fascination with him. You guys have never been like this before over someone you don't even know, someone you can never have."

Oh, Amy, you just don't understand, I thought. Real men are nice, don't get me wrong. Everybody needs a real man. I was more or less desperately seeking one myself, what with the online service and all. But the other ones – the married ones, the ones you don't know, the historical figures, the movie stars – sometimes they are just so much more desirable. Sometimes what a woman can imagine is so much better than real life. Especially if a woman has a little extra-natural help.

I thought that Amy and Darlene were actually in complete agreement, even though they didn't seem to realize it. Amy was right – we were projecting the best parts of all the men we'd known onto Wes. And Darlene was right – we were doing this because he was the best looking man we'd ever seen.

Because of my online dating failures thus far, I just couldn't picture another real relationship happening any time soon for me. It hoped it would happen someday, lest I give in completely to my nascent addiction to Iris's potion. But in the interim, married Wes Thomerville's sexy video would be an especially delectable addition to my collection of cinematic fantasies. I wondered if I had enough candles.

A chiming noise went off in Amy's purse. She folded her study questions in half and stuck them in the side pocket, then retrieved her phone. She glanced briefly at the text. "Is it okay if I have my friend Alex pick me up here, Rae?"

"Of course," I told her, and gave her the address.

"Who's Alex?" Darlene asked.

Amy smiled shyly as she texted my address to her friend. "Oh, he's just a guy. He came into the store." Amy worked at *Starbucks*. "We've been talking for a week or so. We went dancing last Saturday." So Amy did know about dancing. "I thought it might be time for him to meet my friends." She smiled at us each in turn.

"What's he look like?" Darlene wanted to know.

I watched Amy's shy smile morph into a sly grin. "Oh, he's . . . I don't think he looks like anyone you guys know. At least not personally. At least not very well."

No one had a response to that, so we sat in silence for a few heartbeats. Then Dani asked if I would like to see the debut portion of *Rolling Blackout's Hometown Debut.*

"You'll get to hear Wes talk more," Paige said.

I told them that I'd love to see it. Darlene sat back down on the couch and turned the television on. She pushed a few buttons on the remote and was ready to push play and start this epic when the doorbell rang. Amy arose from her seat on the arm of the couch and turned on the lights. She opened the door and admitted Alex. She gave him a little kiss on the cheek, then took his hand and brought him a little farther into the living room so her friends could get a better look at him.

Darlene, Dani, Celine, Gwen, Paige, and I gaped. We couldn't help ourselves. Alex looked like he could be Wes Thomerville's baby brother. The same blue eyes, the same jet black, wavy hair. He was a little taller than their favorite singer, and perhaps eight or ten years younger, but the resemblance was uncanny. Wes Thomerville might not look like anybody else, but this kid definitely looked like *him*.

"I'd like you to meet my best friends, Alex," Amy said and went around the room. Before she got to us, I shut my own mouth and pushed Darlene's chin up. She looked at me and blinked.

We all said it was nice to meet him, then silence reigned again, as the six of us stared in disbelief at Amy's Wes Thomerville knock-off. Just as he was about to become uncomfortable with our wordless, dumbfounded looks, Amy said, "Well, I guess we'll be off then." She glanced at the television. "You guys enjoy your movie."

Alex said it was nice meeting us. He didn't have the same voice, but then Amy never had been overly partial to the way Wes sang or talked, now had she? She claimed to not be partial to any part of him, had told us over and over how average he was, how she couldn't be interested in someone she couldn't have. Yet she had snared someone who looked just like him. Amy wasn't going to have to project anything. *Well, I'll be a son of a bitch*, I thought. *I wonder what his daddy looks like.*

Amy's new beau gave me renewed hope, and I itched to get back to my OkCupid queue, to see if I had any new messages. If Amy could find one that was just right, perhaps there was one out there somewhere for me, too. It only followed. If there were young, single Wes Thomerville look-alikes walking around our humble town, perhaps there were a couple of older ones, too.

Amy and her adorable new boyfriend departed, and we sat in stunned silence. Then everyone started talking at once.

Celine, stating the obvious: "He looks just like . . ."

Dani: "I wonder if he plays guitar?"

Gwen: "But she doesn't even *like* . . ."

Paige: "I need to get a job at *Starbucks*."

Darlene echoed my own sentiment: "I'll be *goddamned!* Where did she? *How* did she?" She looked at all of us and smiled. "If she wasn't my friend, I'd hate her utterly."

"Just like you hate Wes's wife?" Dani asked.

"Worse. I don't know Wes's wife." Darlene shook her head. "I think we're going to have a few questions of our own the next time we see her." She grinned at her friends. "Can I get an amen?"

We all testified.

"What does he smell like?" Dani said.

"How does he kiss?" Paige piped up.

"Does he look as good naked as he does dressed?" Gwen said and we all laughed nastily.

"Can he back up those looks in the dark?" Celine added.

"I'll be damned!" Darlene said again.

I wondered if Amy was the type to kiss and tell. Judging from her peers and their willingness to share, I imagined that she'd have no trouble regaling her drooling friends with every detail they wanted to hear. If Alex was a washout, if all that tallness and those dark blue eyes were all there was to him, I wondered if Amy would tell them. Nobody knew better that me that one cannot always judge a book by its fine cover, after all, and Amy had led us to believe that she hadn't been impressed with Wes's looks, so perhaps there would have to be more to Alex, too, to impress her.

This wouldn't be the case with her friends. If Alex was their beau, just looking at him would be enough to get them there for quite a while, I thought. Enjoyment of a man is primarily between the ears for women, and I thought that my young friends' imaginations could wear out many a Wes Thomerville fantasy on young Alex before they would tire of him, even if he was artic in his cold fish-ness.

The thought that he might be all looks and no substance had not crossed their minds. There was not a sour grapes' bone in their bodies. They all believed that Amy had hit the jackpot — how could anybody that looked so much like their idol be anything but fantastic? It was the oldest trap of humankind, a biological imperative, the one aspect that has kept us mostly a beautiful species: we respond to attractiveness before wit, intelligence, money, power, wisdom, skill. I knew that all my young friends would be more than willing to audition Alex for some months, whether he was worthless or not, just because of the way he looked.

If I wanted validation of this theory, I had to look no further than Devin. He had been an utterly useless human being, not just because he'd been too young for me, not only because it hadn't worked out. I pitied the redhead: Devin had no drive, no ambition: all he ever wanted to do was sit around the house and watch television, stay up all night drinking, sleep 'til two. But he'd sure looked good doing it, and that was all I noticed for the longest time.

I wish he'd get a job, I remembered thinking, *I wish he'd stay sober.* But then Devin would smile at me, or hug me, and then I could smell him, and the desire for all the trappings of responsible adulthood that I wished he'd adopt would dissipate into the air like steam. It took a long time for my intellectual resentment of Devin's irresponsibility to assert itself over my emotional and physical appreciation of how damned cute he was. And I was old enough to know better.

I believed I knew better now. That's why I had sworn off young and cute and *I'll make you feel good* on the dating site. Yet I wondered how I would react if I found a forty-year-old Wes Thomerville knock-off on OkCupid – how would I react if I found out he was a drunken deadbeat, like Devin? Would I overlook that again, support him, put up with his bad habits, just because of the way he looked? Was I really steadfast in my promise to myself – to find a good, decent, hard-working companion, even if he was dumpy or bald? Or would another pretty face turn my head again?

That way lies madness, I thought. Time was running out. If I was going to find a good, real man, a companion for my dotage, as I'd told Iris – then I just might have to lower my standards, at least in the looks department, and stick to my guns. There had to be more to the next book than just an attractive cover. Time was running out.

EIGHTEEN

I felt restive all week. Troy was on vacation, so I didn't even get the pleasure of saying hi to him. Neither was I in the mood for Iris's potion and my usual cavalcade of 1980's leading men. Darlene called on Thursday to give me the not even vaguely surprising news that Amy wouldn't we joining *The Every Friday Night Wes Thomerville Fan Club* on their pilgrimage this week. The other news was that apparently Darryl was through studying and had overcome his boredom enough to once again accompany Darlene to *The Beachcomber* on Friday.

"I knew he'd come back around," my niece said smugly.

The thought crossed my mind that perhaps Darryl was smarter than Darlene gave him credit for. Perhaps he *had* needed to study, and no doubt Rolling Blackout *did* bore him. There might even have been a very real jealousy factor – I didn't imagine that Darlene, young as she was, was very adept at hiding her obvious affection for Wes Thomerville, even in the presence of her strapping blonde boyfriend. All that could be hard on a young man's ego.

On the other hand, Darlene's undisguisable yearning might not bother Darryl that much – even he couldn't help but see that the singer from Rolling Blackout was only slightly more accessible to Darlene than Jim Morrison, staring smokily out of his poster at her every time she entered her bedroom. Wes wasn't dead, but that was the only difference. He was obviously very much in love with his wife, was not in the least interested in his eager groupies.

So I reflected that maybe Darryl wasn't jealous at all. Maybe Darryl was more than just a little bit willing to take all that excess affection his girl was feeling for Wes right on off of the singer's hands for him. Someone should take advantage of it. It would be a shame to let it all go to waste.

Darlene herself was not unaware of these facts, it seemed. She'd said, "Darryl is no Wes Thomerville, but he's better than nothing."

She went on to tell me that Paige and Gwen had also scared up dates for this Friday. I worried that the fan club might be breaking up in favor of real life adventures, but Darlene assured me that it was not. "We'll always go to see him," she said. *Always is a long time,* I thought.

I told Darlene that I was glad that she called, because I could therefore tell her that I wouldn't be able to make this week's gig either, because I'd been invited out to dinner with my friend from the occult bookstore. This was an untruth, of course. I hadn't seen Iris for a month, had only exchanged the merest of texted pleasantries with her in all that time. But I didn't want to go with the fan club, and feel like a third wheel with dateless Dani and Celine.

Darlene said she'd miss me, and that she was sure that Wes would miss me, too. That part made us laugh. Wes was only marginally less aware of my existence than he was of Darlene and her crew. I imagined that he might know their names – he'd certainly written *To Darlene, thanks for all your support* on enough bar napkins and the back of her copy of his movie – but if he didn't have a knack for recalling names, I doubted if he remembered hers.

Thinking of *Rolling Blackout's Hometown Debut* made me remember the video to *My Disgrace,* and Wes-who-didn't-know-me-nor-I-him's lusciousness in it. I asked Darlene to pick me up a copy.

"I'll have him sign it for you!" she said gleefully.

"You do that," I said. *It'll give you an excuse to talk to him.*

Darlene said she'd drop by on Saturday to bring my movie to me and report on the festivities. I told her thanks and hung up.

NINETEEN

The next evening after work, I stopped by *Mohini's House of Dreams* to see Iris. Thinking of Darlene's promise to *report on the festivities,* I was curious to hear about how my statuesque blonde friend was getting on with her online beau.

Iris was glad to see me. She came around the counter and gave me a big hug, told me that she'd missed me. I told her that I'd been going to see a real man, albeit an unavailable one. I promised to lend her my copy of *Rolling Blackout's Hometown Debut,* but added with a leer that it probably wouldn't be anytime soon.

"So you're thinking about returning to the magical realms for masculine amusement again?" she asked.

"At least for one little visit. The thing is only three minutes and thirty-five seconds long."

"With the right man, that can be long enough," she replied. "At least for the first time."

"And what about Gerry, Iris? Is he the right man?"

Iris smiled and said she wasn't sure about all that. She told me that Gerry had confessed that he was not indeed thirty-nine, but was only thirty-five, just like I'd suspected. Despite his youth, Iris related that Gerry was very demonstrative, very capable, and his apartment was immaculate. She said she thought she detected a woman's touch, but he said that his sister visited him a lot.

His sister. Right.

Iris seemed to read my mind, because she frowned and said, "Indeed. I told him that if we were going to continue this thing, it would have to be monogamous. Tyler Durden might belong to the world, but my real man can belong to no one but me." Still Iris didn't smile. "He gushed, positively protested his affection for me and me alone, Rae. He deleted his OkCupid profile in front of me, so I also deleted mine."

Such things are easily restored, I thought, but I also reflected that perhaps I was being overly cynical. Perhaps I was just jealous of Iris's easy success.

TWENTY

Iris had a date. Darlene had a date. Paige and Gwen had a date. Everybody had a date but me, and I went home and opened up my computer with hope in my heart that the OkCupid robot might've found me one, too. It had found three, but I never looked at the second two, because the first one was attractive, forty-five, and local. He had posted an adorable picture of himself with a baby elephant, its trunk wrapped affectionately around his head. He'd also posted a shirtless picture of himself in a pool, with some exotic, Acapulco-looking place in the background. He was just what I'd been hoping for: age-appropriate, yet still trim and sexy.

He's also too good to be true, my rational mind said.

But I didn't listen. This one was cute, the right age. His profile said he worked for a non-profit that helped disadvantaged youth. That was a little selfless for me, but he looked a little like Dean Cain from the old *Superman* series. Though not blue-eyed, he was dark-haired, quite fit and very attractive; maybe this could be my own age-appropriate Wes Thomerville knock-off. His profile said I should message him if *You want to meet for coffee and or an ice cream and chat and see if we have some great chemistry. We can write or type or text all we want, but you can never know much about a person until you talk and meet eye to eye!*

It was the very sentiment Iris had expressed, and look how well she was doing. So I send him a message. Ever the poet my own self, I said *Hi.*

He wrote back a few minutes later, said that he liked my smile, told me his name was Robert. He said he was a painter, in addition to his social work. If I'd send him my email, he'd send me pictures of some of his paintings in the morning. I hesitated. But the internet was anonymous enough – it wasn't like he was asking to get that ice cream right now – so I sent him my email.

Darlene showed up about noon on Saturday with not-so-dumb-after-all-Darryl in tow. They were all kissy-face and affectionate, holding hands and giggling: Wes Thomerville had worked his own brand of magic for all concerned. I imagined that Paige and Gwen and their dates were off somewhere just as satisfied, and I wondered if the blue-eyed singer had any idea whatsoever that he was the agent of so many contented cominglings.

All the happy couples were set to reunite for lunch, and, ever gracious, Darlene asked me if I'd like to join them. I declined, saying that I'd already eaten. It was true. I had devoured a ham sandwich earlier, waiting impatiently for Robert's email. Darlene said maybe next time then, and gave me my copy of *Rolling Blackout's Hometown Debut*.

I turned it over. Darlene had gotten the singer to autograph it, just like she'd promised she would: *To Rae – Thanks for all your support! Your friend, Wes Thomerville.*

"He asked which one you were," Darlene told me. "Maybe he thought you were too shy to ask for his autograph yourself." She grinned at the *as if* of that. "I told him that you were unable to attend last night, but I promised him that I would introduce you the next time they played."

That would give Darlene yet another excuse to talk to him. I grinned back at her, thinking my friend Wes Thomerville and I would be quite a bit more friendly by the next time they played, at least in my head. I told my niece thanks for the extra effort, which I knew had been no effort at all for her. She and her smiling beau departed.

Not long after, Robert at last contacted me. The email he sent contained more pictures of himself with a big family: elderly Mom and Dad, a couple of brothers, a sister, and two young women about Darlene's age who were obviously someone's daughters. *How cute,* I thought.

I scrolled down the email, eager to see his artwork. There were three pictures of abstract paintings photographed in situ: one was above a fireplace and the other two were beside a sliding glass door with a slice of the ocean visible in the background.

I promise to do an abstract of your face as a present from me soon, Robert had written beneath the pictures.

That would be absolutely awesome, I thought, using Darlene's favorite word. I had never had my portrait painted before, abstract or otherwise. I discovered that I was feeling quite enthusiastic about Robert already. Perhaps I, too, had hit the jackpot, just like Iris, just like Amy.

Next was a picture of a painting of a stately, big-eyed Spanish woman. It was striking. This was followed by another picture of another painting, this one a pastel of horses. These photos were of just the paintings themselves. Where they were hanging was not discernable.

OMG, he's wonderful! I allowed myself to think. Cute, and so talented. And he liked my smile. I was again thinking that this guy was just the one for me. I pictured those windy walks holding hands, visits

84

to art galleries. My imagination swung into high gear as I looked at the lovely artwork Robert had sent me. I could see his studio, smelling of oil paints and turpentine, and me sitting in a shaft of natural light while he captured my likeness for posterity. He seemed just right. I thought about what I'd write back to him, about what quaint and romantic, candlelit bistro I would suggest for our first date. I was speculating about how long my ladylike veneer would last before I just brought him home . . . Then the rational part of my mind spoke up again: *he's too good to be true*, it repeated. *Look closer.*

Something struck me as odd about the paintings he had sent, then – the styles seemed entirely distinct from one another. The abstracts looked similar, but then again, all abstracts looked the same to me. I was no art buff, but the other two, the lady and the horses, were completely unalike, from each other and from the abstracts. They didn't appear like they could've been done by the same hand, even to my uneducated eye.

I might not be the most technologically savvy person in the world – I sometimes push the wrong button on my cellphone. Ok, I frequently push the wrong button on my cellphone. But I know how to tap into the incomprehensibly vast pool of information that is the internet. So I listened to my rational mind, and copied the photos of the lovely Spanish woman and the horses onto my desktop, and called up Google Image Search, which allowed me to put a picture file in as the search condition. It then returned all the places where the picture could be found on the internet.

With the speed of megabytes per second, I discovered that the portrait of the lovely Spanish woman had been painted by a German named Christian Schad. In 1928. It was called *Sonja*. The horse painting turned out to be by Franz Marc. One could purchase a copy of it on *AllPosters.com*.

I tamped down the derisive laughter and righteous outrage of my rational mind, and again decided to take the high road. Maybe Robert wasn't trying to sell me the Brooklyn Bridge. Maybe he wasn't trying to tell me that he had painted these pictures. Perhaps he was just showing me the kind of art he liked.

So I wrote back: *I think your paintings are wonderful. I don't know a lot about art, but I have always liked abstracts because I think they allow the viewer to imagine almost whatever they like. The portrait of the lady made me think of a Pre-Raphaelite somewhat. I've never heard of Christian Schad, but I think I'd like his work.*

I'd taken an art history class with Corrine once, and the Pre-Raphaelite style was the only one I could think of at the moment. That and cubism. *Sonja* was of neither style, but if Robert was a real artist, he would correct me.

His answering email was a little bit more disjointed and poorly written than the previous one. *All the arts I sent you were my personal knowledge. The woman I did was a bank director. She wanted me to give her something splendid so that was why I gave it the look of Pre-Raphaelite. I hope you can have time someday so we chat directly as writing is not just enough for me to explain myself. You are always in my mind and I need this relationship we are creating more than life. I want to rock your world and make sure I give you unconditional feelings you would never forget.*

Robert was a liar, and didn't write English well. The fact that he had recycled my own term in his email stung me. The font on the word *pre-Raphaelite* differed from the rest of the email, so it was obvious that he had cut and pasted it from my response.

Still, I wanted so badly for him to be real. He looked just right. So I rationalized. Perhaps he wasn't American, and that was why his grammar was so poor. The older gentleman in the picture looked white, but the older lady, and the younger ladies, and some of the brothers looked like they could be of Latin stock, so perhaps English was not his first language. Maybe we were just misinterpreting each other; perhaps there was a slight language barrier. But Robert looked like he would be fluent in the universal language, so I wrote back, not accusing him, just asking for a little clarification.

I must be misunderstanding you a little. The painting I was talking about was this one: and I put in the link to the Schad painting, hanging in some museum in Berlin. *Maybe you were talking about a different one that you painted yourself.* He hadn't told me he'd painted the Mona Lisa, after all. I'd never heard of Schad, nor Franz Marc either, *AllPosters.com* be damned. Maybe it was all just a miscommunication.

He wrote back: *I read your emails over and over, joy filled my heart and wondered if in this little time you can get a lot of things about me so right. I must say you are a darling to the core. Sorry, I thought I attached the sculpture and painting I did for the woman I mentioned. You just sit down and see beyond the sky where only people with great vision can see. Your existence is becoming a testimony to not just my life but to my world and existence.*

But he didn't send the correct photos. Now, it was not only a painting but a sculpture, too. How eclectic he was in his lies. Was he trying to confess to me in his broken prose that I had found him out? *You can get a lot of things about me so right.* Was my existence becoming a testimony to his own because I could tell a hawk from a handsaw, because I knew how to use Google Image Search?

The next paragraphs of his email dragged the Almighty into the scene: *I truly feel so much joy having met you and would like you to know that my mind, heart, thoughts and feelings are all with you and can only say thank you to God for this opportunity he has given me to know you more and more. God alone can be the rewarder for every impact you created in life. I like to follow my instinct and they have never failed me completely. When I first wrote to you, my inner mind convinced me that I am befriending an angel and it is turning out to be so true.*

I hope God's angels are right there giving you protection that no one else can offer to you. Something again is telling me that we can grow bigger together if we allow God's intervention to lead the way for us. Please, I can't automatically read your mind, I want to be so open and let you know that you caught every feelings that I preserved for that special person who I intend to unconditionally love and care for. Again, I have held you in high esteem ever since we started this communication and will forever reserve this holy place in my life for you if you choose to live and dwell here.

Right, I thought. *God and his angels guard your sacred throne and make you long become it!* Except Robert was obviously grammatically incapable of quoting Shakespeare, whether through foreignness or ignorance or both. At least I was spared that.

Robert was a liar, and while my rational mind guffawed at how close I'd come to being sucked in to his lies, I felt as betrayed and outraged as if he'd lied to my face, instead of just anonymously. Electronically. I'd allowed myself to have quite a little hope about this one, had imagined a cute-couple-ness, something that existed outside of the bedroom, which was the core of what I was seeking from a real man. And he'd turned out to be worse than the horny boys and the long distance lonely hearts looking for money. He was a liar, spinning so much more than just little lies about how old he was, like Gerry had done. Robert had spun monumental lies, claiming art from dead Germans as his own. The smiling, sexy man in the pictures probably wasn't even him, wasn't the person typing the rambling, disjointed, worshipful gobbledygook of the emails.

I was disgusted with Robert, whoever he was, whatever he really looked like, for thinking that anyone could be so stupid as to not figure out he was a fraud. But I'd gone for it, just because I wanted to believe that such an interesting, good-looking man could exist in the real world. Not only could he exist, it seemed, he was available. If I wouldn't have Googled those paintings . . . I was disgusted most of all with myself for almost falling for it. I was disgusted with myself for feeling so much hope, so completely, so quickly. The idea struck me that perhaps all the good men were already taken by the time they reached my age. All that seemed to be left were scamsters and weirdos. I was too smart to be a victim, but because I was their age and single, did that mean I was a weirdo, too?

My phone rang, and I answered it, at the same time deleting all the messages from Robert as quickly as I could, as if they might infect my computer somehow. It was Iris on the phone, and she asked me if I might come over and visit her, if I wasn't busy. Gratefully, I told her that I would be right there.

TWENTY-ONE

On the sidewalk about a block from *Mohini's*, I just happened to glance over at a newspaper box, and was amazed to see Gerry's picture on the front page. I bought the paper and continued on to the occult bookstore. When I entered, I smiled at Iris and again asked her how things were going with her new boyfriend, just to see whether or not she'd heard the news.

Iris sighed, looked at her blue-nailed fingertips. "Things with Gerry didn't work out," she said and sighed again, met my eyes. "It turns out that young Gerry is married."

I blinked rapidly, attempting to hide my shock. *"Married?"*

Iris pursed her lips and nodded. "I was supposed to meet him after nine last night, but I was in the neighborhood before then – he lives in *The Palms Apartments*, over there by Mt. Rubidoux. I thought I would surprise him by showing up a little early. As I approached his door, I saw a very pretty young woman leaving his apartment, and I thought I was finally going to get to meet the sister he'd talked so much about.

"I smiled and said hi, asked if she was indeed Gerry's sister. She told me that Gerry didn't have a sister – she was his wife, and they'd only been married for about six months. Without a trace of suspicion, the poor thing asked me how I knew her husband. I thought fast, Rae, and with hardly a pause or stammer, I immediately came up with a foolproof lie.

"Her husband had ordered a gift for her, I said. I'd thought that he'd said it was for his sister, but now that she told me he didn't have a sister, I realized that of course, he must've said that the present was for his wife. The old hearing just isn't what it used to be. Her gift had come in that very day, and since my business is small, I told her, I make all the gift deliveries myself. I told her I was just making sure that I had the address correct; I'd left the bauble in the car. But when we went back to the car to retrieve her husband's thoughtful present, I discovered to my embarrassed chagrin that I'd somehow left it behind at the shop. Silly me.

"The young woman said that it was okay. She'd only stopped in home for a few hours today, and she was now leaving town again. She thanked me for my pains and told me she was sure she'd be delighted with her present when she came back. She told me she was frequently out of town because she was a stewardess."

"A flight attendant," I corrected gently.

"Whatever." Iris sighed. "When Gerry called me later that night, wondering why I hadn't shown up for our date, I . . . broke it off."

"Seems like it's been a bad weekend for Gerry in a lot of ways," I said, and held up the paper. Below the fold was a picture of Gerry in a hospital gown, accompanied by the headline, *Local Man Claims Coyote Attack.*

I read the article to Iris. "'A Riverside man was hospitalized in serious condition after what he claims was an attack by three coyotes in the 4500 block of Palm Avenue at approximately 9:45 last night. Gerald Adkins, thirty-two, told police and paramedics that he was attacked by the three predators as he went to enter his car, parked on the street. "I heard a howl, and then a couple of yips, then another howl, and then they jumped me," he said. "They came out of nowhere, and they were biting and tearing at me. If I hadn't already had the car unlocked, they would've killed me. I know it."

"'Adkins managed to get inside his car and call 911. He was treated for lacerations to his shoulder, arm, thigh, and groin area, and blood loss resulting from the bites. Doctors are also performing tests for rabies.

"'A spokesman for the Riverside County Department of Animal Control stated that Mr. Adkins must be misidentifying dogs for coyotes. "There haven't been any coyotes in that area since the construction of the Ryan Bonaminio Park at the bottom of the hill. Many breeds of dogs can be mistaken for coyotes. I'm sure that in the danger of the moment, Mr. Adkins just made a mistake." The official said that a sweep of the area turned up neither dogs nor coyotes, but that more sweeps would be initiated in the coming days.'" I looked up at Iris.

"That's ridiculous," she said. "There are still plenty of coyotes in the river bottom. They've just moved a little farther on, since the park was built. All one has to do is call them." When my eyebrows went up in surprise at that, she continued quickly, "Well . . . what I mean is . . . coyotes are known for their perception. Perhaps they could smell what an utter waste of humanity Gerry was and decided to do us all a favor by dining on him."

I considered that, mourning the fact that I didn't know where Robert lived. He was another utter waste of humanity. "Perhaps this experiment in online dating is a failure after all," I said. "You got a flesh and blood adulterer, and all I get are boys and thieves and liars." My phone beeped, and I handed the newspaper to Iris. She set it aside without looking at it. I took my phone out of my purse. "Speak of the devil."

"It's not often wise," Iris replied.

I had no response to that, so I opened the text on my phone. OkCupid was informing me that I had a new message. I looked at it. It was the last straw.

The picture was of a fresh-faced, smiling young man, probably no more than thirty-two, as had been our lying, cheating, now-bit-in-the-groin-by-called-coyotes Gerry.

Hello, how are you? I'm Andy and am incredibly intrigued! I was wondering if you might be the kind of woman I am hoping to meet? Not only are you amazingly attractive, but you seem like the type of person I am drawn to: intelligent, fun, mature, passionate and who has class. I LOVE that you're a fire sign! I hope that means you have the personality that goes along with it: assertive, take-charge, ENJOYS being in control, a powerful alpha female . . . dominant ☺ is this you?

"In fact," I said to Iris, "as soon as I answer this one last message, I'm through with this experiment. What about you?"

Iris nodded.

I wrote back to Andy: *You look entirely too cute to be on this site. Could it be because you're a pervert? I haven't had any messages from any out and out freaks yet, so yours gives me pause – are you looking for a dominatrix? Because you are most assuredly barking up the wrong tree if that's the case. I'm looking for a man that has more guts than me, not the other way around. Is that you? If not, I understand there are sites exclusively for sniveling little bastards such as yourself. I don't think they're free, however. Why don't you go join one of those and leave normal women alone?*

Not only did Andy not reply to my message, but OkCupid regretfully informed me a few seconds later that he had deleted his profile. He would probably create another one, just like Gerry undoubtedly would, as soon as he recovered from the coyote attack. And Robert would send pictures of his purloined artworks to other dupes.

Just what is their motivation? I wondered. Perhaps other women didn't have as rich and varied and complete a fantasy life as Iris and I were fortunate enough to have. Perhaps most women wanted to believe these fanciful lies so much that there were more than enough men out there to supply them. But my fantasy dance card was full, overflowing. I was appalled and disgusted by all these men willing to tell me everything that they believed I wanted to hear – how wonderful I was, how wonderful they were – was it all just a game to solicit money or some kind of sexual encounter?

91

When I signed up for this, I figured that sex would result eventually, but that hadn't been my initial goal – I'd just been looking for a regular guy, someone normal – not too young, not too old, not an artist or a movie star or a poet – just a regular guy, just like I featured myself to be a regular gal. For friendship, companionship, maybe even love. But it was not to be. These guys were all out for the quick lay or the fast buck and they would say anything to accomplish it. I was through. The experiment was a failure.

"Goodbye, OkCupid," I said to Iris and deleted my profile.

"Goodbye, real men," Iris replied, then added, "and good riddance."

"Speaking of which, I have something I want to show you. Do you have a laptop?"

"In the office."

"Go get it. This'll only take three minutes and thirty-five seconds, but it's . . . *it's awesome.*"

I played the video to *My Disgrace* for Iris, and when it was over, she just blinked her big eyes at me, expressionlessly. Seeing that I expected some reaction, she said, "It's really not my kind of music, Rae. I'm–"

"Not the music, Iris! The man!"

"Oh!" She looked at the laptop. "Perhaps we should play it again."

I ejected the disk and returned it to its case. "It's okay. If you didn't get it the first time, there's no sense making you sit through it again." Iris was no more impressed with Rolling Blackout's singer than Amy had been.

"The place looked familiar," Iris said hopefully. "But the man . . . he's not really my type, Rae. I prefer them a little bit more slender. Maybe a little taller. Fair-haired. Like–"

"Like Brad Pitt in *Fight Club*. I know." There was absolutely no point in arguing with Iris over the merits of world-famous, skinny, chipped-toothed, insane anarchist Brad Pitt in the Oscar-nominated *Fight Club* vs not famous, leather-jacket clad, snakeskin-boot shod, guitar-playing, black-haired, absolutely luscious Wes Thomerville in the hometown production of a cheesy music video that perhaps only his wife and a handful of diehard fans had ever seen. It would be like trying to teach a pig to sing: it made you look foolish and annoyed the pig.

"Would you like a drink, Rae?"

"It's four o'clock in the afternoon, Iris."

"But it's Saturday, my friend, and the sun is over the yardarm." She gestured around the store. "This place is dead. There's a nice little bar down the street called *Mickey's*. Very friendly."

92

"Mickey's?" I held up the DVD case and pointed at the back.

"Yes. That's the place."

"They filmed this there. The video, too."

"I thought the setting was familiar." Iris looked at me in alarm, as if she thought I might make her watch the video again. "Do you want to see it? Get a drink?"

I nodded. Then just to irk Iris, I added like a schoolgirl, "You don't suppose he drinks there, do you? Since that's where his band started out?"

"I've never seen him there."

I grinned at her. "Would you remember him if you had?"

"Oh. Yeah. Sure, Rae. He's attractive. He's just—"

"Not your type. I know."

Mickey's was a bright, airy bar, several steps above *The Beachcomber* on the ladder of success. I wondered why Rolling Blackout played there instead of here, but on further consideration, I figured that while the thirty or so people on hand for their sets at the smaller place seemed like a crowd, it would've been a meager gathering in this larger bar.

A bubbly, lovely young waitress kept 'em coming, and Iris and I got drunk. We talked of the mistake that had been our foray into the online dating world, the world of real men. We talked of the real men we had known, the Devins and Jays and Chets and Florida coast pirates, the Troys and Wes Thomervilles and all the good ones that we'd let get away. We toasted the Great Mother, and I had to stop Iris from pouring a libation onto the floor.

Then suddenly, out of the blue, Iris and I reconsidered our reconsideration of real men. Behind us, seated at a table with his not-attractive fellows was a veritable silver fox, tall and slim. He arose and traveled to the back of *Mickey's* probably three times in the space of an hour and a half. Each time he smiled and nodded at us, and Iris and I smiled and nodded back.

"Where is he going?" Iris asked me. "Is there gambling in the back? An opium den, perhaps?" She giggled and sipped her drink.

"The only thing in the back are the bathrooms," I said, as I had visited the ladies' once already myself. My uncle, he of the fondness for Grasshoppers, had often said, *You never buy beer, you only borrow it.* But I reflected that three visits in so short of time was excessive, even for a beer drinker, and I wondered aloud to Iris if the handsome gentleman might be afflicted with prostate problems.

I told her that I'd had an anatomy teacher that had informed the class that if I man lives long enough, the organ would mean his end, eventually. This elicited another giggle from Iris. "Yet another reason for us to forgo them in the flesh." She gestured at the man as he passed us again. "Could you imagine having to put up with that?"

I thought about Devin, a young man unable to drink, and Chet, a man my own age who couldn't get it up, and this man, a little bit older than me, who had to visit the bathroom more often than me. All these realities were quite tiresome to me.

"Father Time brings them all low in the end," Iris said, and picked up her glass. "Shall we drink to that irony? To a problem we shall never have?" We clinked glasses and shared a somewhat ill-mannered laugh.

Iris and I had a great time. We didn't close the place – we were far too old for that, and we had started drinking at four in the afternoon. By nine, we weaved back up the sidewalk to *Mohini's*, completely plastered. Once inside, Iris called me a cab. I wouldn't be driving anywhere in this state.

"No ritual tonight," Iris advised with a slur and she poured me into the taxi. "The invisible realms require an un-fuddled head."

"No ritual tonight," I repeated in agreement. "I'd burn the house down."

The cab stopped in front of my house and I threw a couple of twenties at the driver. I bumped unsteadily inside, then up the steps to my bedroom. I stepped with exaggerated caution over the chalked lines on the floor, then collapsed onto the bed fully clothed, thinking it would be easier to get undressed if I was lying down. It wasn't, but I managed somehow. I looked over at the fiasco on the night table, saw two bottles instead of only one. Iris was right. No potion tonight. I rolled over onto my stomach as a good drunk always should, and immediately passed out.

Somewhere near dawn, Wes Thomerville came to me in my dreams. Everything about our brief encounter was intensely real – it was as if I had indeed taken a draught of the magical potion. Wes looked like himself and smelled like Devin and kissed like Jay and fucked like something I'd never experienced before, like something out of this world. The dream was the best, most life-like, most astonishing thing *ever*, better than real life, better than any previous sex dream, better than anything gotten through Iris's potion. Mere words fail to address the unimaginable ecstasy, the ultimate release. I woke up out of breath, panting, feeling like I was twenty-two again, disbelieving that something so powerfully lifelike and satisfying had been the product of my own mind and body, innocent of any magical preparations.

All the wonderfulness lasted until I blinked at the sunlight and the hangover hit me like a freight train, an avalanche, a ton of bricks. Any and all heavy-object clichés. A ball-peen hammer beat erratically in my head; my brain was a shriveled cabbage floating in acid, banging painfully into the suddenly angular insides of my skull every time I moved my head. There was a reason why I didn't get anywhere near the neighborhood of falling-down drunk anymore, and this was it.

I crawled to the bathroom and swallowed three aspirins, added another one just for good measure, then staggered to the kitchen for coffee. It was not until several hours later, when the worst of the hangover had subsided, that I allowed myself to contemplate the incredible dream.

Had it been induced by my unaccustomed alcohol intake? I thought not. There was a latent fuzziness to it that I imagined wouldn't have been there had I not been drinking – it might even have been more spectacular had I been sober. I wondered if the potion had somehow accumulated in my brain, like some kind of reverse tolerance – was I going to be able to experience these things without it now?

The dream had appeared randomly. It wasn't like I'd been concentrating on Wes before I'd fallen into drunken unconsciousness. Maybe it was just my turn for a great sex dream. They were as rare as hen's teeth: I'd enjoyed perhaps only five of six in my entire life. None as great as this one, admittedly, but it had happened before.

I sat around the house all day, immobile from the lingering effects of the hangover, remembering the incredible dream. But of course, some things – like sex and sex dreams and fear and a good meal – can only be remembered. They can't be relived. That's why there are so many people in the world, and why Hollywood keeps making the same horror movies over and over, and why there are so many fine dining establishments. One can remember that one enjoyed such things, but it's impossible to call up the actual, visceral experience, no matter how well the details are remembered. And just like with any dream, the details of this one were already beginning to fade.

I didn't perform the ritual that night. I had to go to work in the morning after all, and I was sticking to my plan of only indulging on Friday and Saturday nights, even if the online dating trip was no longer going to interfere with my fantasy life. I wanted to make sure all lingering effects of my binge drinking spree had dissipated, too, before the next time. I made up my mind to wait all the way until next Friday night, and looked forward to the experience all week with as much relish as if I actually had a date with Wes Thomerville in the flesh.

Who needed real men, after all? It seemed that at this stage in life, they were all freaks and perverts and liars, anyway. At least the ones that wanted to talk to me. I still experienced a very real discomfort when I thought about being all alone for the rest of my existence on this plane, but by the same token, I wasn't prepared to settle for a weirdo, just to keep from being alone. And I had friends and family, did I not? And I had Iris's potion and my own spectacular dreams to keep me warm at night. Maybe that was just going to have to be enough.

TWENTY-TWO

On Thursday, I called Darlene and told her that I would be a no-show at *The Beachcomber*, due to dinner plans with Iris again. She asked me if I might want to bring my friend along some time, and I told her that unfortunately, Iris and Amy were of a similar mind about Wes and the video to *My Disgrace*.

"There's no accounting for taste," Darlene said.

The night that Amy had introduced us to surprisingly-familiar-looking Alex, the girls and I had watched *Rolling Blackout's Hometown Debut* in its entirety after she left. I noticed that the drummer in the movie and in the video to *My Disgrace* was not the same guy that performed with them now. I worked the conversation around to this, my mind on the possibility of accidental demon-summoning when I played the video from within the sacred circle. Darlene said she didn't know what had happened to the original drummer, but Paige would know. She was the resident expert on Rolling Blackout, had interrogated the bartender at *The Beachcomber*, had researched the director of *Rolling Blackout's Hometown Debut* on the internet. She'd even dared to say a few words to Mrs. Thomerville. If anyone would know it would be Paige.

She gave me Paige's number and I texted her. I said hi and told her I'd heard she had a new boyfriend. She wrote back that he hadn't worked out at all, and I told her I was sorry to hear that. I didn't have to wait long for her to bring up her favorite band.

Are you coming with us on Friday?

I'm gonna have to miss one more set, I wrote back. *But I've been watching the movie, & I noticed that the drummer in it is different than the one that plays w/ them now. Do u kno what happened to him?*

Paige did not disappoint. *I asked Wes about that once, and he said they all work together, and the guy from the video got transferred to a different town so they had to get a new drummer.*

Awesome, I thought. So the guy wasn't dead, and therefore there was nothing stopping me from using the cheesy video in the rite to my heart's content. I told Paige that I would no doubt see her next Friday.

TWENTY-THREE

So with extra anticipation, I touched up the chalked circle, lit the candles, invoked the beneficence of the Great Mother on Friday night. I swallowed a healthy dollop of the potion and put Wes Thomerville's video on repeat. The ensuing vision was spectacular as always. I had not one criticism. Except that it wasn't anywhere nearly as glorious as the dream which my mind had created the week before, on its own, sans potion.

I visited Iris bright and early the next morning, and after all the customers had left the store, I told her that I had a complaint about one of her products.

She blinked expressionlessly at me. "I'm just kidding, Iris," I said, "What could I possibly have to complain about?" I explained about the dream I'd had after we'd celebrated our freedom from the bonds of online dating. I compared it to the same subject matter under consideration via her potion the night before, and told her that I'd found the latter experience lacking.

Iris shrugged. "Alcohol also opens the doors of perception, Rae, albeit not as profoundly nor as consistently as ritual. How many of our greatest poets, authors, artists, conceived their visions while blitzed out of their minds?"

"In your professional opinion, are you recommending that I give up the ritual and become an alcoholic?"

Iris smiled and shook her head. "The chances of your singer returning to you in your dreams again just because you're drunk are slim. Like you say, maybe it was just your turn for a good one, all on your own."

"But—"

"Here's what we learn about these things in Witchy 101," Iris said and grinned at me. "Try this exercise. Once you've lit the candles and invoked the Goddess, once you are within the sacred circle, just picture your consummate mate. Your already know what he looks like, right?

"Because you used the sobriquet *awesome,* I'm going to assume that it's that dark-haired guy? From that blessedly brief video? I'm going to assume that you've at last moved into the modern day, that you've decided to forego the 1980s?" Iris smiled at me. "You know what he looks like, how he sings, right? Now picture how he'd sound if he whispered to you, how he'd taste and smell. Open your mind to all the possibilities – allow your mind to build him for you. Skip the audio/visual aids for a while, Rae. See what your subconscious comes up with."

What Iris was suggesting was just like Amy's little exercise. She smiled at the thoughtful look on my face. "Give it a try. I guarantee results, or your money back."

That night I did the ritual again and concentrated on the perfect man, who resembled Wes Thomerville quite a bit. But Iris's suggestion produced no results. Zip. Zilch. Zero. Nada. Nothing. Her iron-clad guarantee was as good as the paper it was written on. I woke up in the middle of the night, dreamless. I worried that the potion might be losing its effect. Then what would I have? No real men and no fantasy men either. The candles had gone out and I spoke aloud into the darkness. "I would sell my soul for another dream just like–"

"Don't say that. Don't ever say that." The voice seemed to come out of the very air – dark, rich, deep, like spiced mead. It caressed my ear, warmed that soul I'd just been ready to put up for sale.

Once upon a time, I would've thought I was losing my mind, hearing voices in the darkness. Or I would've been petrified with fear, believing that there was an armed intruder hiding in the shadows. But from the glimpses of other planes that Iris had shown me, I knew that the voice was neither in my head nor did I have anything to fear, as long as I remained within the sacred circle.

But I was sure that I'd been circumspect in my research – could I have missed a dead actor? But, too, it had been a few weeks since I'd lit the candles and performed the ritual with any old television shows. Perhaps the original drummer in Rolling Blackout's video had come to some unfortunate end after all – perhaps Wes had lied to his fan about what had happened to the guy. Perhaps I had again summoned an annoying, destructive demon. But wouldn't it have manifested this morning, instead of waiting until now?

And the first one hadn't spoken to me. Iris had said that it might, might say unkind things in a raspy, demonic voice. But this voice was like honey: smooth, full – I could listen to this voice forever. And it was not saying unkind things. It was warning me not to offer up my immortal soul in exchange for a sex dream. Which *had* been a little impulsive of me, I reflected.

I was not religious, and was not quite clear on the concept of my soul, anyway. Could I really sell it? Could I buy it back? If I decided that I didn't like the deal, was there a three day period in which I could change my mind and ask for its return? What changes would I notice in everyday life if I was walking around, no longer in possession of it? Perhaps I should've considered all these things, found out the answers to these questions, before I had so cavalierly offered the thing up for sale.

But I hadn't sold it, had I? No buyer had appeared, no deal had been struck. Because the mellifluous voice in the darkness had stopped me.

The Caterpillar from *Alice in Wonderland* came to mind. I said, "Who are you?"

"Would you believe me if I told you?" the voice replied.

Could it be . . . Satan? Dana Carvey's Church Lady said in my head.

"Try me," I said.

"What is *thy* name?" the voice asked.

"I asked you first," I said. Iris had warned me about giving too much personal information to incorporeal beings. Sure, I liked its voice . . . but God only knew what it looked like. *That was a unique turn of phrase in this situation,* I thought. I was talking to an extra-natural being, something I suspected was another demon, similar to the one I'd inadvertently called the first time. I believed in demons, had seen one with my own eyes. But did I believe in God?

"Who has led thee to this sacred circle?" the voice asked. "Who is thy teacher?"

I wasn't going to give up Iris's name, either. Then the thing might go and pester her, for all I knew. Then she'd be pissed with me. She'd probably have to do all sorts of banishing rituals, taking time away from her business and her own traipses down the potion-fueled lane in order to rid herself of the thing.

"Who are you?" I asked the voice again.

"I see you are ignorant about a great many of the things with which you meddle," the voice said, with just a touch of exasperation. "But I can also glean from the craft of your circle that the one who is thy teacher is not another novice like thyself. Tell that one that a minion of Asmodeus has spoken to you. Your teacher will explain." The voice laughed then, a rumbling, throaty sound. "If you feel froggy after learning who I am, and feel inclined to jump, simply ensconce yourself again within this ring of safety and invoke my presence. Perhaps I will even allow you to see me then." The thing again laughed. "In the meantime, go with God."

The atmosphere in the darkness seemed to alter, and I knew that I was once again alone. The conversation was anachronistic: all thee's and thou's and then that remark about being froggy and feeling inclined to jump. I was curious as to what the thing was.

I was a little bit afraid: Iris had said that there were beings that could definitely harm me in the invisible world, but this one didn't seem like one of those. But then Robert had seemed like an okey-dokey dude until I discovered his lies. I hadn't seen this thing, didn't know why it had spoken to me, where it had come from. I couldn't imagine what its intention toward me could possibly be. But still I was curious.

TWENTY-FOUR

I again appeared at *Mohini's House of Dreams* first thing in the morning. Again I waited until the shop emptied of customers. I stood at the counter and blinked silently at Iris.

"Have you come to tell me of the glories of your subconscious mind unbound?" she asked. "Did you see your perfect man?"

I shook my head. "I didn't *see* anything. Question. Who is Asmodeus, and who are his minions?"

Iris's mouth fell open and now *she* blinked silently at *me*. Then she regained her composure, and playing it close to the vest like she always did, she answered my question with a question. "Why do you ask?"

"The potion was a washout last night. I did what you said, entered the circle and concentrated on all the details of Mr. Right. But there was no vision, no dream. I woke up in the middle of the night, somewhat disgruntled, and wished that I could have that one dream again."

Iris seized on this confession. "You spoke your wish? Out loud?"

I pursed my lips. I guess I was gonna have to tell her exactly what I'd said. If she then tried to convince me that Satan himself had manifested in my little bedroom, I was prepared not to believe her. I was fairly prepared not to believe her. "I said, *I would sell my soul for another dream just like* . . . but before I could finish the sentence, a deep, masculine voice told me not to say that. Not to ever say that." I looked fearfully at her. "Was it . . .?"

"Of course not," Iris said immediately, dismissively. "The Prince of Darkness is not waiting around in the wings of every suburban housewife's bedroom, hand cocked to ear, waiting for a chance to bargain for souls. You've seen too many movies, Rae. Too much of *The Devil and Dan'l Webster*. Too much of *The Picture of Dorian Gray.*"

"Well, that takes a load off my mind."

"Damnation isn't about selling your soul, Rae. It isn't really about you at all. It's about the crimes you commit against others. If you know in your heart that something you've done is wrong, then that's a step on the road to damnation. If you accept that it's wrong, but you don't care, that's another step. If you repent, atone, then that's a step back."

She waited for me to say something to that, and when I didn't, she continued. "Surely, there are devils and demons and evil people in life, pointing you in the wrong directions, trying to get you on the path to damnation. But you have to go there on your own, Rae. You're not tricked, not duped. Not generally. Because if you take a false step, then you can always repent, atone, show remorse. But if you make a decision that hurts someone, and you make it consciously . . . then you're on the road to damnation."

I blinked at her, nonplussed. "You mean like breaking the Ten Commandments? The seven deadly sins?"

Iris shook her head. "Some of those are universal truths – *Thou shalt not murder*, for example. But not all of them are universal – you have to take the wheat with the chaff with all religions, in my experience. Many aspects are more for keeping the congregation in line than for saving their souls. There is the patriarchal nature of most faiths, the core idea of most that women are possessions, to be taken and owned and protected from thieves of chastity. Your chastity belonged to your father, then your husband, Rae. Some admonishments and prohibitions are just ridiculous, nowadays, wouldn't you agree? I believe you've already dismissed the one about coveting thy neighbor's husband. I don't believe that you consider that wrong, a sin, to lust over your young co-worker in your heart and mind."

"I do not." Because I did not. I wasn't hurting anyone having a warm feeling for Troy. What we may or may not have done under the influence of Iris's potion, all unaware, was pushing it a little bit, perhaps, but I'd repented. I felt remorseful about that. I'd never do such a thing again. "I don't believe that lust, in and of itself, is sinful. It's a motivation of the species, just like hunger and thirst."

"Of course lust isn't a sin," Iris said, "because there's not a damn thing wrong with it. There are no commandments against in specifically, now are there? But what about actions motivated by lust? That's why there's the commandment against coveting, and the one against adultery – to keep the sheep in line. Thou shalt not covet, because coveting in the weak can lead to adultery – if you set out to steal this young man away from his darling little wife as a result of your lust and covetousness, if you were a homewrecker, an adulterer, how would that rate on your Sin-O-Meter?"

"That would be wrong," I agreed.

"The adultery – not the lust or the coveting."

I nodded. "I didn't always feel that way. Once upon a time, I used to think, if some woman couldn't keep her husband at home, that wasn't my fault. But now . . ."

"You'd feel guilt, were you to purposefully break the seventh commandment? In your dotage, you agree, thou shalt not commit adultery?"

I nodded.

"Guilt is the most reliable marker of sin, Rae. If you feel guilty, if you feel like you've hurt someone in some way, then you probably have. If you feel sorry about what you've done, if you atone . . . then your soul won't be damned." Iris grinned in delight. "I've basically distilled all of Christianity for you with this one principle."

"The Golden Rule? Do unto others as you would have them do unto you?"

Iris nodded. I reflected. My guilt level was at an ebb at present. I didn't feel as though I'd unrepentantly hurt anybody lately. "What has all this got to do with the voice in my room last night?"

Iris shrugged. "I was just illustrating for you why the Devil isn't hanging around, waiting for you to offer to sell your soul. It just doesn't work that way. It wasn't Satan that spoke to you."

"He said he *was a minion of Asmodeus.*"

"Indeed?" Iris grinned and held up one blue-lacquered fingernail, then disappeared behind the velvet curtain into the office. She returned with her laptop. "Let's see. Asmodeus. Classification of demons . . . seven deadly sins . . . here we go. *Asmodeus is the demon of lust and is therefore responsible for twisting people's sexual desires. Demonologists asserted that his zodiacal sign was Aquarius but only between the dates of January 30 and February 8. He has 72 legions of demons under his command. Asmodeus' reputation as the personification of lust continued into later writings, as he was known as the 'Prince of Lechery' in a 16th century romance. The 16th century Dutch demonologist Johann Weyer described him as the banker at the baccarat table in Hell, and overseer of earthly gambling houses. In 1641–*"

"Where are you getting all this?" I asked. "And what does it have to do with me? Are you saying I summoned – "

"No. Not any more than you summoned Satan himself." Iris turned the computer around and showed me the entry for Asmodeus on *Wikipedia.*

"I was expecting a little more eldritch a reference," I said doubtfully.

Iris looked at me in surprise. "The *Malleus Maleficarum* perhaps? The *Witches' Hammer?* It's all right here, Rae. *Wikipedia* is a great compendium. They don't miss much. Here you go: *in the Malleus Maleficarum (1486), Asmodeus was also considered the demon of lust.*"

"What are you telling me, Iris?"

"Besides advising you not to barter your soul, what else did this voice say?"

"*Tell your teacher that you have spoken to a minion of Asmodeus. Your teacher will explain.* You're not explaining."

Iris laughed, looked down at the counter, shook her head. "You're something, you know that, Rae? You've come in here all along, just asking me questions – you've always been game. Never afraid. Just curious. You're an innocent in your lack of preconceived beliefs. You're just natural demon-bait."

"Demon-bait?"

Again she shook her head in amazement. *"A minion of Asmodeus.* Some women go their whole lives, their whole magical careers, wishing, hoping, praying. Doing rituals, sacrifices, invocations. Studying the ancient writings, pledging their souls . . . Quite without even trying, you've summoned an incubus, Rae. You lucky, lucky girl."

"You can't be serious."

The bell over the door tinkled. Three quite witchy looking women entered: one was fifty if she was a day, and fighting Father Time every step. She wore a purple turban and matching muumuu. The other two were probably a few years older than Darlene. One of them was holding an adorable, red-headed toddler. Iris greeted them, then she said to me, "Here, take the computer. Go sit in the window. I'll be in the back for a few minutes. Google it. I-N-C–"

"I know how to spell it."

"After they leave, you can tell me what you've learned. The internet is a far more comprehensive teacher than I could be."

I might be an innocent, I thought, and *demon-bait,* whatever that was, but I'd heard of an incubus before. *Dictionary.com* confirmed what I already knew: an incubus was *an imaginary demon or evil spirit supposed to descend upon sleeping persons, especially one fabled to have sexual intercourse with women during their sleep. In the Middle Ages, their existence was recognized by law.*

A Google search for the term returned about 5,510,000 results in 0.13 seconds. I heard laughter from behind the velvet curtain – but Iris wouldn't be talking about me, would she? I was just imagining that they were talking about me. Iris wouldn't be telling strangers that I was *demon-bait.* Would she?

By scrolling through just a few pages of the search, I was able to skim the surface of the five million results. The pertinent info on the *imaginary demon or evil spirit* could be divided neatly into four categories.

One – there was the fiction, tales about various and sundry undeniably irresistible demon lovers. I skimmed – the excerpts were all just romances, bodice-rippers with leathery wings and forked tails. I didn't need idealized, love-story fiction; I was *demon-bait.* I needed to find out what I had inadvertently summoned.

Two – there were the unemotional, scholarly treatises. *Wikipedia* cited sources and etymology and said *Religious tradition holds that repeated intercourse with an incubus or succubus may result in the deterioration of health, or even death.*

But what a way to go, I thought churlishly.

Psychology Today explained the entire phenomenon away as sleep paralysis. In those twilight moments between sleep and wakefulness, people sometimes imagined that there was an entity sitting or lying on them, and coupled with natural, physical cycles of sexual arousal during sleep, fear and cultural guilt – there was your sex demon. The same phenomenon supposedly was at the root of alien abduction stories. But I hadn't been paralyzed, nothing had sat on me, nothing had tried to abduct me. It had only spoken to me, in that dark, deep, beguiling voice. I had felt neither afraid, safe within my circle, nor guilty in the least.

Third was the religious take. The page I landed on told the anecdote of a godly matron. Alone in her bedroom one night, sexy thoughts suddenly invaded her mind. The thoughts turned downright vulgar. And then, before she could even offer up a chaste prayer of repentance, filthy speculations, sexual questions popped into her head – the demon was manipulating her mind, talking dirty to her. Before she knew it, the incubus manifested, all black wings and blue skin, and raped her repeatedly, violently.

Another church-going young wife awoke in the middle of the night, thinking her normally reserved husband was feeling uncharacteristically forward – but oh, no! It wasn't her husband! It looked a little like him, but it was demonic in its ardor, its roughness! It laughed when she screamed!

Then the analysis seemed as though it was talking directly to me. First it chided the scientifically minded – saying that those of us who believed in evolution or the Big Bang – we could believe that everything came from nothing, but we balked at believing in evil spirits that had intercourse with people?

Okay, Reverend My-Way-or-the-Highway-to-Hell. You've got my attention. I never believed in any of this stuff, once upon a time. But I've danced with the dead, have experienced preternaturally enhanced fantasies. I've seen one demon, and I've definitely heard something else. Proceed.

He explained how evil ancient cults once used rituals to achieve sinful sexual ecstasy. Nowadays, these things were reached through the use of technology – the internet, television, movies. But it was really all the same godless thing. I wondered what he would think of the combination of ancient rituals *and* modern technology that I used.

He stated simply that those of us sinners who spent an evening viewing pornographic material (well . . . I wouldn't consider *MacGyver* exactly pornographic), those of us who attempted to enhance this activity with a few drinks, or Lord have mercy, drugs – we were all damned. Because attempting to achieve any kind of sexual feelings that were not within the bonds of holy matrimony was a sin. And the proof was what happened after we attempted these solitary fantasies. If we should be fortunate enough to afterward have incredible dreams, if we woke up hot, sticky, drained – he didn't say *feeling good,* but I supplied that myself – it was a good chance what we'd experienced weren't dreams at all – we had actually been defiled by a phantom, a demonic entity.

Not yet, I thought.

My fantasies, which I'd been enjoying since I'd been old enough to think them, were in reality dark and unacceptable sins, according to the pastor. Such thoughts were the wrack and ruin of a sterling character. An exercise in which good, upstanding, God-fearing people simply did not engage. My fantasies were what had brought me an incubus, and I must needs repent immediately, lest my immortal soul be damned by my own hellacious, though completely imaginary, appetites.

The demons are real, the pastor told me – they're out for my soul, because I'm a sinner to start out with. My only path to redemption was to give up these evil dreams, to take the chaste and repentant road to Heaven.

Whatever. The reverend was selling, but I wasn't buying. My journeys in the world of fantasy had never hurt anyone, me least of all. I reflected that the pastor would consider me a lost cause – not only wasn't I game to give up my fantasies, I'd almost offered up my soul for a chance at a repeat of just one of these sinful dreams.

My evil fantasies had first led me to my evil occult friend and her extra-natural means to achieve even better fantasies. And all my longings for a repeat of the out-of-this-world sex dream had led me to think of bargaining with that soul that I wasn't sure I even possessed, or would miss if I sold it.

But on the other hand, it hadn't been some sanctimonious pastor's voice that had stopped that transaction. It had been something else entirely.

Perhaps the reverend was right after all. Perhaps all these dabblings had indeed summoned an incubus, Asmodeus's minion. A sex demon. Iris surely thought so.

Well, hot damn.

I couldn't see anything wrong with that just yet; I actually thought it was a pretty cool trick, seeing as how I hadn't even been trying. Iris had said that not all of the entities that approached the sacred circle

107

were out to hurt me. I just had to ascertain what the give and take was. What did the dark silky voice want from me? Was I willing to give it?

The fourth category of thought on the sex demon debate came to me courtesy of the Church of Satan. Their site provided invocations for summoning your very own incubus or succubus. Once summoned, the entity could become one's lifelong companion, it said. The demon was no harder to call, no harder to bid and to keep, and no more dangerous than the family dog, according to them.

I agreed with the Bible-thumpers and the Satanists equally on one point: these creatures were real. I hadn't imagined that flaming-headed thing, and I surely hadn't imagined that honeyed voice in the darkness. After that, my opinions diverged. I felt absolutely no guilt about my dirty thoughts, so if such activity had led me to this creature, then perhaps I had lucked out, as Iris had indicated. But I doubted if it was entirely roses and orgasms as the Satanists wanted me to believe, either – perhaps there might be a little more to the care and feeding of an incubus than there was to the family Chihuahua.

I closed the computer and waited for Iris to conclude her witchy convocation in the office. I was sure she'd show me the middle ground. The truth. Not long afterwards, my teacher emerged with the three women, all still laughing and talking. She bid them farewell, and they didn't look curiously at me as they passed out of the store. I'd been being paranoid in thinking that Iris might have been talking about me.

"What have you learned?" she asked from behind the counter, across the store.

I left the window seat. I wasn't going to shout across *Mohini's* to her about this, even if the place was empty. "I learned that you and I are damned, because giving in to one's fantasies is a sin, and how much more of a sin must it be to cultivate them the way we do? With potions and television?"

Iris smiled and quoted Oscar Wilde: *"It is not good for one's morals to see bad acting."*

I returned her smile. "Apparently, this cultivation that I've done, this pruning and weeding, this perfecting, this honing with the aid of your potion – my folly, if you will, of continuing to enjoy this sinful pastime – has led me directly to Hell's door. It's led me directly to a sex demon."

"And again, I must commend you on your good fortune. So you're not going with all the claptrap about the danger to your soul from harmless fantasies? You're comfortable with the idea of a spirit to share your bed?"

108

I shrugged. "Just exactly what it is, though, Iris? What exactly does it want?"

"There are several thoughts on the origins of incubi, Rae, as myriad as the concepts of sin, probably. Some say they're fallen angels, corrupted by the comeliness of womankind, unable to help themselves, consumed by their own sinful lust." She shrugged. "And then there's the idea of cambions – demons made flesh – you can always tell them by their webbed toes."

I snorted in disbelief. "My cousin has webbed toes, Iris. I could hardly imagine him as a sex demon."

"It's like squares and rectangles, oh, ye of little faith," Iris said and grinned, showing all her little teeth. I could tell she was enjoying every second of going her roundabout way in telling me what I needed to know about this. "All men with webbed toes are not of the brotherhood, but all of the brotherhood have webbed toes. It is a marker, so that we may recognize them. Those incubi of women born do not necessarily know of, believe in, nor embrace their legacy. But they are just as irresistible, just as addictive as the spiritual kind.

"It's the spiritual kind that spoke to you; the demonic kind. He was once a man, Rae. He's been damned to this existence."

I decided to enjoy the scenic journey of Iris's explanation, to not try and rush her to a point. "What does it want, Iris?"

"It's not an *it*, Rae. It's most definitely a *he*." Iris giggled. "A masculine, heterosexual demon, who came to be so because of his proclivities in life. He wants to . . . do I really need to draw you a picture? Apparently you've done something to deserve this treat, so I say . . . Enjoy!"

"Can it – he – hurt me?"

"Only if you want him to," Iris said and winked. "Talk to him, Rae. Be on your guard no more or no less than you would with any other stranger. He doesn't want your soul."

"That's all the advice you have for me, Iris? You tell me I've been contacted by an incubus, *Asmodeus's minion*, and that's all you can say? *Talk to him?*"

"When you get a minute. In between . . . you didn't see him, you said?" I shook my head. "Like I told you, some women work without success for their entire magical lives, trying to entice an incubus. And somehow, you've succeeded where more experienced others have failed."

Iris smiled gleefully at me. "We may say that this man or that man is a demon between the sheets, Rae – but this being that has visited you *is exactly that.*" When she saw that I expected more explanation from my *teacher*, she added, "Make no vows, utter no oaths. Prick not your finger and sign any contracts in blood." Iris's flawless blonde eyebrows rose at the ridiculousness of her own statements. "I can't really say anything more about it, Rae, not until after you've at least . . . seen him," she insisted. "Maybe he won't even come back. Maybe he was just in the neighborhood. To warn you against attempting to sell your soul." Iris's purple-blue eyes sparkled. "But if he does come back . . . I want to hear all the details!"

She made me feel like I had a date with the prom king. "How do I . . . what did I do to summon him in the first place?"

"That really is the question, isn't it? Just repeat whatever you did before you woke up and he started talking to you." Iris shrugged. "Maybe it'll work. Maybe it won't. Maybe he won't come back."

"Thanks for all your help, Teacher," I said and smiled at her. "I'll let you know how it turns out."

"I can't wait."

TWENTY-FIVE

When the time for slumber rolled around again, I took to my bed and considered: what had I been doing before the voice spoke to me from out of the darkness? Besides offering to sell my soul?

The night before had been my viewing of Wes Thomerville's cheesy video to so-so results. Then Iris, my most dubious of teachers, had advised me to leave off of the technological aids the next night, to just let my subconscious flow. "Just picture the consummate man," she'd said. He hadn't materialized in my dreams, and I'd been sorely disappointed. I'd started to make that most dramatic of statements . . . then the disembodied voice had intervened.

So perhaps it had been my attempt to imagine the ideal man that had attracted the thing. So even though I had to go to work in the morning, I lit the candles, said the words, drank the potion, commenced the ritual.

And this time, when Wes came to me in my dreams, it was him – but it wasn't quite him. He was a little older than he was in real life, a good, solid, prime thirty-eight, instead of the still boyish thirty-three or thirty-five that he actually was. And he was a little taller, too, probably six-two or three compared to Wes's certainly-tall-enough six foot, and his hair was just a little longer, a little curlier, but still just as black. Besides these subtle differences, these subtle improvements, the dream progressed as it had the previous time, through astounding and amazing, surpassing incredible.

But perhaps the most noteworthy thing about the dream occurred when I opened my eyes, panting, out of breath, feeling like I was twenty-two again. Where on the previous occasion, the sun had speared my eyes, and I had reeled from the hang-over, I had still been most definitely alone.

This time, the sun had just barely began to illume the room – my alarm hadn't even gone off yet – but I wasn't alone. Beside me was the man I'd thought up, the perfect man. The incubus. He offered me a crooked grin and said, "What is thy name?"

"How did you? The circle . . ." I panted. "I didn't invite you inside the circle!"

"Not in so many words," he replied in that dark, fluid voice. "I invited myself, actually. I heed neither priests, nor exorcists, nor tearful entreaties. I'm impervious to such foolishness as charmed circles." He grasped the Eye of Horus pendant that still hung around my neck, ran his thumb thoughtfully over it as Iris had, then let it fall again. He smiled in amusement.

"But when you spoke to me . . . I thought the circle prevented you from . . ." But I couldn't really be bothered with all that. This was either the most spectacularly fantastic hallucination ever, or I was in bed with a supernatural being. "Are you . . . real?"

He laughed, that low, throaty, musical rumble, and took my hand, pressed it against his hot flesh. He was real, all right, at least for the moment. "What is thy name?" he asked me again. I told him my name and he commanded, "Kiss me, Rae."

I did as I was bid and in the middle of it, the alarm went off. I opened my eyes, but he was still there, as impervious to the foolishness of the clock's braying annoyance as he was to the magic of my enchanted circle. But I was not impervious to it. It was diverting my attention from kissing him, so I broke off and silenced it. He again smiled at me, and I was amazed at how much he looked like Wes, but still was not Wes. I didn't know Wes, after all, but I felt as if I knew this creature, had known him forever. I'd dreamed him up, had I not?

I said to him, "What is *thy* name?"

He growled laughter and kissed my neck. "Call me Chanticleer, for I'm as proud as a—"

"A rooster?" He looked up at me and I said, "Kiss me, Chauncey."

I stayed in bed with the incubus until noon, pausing only to call in sick at work. His every move, his every breath was sublime – I wondered vaguely if the soul-selling had indeed taken place, because nothing could ever equal this.

Eventually, I fell asleep, from sheer exhausted bliss. When I awoke, the sun slanted in from the west and I correctly guessed it to be mid-afternoon already. A glance at the clock revealed it to be three-fifteen.

Hot damn, what a dream! I thought, but then Chauncey shifted in his sleep, and I realized that whatever this was, it was no dream. There was still something, *someone* in bed with me. Someone, *something* that hadn't been there the night before. Not someone that I'd picked up at a bar. Someone who had apparently congealed out of my subconscious.

I crawled gently out of bed, then turned to look at him. He was sleeping on his stomach, head resting on his arms, curly black hair falling over his eyes. His shoulders were broad, like a swimmer; I was surprised to see that there was a jagged white scar a little to the left of his right shoulder blade. I longed to run my hand down his bare back –

but I didn't want to wake him. The sheet covered up the rest of him, but I could remember. How could anything so splendid be evil?

I threw on a robe – I had company, after all – and crept downstairs to make coffee. While it brewed, I stared dumbly out the window. *What were the rules to this?* I wondered. *Talk to him*, Iris had said. *In between . . .*

I made myself a cup of coffee, and one for my demon lover, and carried them upstairs. *If there's no one there*, I told myself, *I'll just drink them both.* I'd pretend that I'd never actually believed that he was really there in the first place. I'd had quite realistic hallucinations before, thanks to Iris's potion, but nothing like this. Nothing that I'd perceived to be real. Nothing that I'd called in sick over. Nothing that I'd made coffee for. When I entered my bedroom and there was nothing there, I thought, maybe it would be proof positive that it was time to cut back on these pursuits for a while. There weren't going to be any real men, it seemed, but when I started to believe that the fantasy men had actually manifested . . .

But Chauncey was still there, still asleep, still just as flawless and appealing as any Adonis. I sat on the edge of the bed and nudged him with my elbow. He opened his eyes, just as blue as a summer day, and looked rather expressionlessly at me.

"Coffee?"

The black eyebrows went up in surprise, and he sat up. "Yes," he said finally. I handed him a cup and watched him sip it. "Thanks," he said.

"It is absolutely no trouble at all," I said, still nonplussed that he was actually there.

"I'm not used to such continuing welcome, once the sun is up," he replied.

"I'm not used to such . . ." I said. "So you're an . . . incubus?"

He set the coffee cup on the night table, and reclined back in the bed, his hands behind his head. His arms and chest were as if carved from marble, the glorious masculinity of a Greek statue. Just looking at him made me breathless.

"I am *doom'd for a certain term to walk the night, till the foul crimes done in my days of nature are burnt and purged away.*" He grinned most deviously at me. "So, for lack of a better term, suffice it to say that, yes, I'm an incubus. A sex demon. *Your* sex demon."

"Why me?"

He squinted playfully at me. "Why not?"

"I'd just like to know why I merit such largess."

"I've driven those who would deny the sinful, clandestine lust in their hearts and minds – or would not deny it – I've driven them to ashamed and heartfelt repentance, when their simple, pious minds couldn't stand the heat of their own hidden desires made flesh. After a night with me, they get themselves out of Hell's Kitchen, so to speak, and get themselves to confession." He grinned. "I've answered the secret prayers of matrons whose fat, impotent husbands snored worthless beside them. I've visited lamenting brides on their wedding nights, after they'd discovered the ignorance of their fumbling, bumpkin grooms. I've even deigned to appear to the rare witch whom I've considered deserving, reveling in her complete amazement when that which she begged and pleaded for finally manifested.

"But you tried to conjure me out of your mind, without artifice, unaware that I already exist. So how could I not show myself to you? And no one, not in four hundred years, has ever made me coffee. Come back to bed, Rae," he said, with that scintillating whisper of command. "Let me demonstrate my gratitude for your hospitality."

TWENTY-SIX

When next I thought about time, or space, or existence beyond the creature's embrace, the shadows had once again gathered in the corners of the room. I brushed the damp curls back from his forehead, gazed at him tenderly. He returned my look inquisitively. At last I said, "How does all this work, Chauncey?"

"I may come and go at your whim, Rae–"

"Like the genie in the lamp? All I have to do is rub it and you'll appear?"

He ignored my interruption and continued. "Or I may come and go at my whim. It is entirely up to you."

"How real are you?"

Again he pressed my hand against his hot flesh. "How much more real do I need to be?"

I laughed and kissed the tip of his nose, and again he squinted curiously at me. "I mean, can you . . . cook? Clean? Cut the grass? Can you manifest outside of this room? I notice a distinct lack of wings and a tail – can we walk down the street together?"

"I can be your partner, Rae, though I'll not be your servant. No one can see me, except you – if someone should chance upon us, with the incorporeal air would you seem to hold discourse – yet I can act in the corporeal world."

"How long will you . . . stay?"

"Stay? Why, I'm yours to command. Although, be aware, I'll not always answer your charge."

"You speak in riddles, Chauncey."

"It's intrinsic to my charm."

"Will you sleep here beside me tonight? Will you be here when I wake up in the morning?" For some reason, this question was foremost in my mind. While I had surely enjoyed him, I discovered that now I wanted nothing more than to curl myself around his hot flesh and go to sleep. I wanted to wake up with him there beside me. For some reason, this was suddenly paramount to me.

Again he looked at me with that strange curiosity, spoke softly to me. "If you so desire."

TWENTY-SEVEN

I slept dreamlessly after that. There were no dreams left to experience – the man of my dreams had become manifest. I should've set my alarm for an hour earlier – as it was, I barely had time to get dressed and run a brush through my hair. I dashed out the door and still barely made it to work on time.

Once again within the confines of my familiar cubicle, I was able to catch my breath, take stock. Here was the real world, safe, secure, solid, sane – there was my *In* basket; several files needed my attention. I'd get right on all that. Here was my desk phone, red beacon flashing. I'd start with my messages.

The office voice mail was in order of the oldest call first – I listened patiently to the first two messages from yesterday, commonplace requests for me to perform my duties just as soon as I was feeling better and back in the office. I would get right on all that at once, also. How nice it was to just sit here, to look at all the normal things that made up my office, the normal things that made up my life, devoid of mystical circles, all unheeded anyway, and irresistible, diabolical angels from another plane of existence . . . I jumped when I heard his mellifluous voice on the last message.

"Rae, you left your communication contrivance beside the bed. I thought you might want to know. Farewell."

No, I wasn't losing my mind at all. There could be nothing more firmly rooted within the realm of sanity than sitting within the familiar environs of one's familiar office cubicle and listening to a voicemail from one's incubus. Going along with the natural flow of everyday normalness, I called my cellphone. He answered immediately.

"You can use a cellphone?" I asked, unable to escape the obvious.

"It's not the most complicated thing," he said. "I just located the entry under *Office* . . . I told you that I can act in the corporeal world, Rae." He chuckled.

Again I looked around my office. Everything was as it should be. Yet I was talking to a demonic spirit made manifest. Yes, he had been quite tangible, quite . . . solid. And had we not been acting corporeally? "I'm at a loss for words, Chauncey," I finally said. "This is all new to me."

"Your teacher didn't enlighten you?"

"My teacher's only advice was to talk to you."

Again he chuckled. "And we did little enough of that."

"I have to go now. I have to work. Will I see you tonight?"

"If you so desire," he said, and hung up.

The work day progressed, passing in its slow, dreary fashion. I was busy, making up for the day I'd taken off, and I hardly had a second to pause and question my sanity again. Corrine called to invite me to a dinner party at her house two Fridays hence. "Nothing fancy," she promised. "Warren wants you to meet the new guy." She paused. "Well, he's not really new. He just transferred from Sacramento. He's a widower."

So it wasn't Warren that wanted me to meet this guy, it was Corrine, ever the matchmaker, ever the controller. "I don't know," I told her. "I might've kind of met someone . . ."

"You might've kind of? What does that mean?"

"How old is this guy?" I asked, just for something to say.

"Warren says he's very trim and healthy for fifty-six."

"*Fifty-six?* Really, Corrine? Eleven years older than me?"

"You said you were looking for someone age-appropriate."

"Eleven years older than me is not age-appropriate. It's one foot in the grave."

"Will you be there?"

"I don't know, Corrine." Because while I might be crazy, while I might truly believe that I was getting phone calls from sex demons, the loss of my faculties was still a better prospect to me than an evening with some old grieving widower that my brother-in-law had scared up from God-only-knew where. He no doubt came complete with all the health problems that accompany the September of a man's years, just as Iris and I had once discussed.

But it was the thought that counted, and Corrine was reaching out to me, something she seldom did. Even if it was from pity, I supposed it would be ungrateful not to attend. "I guess so. What time?"

"Seven o'clock. I'm sure he's very nice."

Very nice. Chauncey, in our brief time together so far, in our time that had included hardly any conversation whatsoever, had revealed nothing about himself other than that he was what he claimed to be. A sex demon. *OMG, the things he did!* I had the impression that, if I was to learn anything more about him, if there was anything more to learn – *very nice* would not fit into the description.

TWENTY-EIGHT

Iris grinned from ear to ear when I entered *Mohini's*. Before I even crossed the floor she exclaimed, "You must tell me everything!" A young couple browsing among the incense looked up – he looked at me and she looked at Iris. When I didn't shout an answer back, they resumed their perusal of the scents.

Iris folded her hands before her on the counter and looked expectantly at me. "His name is Chauncey," I whispered.

"Chauncey?" Iris wrinkled her button nose in distaste.

"Well, I call him that. He said his name is Chanticleer."

Iris blinked innocently at me. "That's a pun, Rae. A chanticleer is a—"

"A rooster. I know."

"You told him your name?" I nodded. "And you asked him for no other name? Did you ask him his crime?"

"His crime?" I asked incredulously. "You didn't say anything about—"

"Sometimes I think you just don't pay attention, Rae." Iris shook her head. "An incubus is a demon. He was once a man, just like any other. He no doubt committed some crime and he was damned for it."

"What kind of a crime?"

"That really is the question, isn't it? It is a crime that you could live with?"

"If his crime damned him . . ."

"You've missed my point on damnation, Rae. It's not your crime that damns you, it's your attitude about it. If you repent your crime, you'll be forgiven – isn't that what you learned in Sunday School? *Forgive us our trespasses as we forgive those who trespass against us?"*

"I didn't really go to Sunday School, Iris."

Iris shrugged. "You have the internet to make up for the holes in your philosophy. You already know right from wrong. I can't believe that you didn't ask his crime, what he'd done that had damned him to be a—"

"We didn't talk a lot, Iris."

Iris's lip curled. "No. I don't imagine that you did."

I sighed. "He's impeccable, Iris. I've never in my life been so—"

"Moved? Why are you so surprised? He's *supernatural,"* she said emphatically, "above the ken of mortal men."

"He's . . . flawless."

Iris frowned in surprise, shook her head. "You're mistaken about that, Rae. He's *fatally* flawed. Find out his crime, my friend, find out what damned him to this existence." She studied me. "Find out his crime – see how it sits with you. Before you become any more . . . ensorcelled. All this truck with demons is not without its price."

I had no answer to that, so I simply nodded. It was true: I was ensorcelled, and so quickly – manifest a woman's ideal man and set him to work doing what it is he does, and she may forgive many crimes. But I saw Iris's point – if I chose his skills and ignored his crime – if it was something that I couldn't otherwise forgive – then that way led to my own damnation.

TWENTY-NINE

I walked into the house, threw my purse onto the coffee table and called to him. There was no response. And then I got the idea that perhaps it wasn't as simple as that – one did not summon a sex demon as if he were just hanging out in the empty air, waiting to be called. Hell, one didn't call any man so simply. Not any man that was worth calling.

So I closed my eyes and I held my hands out a little from my sides and pictured his tall, lean perfection; his curly hair, his blue eyes, his flawless mouth, his dark, smooth, honeyed voice. I reveled in the memory of him, thought expressly of how much I appreciated him. Then I had to imagine no more, because I felt him manifest, felt him take me in his arms, embrace me.

I put my arms around his neck, opened my eyes. He smiled at me. "My teacher instructs me to talk to you."

"So you have said." He pulled me tighter against him and I could feel every part of his burning, naked flesh through my clothing. This was entirely his intention, because he grinned and said, "Did you want to talk now, or did you want to . . ."

"It is possible for you to in some way . . . cover thyself, Chauncey?"

He released me so suddenly that I almost stumbled backwards. It was obvious that gentleness was not his long suit. There was a sound akin to a muffled thunderclap, and black, leathery wings sprouted from his shoulders. He grabbed the veiny ends and covered himself demurely, as with a cape. He grinned.

"Impressive," I said, genuinely impressed. "But I was thinking more along the lines of clothes, maybe?"

"Would you clothe the David?" he asked arrogantly. I doubted if it had been pride alone that had damned him, although he did possess an abundance of it. It was not unwarranted.

"I would if I was trying to have a conversation with him. Your beauty distracts me, Chauncey. I can't concentrate. Hold on just a minute."

I ran up the stairs to my bedroom, and dug around in the bottom drawer of the dresser. Devin had left behind a few pairs of sweats and even though I was thinking all the while, *Devin who?* I was also thinking that I could cover my demon lover in them, at least temporarily, because it really was impossible to string two thoughts together when he was walking around naked all the time, and the wing thing was not helping either.

But when I returned, Chauncey had dispensed with the wings and was seated on the couch, dressed in some kind of medieval doublet and hose thing, black slashed with blue, contrasted with an open-necked, big-sleeved, white shirt. He was even more stunning so clothed, and I stared at him open-mouthed for some seconds. He grinned smugly. "Of my era," he said. "Residual self-image, if you will. Better? Less . . . distracting?"

He was beautiful, impeccable, and despite what Iris had said, I thought again, *How could something so splendid be damned?* I began to see that perhaps here was the danger – this pleasing disguise might hide a monster, a madman – my costumed Romeo was *a demon*, after all. I needed to find out how . . . why . . . before I became any more accustomed to him being around.

"No less distracting, but perhaps more apropos. My teacher says that I must ask you about your life. How you came to be . . . what you now are."

"She is extraordinary that she would bid you ask me, and you are extraordinary that you would care to ask. Perhaps, if you would tell me her name . . ." His blue eyes sparkled playfully, then he patted the couch beside him, indicating for me to sit. "But, no matter. Though I'm nearly as skilled at conversation, it's not something that I've been called to use much in the time since my . . . fall, shall we say? I remain proud and unrepentant, Rae – when my sad tale is told, you judge whether the punishment fits the crime. Whether the crime of which I'm guilty and the crime for which I'm damned are even the same crime at all. I'll relish a new ear, a modern perspective." Again, the smug smile. "Perhaps you can point me toward the road to redemption."

I got the impression that Chauncey spoke of redemption the way a lifelong smoker speaks of quitting – as if it was something that non-smokers – the not-yet-damned – expected him to do. He didn't seem to be ashamed of his position in the least, was in fact proud of it. Had he not told me his name was *Chanticleer*, because he was as proud as a cock?

"In fair Verona, where we lay our scene, in the Year of Our Lord 1563 was I born, christened William Stephan Thomas Roderick." He paused and squinted playfully at me, then added, "Ninth Earl of Efisga."

"So many names," I commented.

"Call me whatever pleases you, Rae, as it doesn't matter to me."

I studied him; his carelessness, his unconcern. For a being that claimed to be more than 400 years old, he seemed quite indifferent to anything that marked any kind of permanence. Even a name. But what was more important to one's sense of self than one's name? I imagined that he was damned by those names with which he was christened, and perhaps that was why he was so cavalier about them.

But I was fascinated by him. I wanted to know him for what he once was, for the man he'd been, more than for what he was now. What he was now was wondrous, unbelievable, supernatural. But Iris had warned me: what he'd been had damned him. Still, despite this curse, on the surface, he was without defect to me, and I sought more than just this demonic, angelic façade - I wanted to know the most secret parts to him. He was not tender: he hadn't kissed me playfully, nor gently pushed the hair out of my eyes. He hadn't held my hand or hugged me. Yet he wasn't cold, either. Just not . . . *affectionate*. I figured that if, for no other reason than that he was beautiful, someone must've been affectionate to him in life, however. "What did your mother call you?" I asked.

He sighed. "I had four half-sisters, children of my father's youth, of his union with his first wife. Sadly, she died, and in his grief and loneliness, my father took a second wife. She was sturdier, but less fecund. I was my mother's only child, my father's only son. My father's wives – she of his youth and she of his middle age – were fair, as were my sisters. Milk-skinned, flaxen-haired – my mother's hair was the color of champagne in the moonlight, Rae. My sisters were all beauteous, pale, like asphodels, daffodils. All with the eyes of the clearest, palest blue.

"All my family was fair, except for my father and me. He had gone to gray, so I alone was dark. So I was their *Ala Nera*, their *Black Wing;* their *Piccolo Corvo*, their *Little Crow*. Most affectionately, my mother and sisters called me *Corvino. Raven.*"

"I like that so much better than *Chanticleer*," I told him. "May I also call you *Corvino?*"

Again the curious look, as if my simple request was incredible to him. "You may," he said softly. "If you so desire."

I nodded, told him I would like that very much. Again, he regarded me as if I was a strange bug, then continued his tale. "Sisters and mother doted on me. I could do no wrong in their eyes, and so I ran wild, free from even the mildest chastisements. My father would attempt to frown at me on occasion, but he could bear no dolor to touch my mother's mood – if I was the apple of her eye, she was the apple of his, and he would not risk her unhappiness by correcting her beloved son.

"But I was a good, obedient boy, despite all that. Until my fifteenth summer, when the true way of the world was revealed to me, I was studious, pious. Until the path to mastery was shown to me, the path to my damnation, I was guiltless. Sinless."

He smiled slyly at me, and again I was struck by his lack of remorse. It was fascinating. I was impatient to hear the meat of it. But Chauncey – *Corvino* – was turning out to be like Iris in his tale-telling, slow and ponderous, given to much detail and flowery language.

"It was springtime, and as twilight fell, my friends and I were out playing at hunting, following our fathers and older brothers and the hounds through the forest, with borrowed bows. It was doubtful that any of us would close with the stag, but we followed along anyway, believing that such activities would grow us into the men we longed to be.

"But after a long day, we lagged behind, the chase having lost its thrill. As we discussed giving up the pastime all together for the evening, we were confronted with a strange glow, emanating from a yew grove adjacent to a crossroads. My fellows were frightened, fearing sorcery. They refused to enter the grove with me and fled to rejoin our elders.

"But I was curious, fearless. What was sorcery to me? My soul was white, pure – I was sinless. What had I to fear from sorcery?

"So I stepped into the grove, and within the encircling trees, I found a young woman, probably ten years my senior, seated on a stone bench. I recognized two of my father's fiercest hounds, now docile, sitting on the ground on either side of her bench. They would turn and look at her, loll their tongues and smile as dogs do, and she would pat one or the other of them.

"Then she looked up and also hailed me as *Ala Nera, Black Wing*, and bid me come and sit beside her. The dogs growled balefully at me as I stepped forward, but at a terse word from her, again they smiled and begged for her touch like eager pups.

"She was the most beauteous creature I'd ever beheld – fair like my mother and sisters, but with a darker shade to her blonde hair; it was made up of a thousand shades of yellow, worn down her back in a thick luxuriant braid. And her eyes were a darker blue – almost purple-hued, like a Concord grape."

A surprising, hot bolt of something that I could only call jealousy flashed through me: my damned demon lover was describing Iris.

"So, entranced, I sat. She took my hands and told me that I was beautiful, exceptional – these were not unheard of words to me, as my mother and sisters had always called me such, and I believed them implicitly. But coming from her, the compliments warmed me in a manner I'd not experienced before. She asked me the name of my betrothed, and threatened to curse her for her luck in having me.

"'No one maid should be so fortunate, to be alone possessed of such beauty,' she claimed. 'You have charms enough for all, and she is overly confident that you will not share them, allowing you out of her sight to come under my sway.'

"When I blushed and confessed that I was not yet betrothed, that no fortunate maid had yet *possessed* me, she grinned. She had small, perfectly white teeth; a classic, pink, bow mouth."

Again I was struck by how much he seemed to be describing Iris.

"'Then it is I who am fortunate,' she said, and bade me kiss her. When I hesitated, she laughed. 'Never even kissed?' she asked. Again, I blushed.

"And thus did my education begin, Rae. I met the girl in the yew grove at the first thin bow of the moon. I returned nightly, and by the time he grew fat and bright, he was witness to the apogee of my most unspeakably wonderful graduation. It was indeed sorcery, of the most ancient declension."

That ol' black magic, I thought.

"But the golden enchantress didn't only show me the physical ways of love, Rae. She also showed me the secrets of its looks – how gestures and glances give the lie to sanctimonious words. The truth to *Yes, I must*, is in the eyes, the sigh; the *No, I won't* – those are only words, easily brushed aside.

"So by the time the moon was gone from the sky, I was altered forever, a boy no more. The sorceress revealed to me the secret of my own power. She taught me to read the desire plain upon your gender's features. No matter how you try to hide it with blushes and veiled looks, with denials and protestations, ever am I able to ferret it out."

I looked at him doubtfully. "No still means no," I told him.

"Ah, the vaunted woman's prerogative. But I disagree. Assent is assent, no matter what is spoken later. Do not invite me and then attempt to deny me once I've arrived. You are a being with a mind as well as a soul; if you truly don't want me, deny the thought. Prevent it from forming.

"Once I am arrived, I will exercise *my* prerogative," he said darkly. Then he smiled, took me in his arms. Modestly clothed or not, the heat that came off of his supernatural body was palpable, tangible, undeniable, irresistible. "Tell me no," he commanded.

The authority to his tone roused my defiance. "I could tell you no, if I so chose," I replied, but it sounded lame the minute it left my mouth.

"Yet the choice is no longer up to you, once I have arrived," he said. "I am only here because you wished for me to be. Denial after that is not an option." He released me, again, almost roughly, causing me to fall back against the couch. "If you didn't allow yourself the luxury of these thoughts in the first place . . . However, I'm not claiming that I'm irresistible."

"That's exactly what you're saying," I countered. *"Prevent the thought from forming.* I say there is no sin in the thinking. After I've had the notion, all I have to do is say no, whether you have *arrived* or not. Would you rape me, Corvino?"

Now he took me into his arms again, not quite tenderly, but more gently than he had released me. "I do not speak of you, specifically, Rae. I'm talking about those who would deny their own thoughts and desires, once they are made manifest. You're aware of your own thoughts. You don't fear them. You know what you want.

"But still, I charge you." He didn't smile. "You beckoned me from the sum of your desires – once I was here, you claim you might've said no? I say you would not. You cannot. You tell yourself that you can, but you don't. You didn't wish me up to tell me no, and regardless, I would not have taken no for an answer, not even from you."

He kissed me, and I realized it was true, to a great extent. He was unequaled, irresistible. Yet I had to resist him, at least until I heard his story. I saw the danger clearly then, just as Iris had warned me: if his crime was anathema to me, if he had been in life some kind of monster – I couldn't allow myself to ignore it. I couldn't continue to enjoy his beauty and flawless physical prowess if what had damned him was indeed damnable to me. I had to hear the rest of his story.

I let him kiss me, but when he paused, I said, "You're undeniable. It's true, and if I doubted it, I'd have to go no further than to ask you – 'Are you irresistible, Corvino, are you undeniable?' – and you will assure me of it." I grinned at him and he grinned back. "But I do want to hear the rest of your story. So, if you will so allow, I won't say *no*, I'll just say, *not now*, and let you finish."

"As you desire," he said, letting me know again by his expression that my desire was secondary to his own. One is not, in any fashion, allowed to toy with, *to tease*, an incubus. He would take that for which he had been summoned regardless of any last second apprehensions.

"Perhaps you're misunderstanding me – when I speak of exercising my prerogative, it is as I am now. Once I am arrived as I now exist, I'll not take no for an answer. If you suddenly fear some godly retribution for your sinful desire at the sight of me, well . . . that's your problem. But I never forced myself upon anyone when I was a man, Rae." He chuckled. "I didn't have to. You see, after the ministrations of this mysterious sorceress, I was transformed. I now looked upon women, young ones, old ones, and with a glance was I able to ken their desire. It was not that *I* was suddenly desirable, that I hadn't been so before. I'd just been unaware of it until then. I was just now awakened to this power that I held. I saw that women wanted me." He shrugged. "Not all women, of course, as I said. There were women upon whom I made no impression whatsoever."

"But not many," I supplied. I thought of Iris and her complete disinterest in Wes Thomerville.

Corvino shrugged again. "We walk through a crowd, pass a sea of faces, and recall only those that mean something to us. I did not, do not, appeal to all. I was no more than a boy at the time–"

"Ah, what a pretty boy you must've been," I said.

He smiled crookedly. "My mother had always told me it was so. But for the first time I was aware of its effect. I became aware that it only took a smile, a nod, a word – and I'd get back that reaction that signified my power over women. Not all women, I must protest. But the ones that reacted . . . their desire was plainer to me than any words."

"And how did you deal with this power?" I asked. "Were you, like a good king, fair and just? Were you merciful? Did you take pity on those women, not all, but those, like myself, who were powerless before your charm? Or were you cruel, Corvino? Was it your cruelty that damned you?"

"It will be for you to judge. I did not, do not, think myself cruel. Cruelty is not like a round, dead stone, would you say, Rae? Cruelty has arms and legs and voice – cruelty is the result, the net product of other actions. If I lie to you, and you believe my lie and so suffer, then I am guilty of cruelty. If I make a promise to you, and then fail to honor it, then I am cruel.

"But doesn't one of the more famous fables warn us about the nature of things? The one about the frozen snake? As the legend was told to me, the maiden takes pity on the frozen snake, takes him to her bosom and warms him. Once revived, the snake bites her and she dies. What do you see as the moral of this tale?"

I shrugged. "You could take it to mean that some people have no gratitude–"

"No." The demon shook his head resolutely. "The maid knew she succored a snake. And the moral of the story is that neither succor nor honesty nor loyalty nor any other means will change the basic nature of a snake."

"Are you comparing yourself to a snake, Chauncey?" I asked him with a grin.

He smiled at the more playful appellation. "Allow me to tell the full tale, Rae, and, as I say, you tell me what you think. You're the first woman in four hundred years to care to hear it, so I'm really quite curious to hear your judgment."

He kissed me again and then continued. "As you might imagine, the world was my oyster. I was entirely too young to have this jade's skill. Girls my own age: my stammering, blushing contemporaries; their older sisters, their mothers — with a glance I could read their minds. So I allowed them to seduce me. I was quite adept at feigning an innocence I no longer possessed.

"This continued until I reached my majority at twenty-one, when my mother, in equal parts appalled and amused by the stories she'd heard of the willingness of her seeming choir-boy son, took me aside. She told me that the time had come that I cease to be a dupe.

"'I'll allow it's a clever ruse, Corvino. But you're too old to allow these women to think they continue to take advantage of an innocent boy. There is nothing either innocent or boyish about you.'

"I opened my mouth to protest, but she shushed me. 'The time has come for you to take responsibility for these things you do, or at least . . . to take the initiative. I no longer want to hear laughing into fists about how easily you are seduced. It's a man's world, Corvino. It's time for you to be a man.'

"And so I took my mother's advice, or her admonition. I no longer played the innocent. If I looked past girlish blushes to the true desires that lived behind the quick glances and the quick glances away, then I would step up, make inquiry. If, of course, the lady interested me.

"But I made no promises, Rae. This I must stress to you. I made no pledges of love eternal, no vows. I told them all that I was as my name — a crow that is intrigued with a shiny, pretty thing for a moment, or a season."

Again, I felt a small spurt of jealousy. I said. "Am I just a shiny thing?"

He laughed, that melodious, throaty sound. "I am a spirit, Rae, made flesh only because of your desire. You summoned me."

"Will you tire of me in a season?"

127

"How can I tire of someone who wished me out of the air? I am damned. This is my existence." Again he grinned, unrepentant.

"Proceed," I said.

"So, I lived. I became the seducer, no longer the seduced. But the protests were never more than excuses for these women, the right and chaste things that they were compelled to speak, to make themselves feel proper and guiltless. There should be no guilt in attraction, Rae, and never felt I guilty in it. I never judged them for their weakness. They knew what they wanted – I told them they could have all of me, body, mind, soul. But only for a moment. I also warned them that they could not keep me. I made sure they understood that."

"You didn't say heart, Corvino. Could none of them capture your heart?" I felt strange, adopting his lyrical language. But there was poetry in it, in him – I didn't feel there was any other way of expression other than to mimic his old-fashioned phrasing. The way he talked was as intrinsic to his charm as was any other aspect of his beauty. "Did you not love any of them?"

He shrugged. "I loved them for that moment. But they were all transparent. They didn't love me for any longer than that, either. It was all transitory. It was youth. There is no permanence to an infatuation with looks, Rae, with a smile or a wink – none of them sought my heart. If they did, I was unaware of it – I had warned them that I would not be kept, so I didn't cast too many glances over my shoulder, to see how they were faring at my departure.

"I saw no sin in any of this – I may have toyed with what would someday belong to another man or what currently did, but it was a playful kind of adultery. *Thou shall not steal*, it is commanded, and I was no thief. I didn't seek to take anything away from anyone permanently. I just borrowed it for a while." He blinked innocently at me. "But I told no lies. I was not the marrying kind, and I made no claims to be. If any of them became too attached, if any of them sought that which I had not promised . . . They had been warned that it would not occur, so how am I to blame for the lies others tell to themselves?"

Corvino was above reproach in his own philosophy. If any of these girls fell in love with him, it was their own fault. Sooner try to capture the bird on the wing than his love – he'd always warned them of the impossibility of that. There was a major flaw here, but I couldn't quite put my finger on it, couldn't put it into words. If he told them that they could not possess him, then what sin was there in him if they tried? If they knew he was a heartbreaker, was it his fault if they allowed him to break their hearts?

"When I turned thirty, again my mother took me aside. 'You are in danger of becoming a libertine, my child,' she told me. 'Again, I hear unkind words associated with your name. Matrons lock up their daughters at its mention. Husbands then lock up the matrons. It's time to end this errant sampling. It's time for you to take up the mantle of your years. It's time for you to take on the responsibilities you owe to God – be fruitful and multiply – all within the confines of custom and law. It's time for you to choose, my son. It's time for you to wed, to create your own sons to inherit your father's holdings.'

"I made protest. I would not settle for one woman, custom be damned. It was not in my nature. Better to be a bachelor and commit venial sins, to drive maidens and the wives of others to confession, where their own sins would be absolved. I would not take one woman to wife and then make a fool of her.

"'Yet it must be,' my mother insisted. 'You must wed. It's the way of the world. The happiness of your union will be decided by your choice. All women are not as foolish as you believe. You simply must find one, like the ones you've always found – one that understands you, one that accepts you despite your . . . lack of fidelity. Marriage offers its own brand of fidelity. She will have your lands, your title, your sons. She will have yourself, when the whim moves you. If you choose wisely, perhaps the whim will settle on you. Perhaps you will want no other. But if you still seek amusement with the polished trinkets others offer you . . . a properly chosen wife will be satisfied with the other benefits of having you as her husband. She will remember them and be content on those occasions when you may share another's bed.'

"As always, my mother offered me a view of life free from care, from accountability. When, as a boy, I would express dislike of a tutor, or a task, she had always found another tutor, more to my liking. She had always assigned me some other task, one more suited to my mood. And here was she so doing again: her only son was not to be shackled to one woman, as was the custom of our time, our culture, our religion. I could live the carefree, pagan polygamy I'd always enjoyed. if I would only choose that rare bride that would understand and accept me.

"And so the search for such a bride commenced. It was let out that the Ninth Earl would wed, and many of my former paramours lined up for consideration. But as you may imagine, none of them moved me. *Been there, done that*, as the poets say." He grinned at the anachronism. "Their seasons had each passed.

"But eventually, I would be caught. Eventually, came to our town a young widow, returned to her father's house after the tragic loss of her husband. Some misadventure at sea, a shipwreck, all hands lost. So it cannot be said, in the final analysis, that I beguiled some innocent, unworldly maid.

"There was not much beguiling done at all, actually. Her name was Adelle, *of the nobility*. She was twenty-five, beauteous. She had cinnamon-colored hair, burnished with gold, and large brown eyes, black-lashed, like a fawn. But the expression in those eyes was one of sadness. She missed her lost husband – no joy, no desire looked out at me from her soul, and I pitied her the loss of her love. Her sadness touched me, intrigued me. I was challenged by her dolor, wishing to elicit some response from her marble visage.

"'Your reputation precedes you,' she told me, the first time we conversed alone. 'Why do you bother with a vessel already uncapped, left empty by the whim of Fate? Aren't there fresher prizes to soothe your appetites?'

"'Appetites come and go. You say you are uncapped, empty. So I assume you also know the joy of fulfillment.' I smiled at her, seeking her own smile. 'My mother says I must wed. I offer you another chance at fulfillment, as our appetites may dictate.'

At that, her own smile appeared, as I knew it would. She was no maid, Rae. She knew of those appetites of which she spoke, and surely, she missed her husband, no doubt for all the reasons one would miss a spouse, taken from her so early in their bliss. But the smile in her eyes at last told me that she missed not the least that pleasure that could be provided by any man, by me – not just by only that one man that was gone.

"I paid my humble court to her. As I say, there was little beguilement. Adelle confessed that she was fond of me, but I detected no all-encompassing lust – no ungovernable passion for me shone out of her eyes. I was a man, true, and having once been married, she knew of the passions we could mount together. She missed these activities, being young and lonely. But she was not overly anxious to take me up, to have me blot out those memories of another that she still so treasured.

"She told me that she knew that I wouldn't be true. It was not in the nature of men, she said. Even her vaunted love, he for whom she still mourned, had not been entirely free of the sin of adultery, she said. But he had loved her, truly, completely, she said, her eyes misting with tears. And so, secure in that, she had forgiven the suspicion of an occasional, meaningless dalliance on his part.

"I told my mother of these revelations, and she clapped her hands in glee, saying that here was a woman to match my mettle. That rare and marvelous woman who would understand me. 'She has the wisdom to value matrimony for what it really is!' my mother cried. 'The bonds of property and title allow room for mere passing fancy. In the end, she knows that she will be your woman above all others, as she will have your name and your sons to comfort her if you occasionally stray. You must marry her at once!'

"And so I pled my troth, and after some hesitation, Adelle agreed to the union. Again, she said she knew of my reputation, and if I agreed to be discreet, she said that she could ask for no more than that.

"And at first, it seemed that there would be no need for these self-effacing provisions to my baser nature. At first there was no other for me than my beauteous, gallant bride. She was my match in wit and temperament, in action and pride. What could I seek – what was there behind the veiled glance of a passing maid – for there was certainly nothing there that held any mystery to me? There was nothing to seek elsewhere that Adelle was not more than willing to fulfill. We were a matched pair – I desired no other amusements. She was happy with me, and frequently opined that she might even grow to love me someday. Perhaps, she would say playfully, someday I might love her, too.

"And then came the season when Adelle announced that I would have an heir. The joy at the news was marred only by the trouble of the time for her. She was ill, almost from the moment she felt the quickening. As the child grew within her, she became distraught at the changes to her body; she thought herself disgusting and believed herself to be unsightly to me. It was not true, Rae – she was as lovely to me as she'd always been. But she would not heed my protestations – she shut herself away from me, with only the company of Leonor, her maid.

"She'd brought Leonor with her from her father's house. The girl had lived with Adelle and her first husband, and Adelle wouldn't give her up when she married me. They'd been inseparable since childhood – Leonor was the daughter of some servant of her father's – her only task in life had been to amuse Adelle, to keep her company. She was the lifelong vessel of all my wife's confidences, her best friend, her sister.

"Adelle had often extolled the girl's maidenly virtues, regaled me with the facts of her steadfast promises to remain unwed, to devote herself, body and soul, to Adelle's service. My wife hadn't requested this boon, she claimed, and the unnaturalness of such an unlooked for promise assailed me: to me, Leonor seemed no more holy than any other. Although she was always maidenly in my presence, all shy, murmured responses and downcast eyes, when I would sometimes catch her unawares, when her maidenly gaze was not downcast, she looked at me with the same frank appraisal that I'd suspected might be there. She was no more steadfast in her fidelity than any other girl her age. She would've been mine at a word.

"Yet I was quite sure that her speculative inclinations toward me were unseen by Adelle. They might giggle together like girls – they might share all their secret thoughts – but this was one thought I was sure Leonor did not broach with her sister. She would not admit to her friend of an admiration for her husband. It would be unseemly, unmaidenly. But I could see it, nonetheless.

"I bid my mother make discreet inquiries into the girl's habits. If there was a viper in my midst, I would know of it. I was not returned any tales of grave indecencies on Leonor's account. She had a few unseemly good friends among the stable boys, but that was not unexpected. She was not known to be profligate in her . . . *friendships,* but neither was she as virginally devoted to my wife's service as she had led Adelle to believe.

"Leonor was pale and blonde, of fine enough figure, slim, possessed of a pleasing gait. But she was no beauty. She was plain, her features unremarkable, her expression vacant, or sometimes of a slight, thoughtful nature, as if she might be thinking mightily about something, but was ill equipped for the task. At these times it struck me that a touch of madness might hide in her. Her best features were her large, dark-blue eyes. In those, she reminded me of a shadow of the sorceress I'd known in the woods. Those eyes had held all the promise of unrepentant knowledge, and of the affinity for instruction – the deviousness of pleasure received from pleasure taught. But Leonor's blue eyes were guileless, most of the time. Unless I caught her looking at me and I could see that she was attracted to me; or if she was thinking about whatever it was that she sometimes thought about – then there might be a slight artfulness to her expression. But otherwise . . . blankness. I counted myself lucky that my wife should have such a bland companion.

"As her pregnancy progressed, as she continued to be ill, an odd obsession seemed to seize Adelle's mind. Although she seldom emerged from her chamber, although she never gave me entrance to it, still she was compelled to know my whereabouts at all times. Ever was I looking up to see Leonor peeping at me from behind a wall or out of the shadow of a doorway. Yet never would Adelle admit me when I entreated audience. Eventually, I gave up and quit asking.

"Yet still, she had to know what I was about. Various and sundry footmen and loyal servants came to me and confessed that they had been offered bribes by the lady of the manor to report my activities to her, both sacred and profane."

"Was there profanity afoot?" I asked. "Was there a reason that your pregnant wife might want to hire spies, Corvino? Did you bear watching?"

He considered me mildly. "I bore watching no more nor less than I had at any other point in our union. The Lord has blessed or cursed us with free will, Rae. Adelle exercised hers in shutting herself up away from my company, so I exercised my own in the company of others." A slight cruelty marred his expression when he said, "Don't nod sagely and assume that I suddenly loosed my publicized charms on an unsuspecting countryside because my wife had just as suddenly deigned to cloister herself, Rae. If I amused myself with other women, it was only with a smile or a laugh. A meal or a ride in the countryside. I was monkish – there was not a single consummation. Even I was not so base as to betray my wife, indisposed with the bringing forth of my heir, with frolics that would no doubt get back to her.

"I was willing to wait out this strange distemper on Adelle's part. My sisters assured me that it was just a passing fad of pregnancy – once my son was born, my wife would return to me. They'd all had similar fugues, they related to me – none claimed to have so cut off her husband, but they said that they had also felt ugly and undesirable while with child. They promised me that it would pass.

"But still I was vexed. I took to long, solitary, nighttime walks. It was on one of these that I once again came upon that enchanted grove of yew trees. The glow shone forth as it had when I was only fifteen, and once again I stepped inside the encircling trees.

"The sorceress was there, just as beauteous and beguiling as she'd ever been, not aged a day. She bade me sit beside her again, and I did, as enthralled with her supernal majesty as ever I'd been as a youth. I was more aware now of the glories it signified. She chided me for my long absence, again threatening curses on whatever selfish maid had so long kept me from her company.

"I told her that it was only the passage of time and life, and no selfish maid that had kept me away. I told her that I was wed, but that my wife sought not the keeping of me, but my expulsion at this, her time of trial.

"'Then she has cursed herself,' the sorceress said. 'It is more foolish to expel one such as you, than it would be to attempt to keep you all to herself.' And then she leaned forward and kissed me, Rae, and I allowed myself to be seduced. It was sorcery. I was the favorite of an enchantress, and I saw no harm in dalliance with this unearthly angel, after all the months of deprivation I'd endured. I thought it my right – nay, my duty! Such an interlude would keep me honest in the face of the more commonplace women I saw daily, who still bestowed upon me their sideways looks, heedless of my married station. Nor would any word of my congress with this extra-natural being leak through mortal lips and seep back to Adelle. It would all be as a dream. Do you take my meaning, Rae?"

He was of course referring to my own dreams, my extra-natural additives to them. He was referring to my *congress* with him, saying that our couplings, of flesh and spirit-made-flesh were no more sinful than his with the sorceress.

"But I have no pregnant wife at home," I rejoined.

"My wife had rejected me. I didn't rub her nose in sordid neighborhood affairs as I could've done," he replied, again with that whisper of cruelty. "No one would've called me on it if I had, given my previous entertainments. In fact, I think it was rather expected of me. Even my mother marveled at my loyalty.

"I took to visiting the grove on a regular basis. I confess it. These interludes were welcome feminine company, surcease from my loneliness. The golden witch asked nothing of me but my company; she neither asked me to stay, nor inquired if I would return."

Corvino sighed. "At last Adelle was delivered of a healthy boy, my son, destined to be the Tenth Earl of Efisga." He grinned at me, then continued. "I returned no more to the sacred grove, gave up my golden lover, she who had kept me sinless, had kept me from more mundane pursuits during my undeserved ostracism. My wife returned to my bed.

"But I found her a changed woman. Gone was the bold, straightforward match for my wit and mettle, the independent, strong-minded woman of our courtship and early marriage. Somehow, she had been transformed. Now she was become clingy and whiny, prone to fits of crying and fits of rage, during which she accused me of every adulterous pastime imaginable, except, of course, for the one in which I'd engaged. Again my sisters assured me that it was just an offshoot of new motherhood. I would have my wife back again before the moon waxed old.

"By the next moon, Adelle's tantrums and wild accusations had indeed stopped. But the familiar Adelle still didn't return. She became quiet and fearful, peeping at me at meals with the expression of a whipped hound, as if I might strike her. At night she clung to me. Now she professed love for me, saying that it had grown on her during the days of her pregnancy. Now she could not live without me, she claimed: her devotion had become undying.

"This was all pleasant to my ear, as it would be to any man. I imagine that all men desire for their wives to love them. I was fond of

Adelle, Rae – I honored her enough to be faithful to her, did I not? But I wished for the old Adelle back, the one that had joshed me, told me that she might *someday* love me. This love that she now claimed made her weak. It seemed to haunt her, until she became a ghost of her former self, almost as if she was possessed by some unnamable fear.

"The child grew and flourished, while all the while, his mother wasted away, gnawed by some condition of the nerves. Physicians were called in, and priests. Nothing seemed to sooth her. She took to long walks out into the forest at night, attended only by Leonor. I became grateful for her absence – when we were alone she only stared reproachfully at me, or clasped me around the knees and sobbed. She would not tell me why she was so melancholy – so after a while, I gave up asking. I began to avoid her during the day, just to escape her unrelenting depression.

"After the first anniversary of my son's birth, Adelle's mood began to lighten. She again smiled and laughed, but there seemed to be a little edge of malice to it. She became a whirlwind behind closed doors, whispering to me that she had come to understand that the only way to keep me at her side was through carnal pleasures. 'My husband's lust must be served!' she would cry. At first this was a refreshing change from her months of whiny dolor, but after a while, there came to be a certain mania, a certain desperation, to it. If I pleaded fatigue, she would leap from the bed in agitation, dress quickly and fly from the chamber. She would then gather up Leonor and tramp out to the woods, sometimes dragging the boy with them.

"For a season, stories had been swirling, murmurs of unholy goings-on in the forest. It was whispered that witchcraft was afoot. Adelle's name had not yet been attached to these gossips, but note had no doubt been taken of her strange forays late at night, when good wives had no business abroad. Servants have eyes and ears and tongues and listeners. Her jaunts had been curtailed since her sudden renewed interest in our marital rites – only if I denied her would see flee to the forest anymore. But rumors were rumors, and on one such night, just to see what would occur, I pretended to be asleep when she came to bed. I resisted all her attempts to rouse me from my counterfeit slumber, and when she at last alit from the chamber, I followed her.

"I trailed her to that grove of yew where I had once cavorted with the golden sorceress. Again, a light shone forth from between the trees – but it wasn't the otherworldly glow that I'd once known – it was only the sickly, pale light of many candles. From behind a tree, I spied within, and beheld a scene from Hell. Several black-robed women stood in semi-circle around the stone bench, their faces in shadow from the cowls they wore. Candles surrounded them, and they gave voice to murmured chants, the words indistinguishable. Adelle stood at the head of the bench, and Leonor at its foot, both similarly robed. Asleep or drugged, my son lie on the bench between him.

"As I watched, the chanting rose to a crescendo, a ululating, banshee wail, and then suddenly stopped. In the ensuing silence, Adelle raised her hands heavenward and intoned, 'Oh, Unhallowed One! See here my sacrifice, the flesh of my flesh, freely given! His soul is but a trifle to me. Take it and return to me that which I have lost!'

"Adelle reached into her robe and then threw one arm skyward again. In her hand was a dagger, gleaming dully in the candlelight. I leapt forward, covered the insensate boy with my own body, attempting to shield him from his mother's unholy rage. The dagger, already on its relentless path downward, caught me right beside the shoulder blade. It was buried to the hilt, slicing through muscle, nicking bone, puncturing my lung. The pain was intense and I teetered on the edge of oblivion. Then the forest was alive with light, and sound – torches blazed and arrows whizzed over my head. Still I shielded the boy – Adelle dropped to her knees beside me. 'Forgive me, William,' she said. 'I could not live without you.'

"And then she slid to the ground and spoke no more.

"Arms lifted me, and I braced for another dagger thrust. But I was now among friends. As I had followed Adelle, worried servants had followed me. They had burst into the grove just as her dagger had descended, and with crossbows had made short work of the robed women. All were either dead or fled, except for Leonor, who hissed and struggled in the iron grasp of a scowling bowman.

"I instructed one of my benefactors to remove my son from the befouled grove, then braced myself against a tree and bid another to remove the dagger from my back. Again the world swam and threatened to disintegrate into blackness when he did so, but I held onto consciousness. Sweating and bleeding, I turned to Leonor. Before I could form the words to ask her why, she cackled and spit in my face. One of my loyal retainers struck her, but she only turned back to me again, and grinned through her shredded, bleeding mouth.

"'Your bride believed she'd lost your love. She believed only through the intervention of dark forces would it be returned to her. She would sacrifice all to retrieve what she believed to be lost.' Leonor cackled again, choked on her own blood, then spit it out onto the bench. 'I don't know what amuses me more – the idea that she thought she had ever possessed your love, or how easily she was persuaded that she'd lost it! You! *Ala Nera! Cuore Nero! Crudele! Snaturato!*' She spit out another mouthful of blood. 'How she lamented the loss of your love! She had no inkling that you never loved her, that you've never loved anyone! Only yourself! Black, heartless, demon!' She glanced around at her captors. 'Look on him, you men! See what his cruelty and selfishness has led to!'

"One of the servants moved to strike her again, but I stayed him. 'Who has told Adele that I was lost to her?'

"Again Leonor laughed. 'It was I!' she cried. 'Cast your memory back, Black Heart. Recall a young serving girl that you waylaid outside of an inn, once upon a time, as she returned from the well. Recall how you plied her with honeyed words, how you compared her fairness to the blush of spring! Recall how you inveigled her into a shady bower and deigned to shower upon her but an afternoon of your luxurious love! Recall how you left her among the trampled lilies, with naught but a kiss and a fare-thee-well!'

"I watched one of the servants grin at his fellow. Leonor caught the expression. 'You may well smile at my shame. It is a common enough story. But see how your master doesn't smile. He just stands there uncomprehending, bleeding, splashed with the blood of his loving wife, drowning in his own. He doesn't even remember me. Do you, you foul creature? You, who walks around with the semblance and elegance of a man, but who possesses not the fealty of the lowest cur! *Snaturato!* Heartless! You remember me not from that stolen afternoon, but you'll not forget me now, nor my revenge!'

"I nodded at the man holding Leonor, and he dragged her away. It took little magisterial . . . *persuasion* for her to confess to sorcery, although I have no doubt that it was still liberally applied. The Archfiend came from the pit and Leonor had willingly given up her soul to him. My wife had been her partner in sin, had also pledged herself to the Dark Lord. To prove her devotion to Him, she agreed to sacrifice our son. A cautionary tale, to underline the evil that lies in wait for us all on every side. The confessionals were stuffed full for a fortnight.

"I visited Leonor in her prison cell. I was curious to hear from the lips of one damned willingly, how having once been so pious, she'd run afoul of the Devil. I wanted to know why she'd spun such a supernatural tale, why she had not repeated to the priests and magistrates what she'd said in the grove, how it wasn't Satan but I who'd supposedly enchanted her once upon a time. To me, she gleefully dismissed Satan, saying that while he might indeed exist, it hadn't been his influence that had led her to that blood-spattered grove. The only Devil she'd ever seen in this life was me, she spat. She believed implicitly only in her hatred for me. In her eyes, I'd stolen her chastity, then left her like a drab on the side of the road, unable to even remember her when I beheld her again at Adelle's side.

"To this hour, I don't remember any golden afternoons beside an inn, Rae – or more accurately, I don't remember any golden afternoons beside an inn with Leonor, or anyone that even resembled her. I don't claim that it wasn't I who seduced her. But I maintain that she entered into the fray with open eyes. For all I recall, she may have seduced *me*. Regardless of the exact circumstances, I know that I never lied to her, never promised her anything. I never murmured *I love you*, or said I'd take her home with me. Even though I don't remember her face specifically, I have no doubt that the look on it had said she wanted me, so I gave her what she wanted."

"Apparently she wanted to keep you."

The black eyebrows shot up and he grinned. "Indeed. And when I left her with *naught but a kiss and a fare-thee-well*, she couldn't accept the fact of her own collaboration in the deed. She'd assumed that what she'd given to me so freely was a prize without compare, and therefore, I'd forego my sinful ways just to continue to possess it. But I told her beforehand – I told them all – that this would not be the case.

"Leonor couldn't accept that there was nothing whatsoever special about her to me. So in her madness, I became a thief, and she cast herself as an unconsenting dupe, a victim robbed. It wasn't so, Rae. I may have been a libertine, taking my pleasures where they presented themselves, but never was I a liar. As you say, all she would've had to do was say no. Many, knowing my reputation, did say no. Most did not. In life, I never forced myself on anyone – I never wanted anything badly enough to take it. If Leonor sought a husband, she should've waited for one, extracted the requisite vows and promises, the ceremonies and strictures. But she did not. She willingly agreed to an afternoon among the lilies with me, and I promised her naught else but that.

"When Leonor beheld me betrothed to Adelle, unremembered of our tryst, she seethed. She plotted revenge. She first convinced Adelle that I was the most wonderful husband a woman could wish for. She praised Adelle's wisdom in choosing me, admired the love Adelle had for me so thoroughly that Adelle began to believe that she indeed loved me utterly. Then Leonor wove tales of sorcery, that through its means had the one whom Adelle loved so much been cruelly, unjustly stolen from her.

"Leonor of course had no way of knowing that there was a kernel of truth to the tales she wove. I was bewitched – but the enchantress hadn't stolen me from my wife. She'd only borrowed me for a time, whilst my wife shunned me. Never had she sought to keep me from my earthly bride. Leonor's fantasy had mirrored reality, but it was just a coincidence. No one was aware of my trysts with the sorceress, least of all a serving wench.

"But her imagined stories of sorcery hit their mark. Leonor told Adelle that I was on the verge of sending her away, and she believed it.

"It amused Leonor to see the desperation that all her lies engendered, and after our son was born, it amused her further to advise Adelle that the only way back into my heart was through marathon love-making. And when I seemed disturbed by that, Leonor invoked Satan. Her husband had been bewitched, and only through stronger enchantments would I be returned. She convinced Adelle that the surest way to win me back was through the aid of ultimate evil. There were others in the neighborhood who also believed in Satan's power, and by bringing them together in the forest, Leonor convinced Adelle of his presence. If she'd sacrifice her boy to the Unhallowed One, the enchantments would vanish, my affections would be rekindled . . ."

Corvino shook his head. "Leonor believed not in witchcraft, Rae. She believed only in the wrong she felt I'd done to her. By leading my wife to her doom, she felt herself justly revenged on me, and went to the gallows with a smile on her face.

"As for me . . . Adelle's wound proved fatal. As I slowly succumbed to my injury, all the tragedy and bloodshed and revenge of my fast-approaching end caused my mother to suddenly become quite pious. She recanted her advice to me, that a little on the side never hurt anyone." He grinned. "She urged me to confess myself, to seek absolution for what she suddenly perceived as my life of adulterous sin.

"'You've never loved anyone but yourself, Corvino, and that is partially my fault. You've never had one thought for any other above yourself, and I now realize that to be grievous. Confess the sin of your adultery, your selfishness, before it is too late!'

"To please her, I did so. But it was a hollow confession, Rae. I saw little sin in my life. I never took anything that was not freely given. If I had failed to feel as utterly as Leonor, if I had failed to love them as they apparently wanted me to – this was the phenomena that my mother suddenly pointed out to me – I considered that to be a fault in them, not in myself.

"So am I damned, as I will neither confess to nor atone for a sin I do not recognize. Now, whenever maid has an unclean thought, I materialize to answer it. If she finds herself repentant at the sight of me . . . why, that's just too bad. May she all the more fully repent, later.

"Those that would seek to enslave me, such as wishful witches . . . I've been left with nothing if not my free will, and I'm not amenable to slavery, so their experience is fleeting. What could they possibly possess that would enslave me? I, who have known uncounted legions of women, for four hundred years?" He chuckled. "Your gender has witchcraft aplenty, Rae, but there is certainly nothing new in it to me. There is no spell, no charm possessed by mere mortal witches that will enslave me.

"Others wish for me, enjoy me . . . then dismiss me in embarrassment at the dawn's early light. Like yourself, they're not ashamed of their sin, of their dreams of dark, unfettered passion with one built solely for that purpose. They would only be ashamed if their neighbors got wind of it. Amazed at the depths of their own depravity – *my God, it's summoned a demon!* – they're anxious for me to be gone. They counsel themselves to henceforth show some restraint, to not so easily allow themselves the luxury of holding truck with the damned." The demon kissed me on the forehead, almost tenderly. "But no one's ever made me coffee, nor called me *Corvino.*"

"My teacher said that I must understand your crime, must know whether or not I can forgive it."

He smiled smugly. "Or what follows?"

"My own oblivion. If I *hold truck with the damned* as you put it, and ignore your crime – if I give up my own sense of right and wrong . . ."

"And have you? Do you find me justifiably damned for my profligate adultery?"

"I do not," I said immediately. I wasn't the most unbiased of judges, however. I couldn't see why Leonor's tragic overreaction to his trifling seduction should've damned him as it had. It had not ruined her life, other than that she had allowed it to do so.

I would not allow him to ruin my life. He was beyond the ken of mortal men, but that didn't mean I had to feature myself in love with him. I could think of him like Devin, who, except for his own youthful perfection, was basically unlovable. I could keep Corvino no more than I could've kept Devin, in the long run. I could accept that he was unkeepable, that he wouldn't love me, any more than Devin had. I would try my damnedest not to succumb to his skill, to not allow myself to want more than I could have. Didn't I have enough already? Had I not experienced my very own sex demon? Wasn't it asking a lot to think I could keep him, that he would love me?

I could see the poetic justice in his curse: the man who had possessed an inescapable power over women was now doomed to be an inter-dimensional whore for all eternity. He who had never wanted any woman enough to take her was now a spiritual rapist who would show chaste matrons the error of their irreligious thoughts.

But to me, there was something more to him than just his fate. I couldn't treat him like a whore, as Devin had been a whore, as perhaps I had treated *him* like one. And since I'd never deemed my thoughts irreligious, Corvino was hardly a rapist to me. He was proud; he made no excuses for his virility, either in life or in damnation. If I feared the consequences of the pleasures he could provide, then I should not have considered them. I should've *denied the thought*.

But now another idea insinuated itself into my mind, and I shook my head to clear it. The moment that I'd resolved to be okay with the reality of not being able to keep him, the next thought was how much I wanted to do just exactly that. Suddenly I knew that I wanted desperately for him to stay, and everything else was just rhetoric. I wanted to love him – perhaps I already did. I wanted to know him completely, as a man and a friend, more than just physically, as an incubus. I suddenly dreaded what it would be like when he was gone. It was a black terror, loathsome, bottomless.

Insanely, lolspeak emerged from me. "I has a fear, Corvino."

"Be just and fear not," he replied and kissed me. Soon all metaphysical theory was blotted from my mind, all deliberation on damnation and souls and adultery, and silly vengeful girls that loved not wisely but too well. All thought was evaporated from my mind by his fevered, supernatural touch.

Even that dark fear that had glowed in my mind was banished: what means, like poor, deluded Adelle, might I attempt that I might keep him? Would I risk my own damnation, again stake my immortal soul, crawl on my belly like a reptile, that I might always look into the haughty blue eyes, run my fingers through the inky curls, feel the irresistible press of his hot flesh?

THIRTY

"Perhaps I should question him," Iris said, after the incubus's tale was told. "There was never a Ninth Earl of Efisga, Rae. It's not even in Italy. *Efisga* is another name for–"

"Maybe that was just embellishment," I said, remembering the demon's grin every time he'd said *Efisga*. "But the rest of the story . . . why would he lie?"

She blinked her blue eyes at me, nonplussed. Those eyes that were so like the sorceress Corvino had described. "He's a demon, Rae."

I shook my head. "I believe his story. He was damned for a lifetime of prideful adultery, for his unwillingness to take responsibility for Leonor's madness."

"I'll give you that he has no reason to lie." Iris shrugged. "There are universal truths, as your demon lover discovered. It doesn't matter that he sees himself as blameless. The Almighty has deemed him to blame for what happened, and he will remain what he is until he takes responsibility."

I was not concerned with Corvino's responsibility at the moment. I was concerned only with myself, with that nagging fear. "What's my risk here, Iris?"

"You have to be more specific, Rae. Do you want to know if you'll be similarly cursed, just because you agree with his excuse? I would say not. The events were all in the past – the only thing that remains is his punishment. You cannot change what has passed, and if you were moved to condemn him, then your condemnation wouldn't add or subtract from his curse – neither will your acceptance. Only he can repent. Until then, he's damned."

Iris studied me closely. "But if you ask me, what's the risk to you, yourself, in keeping company with him . . . that's something upon which I cannot speculate. You're not married, so there is little sin in having a demon lover. There are no commandments against it, now are there?

"But there are universal truths, Rae," she repeated. "Not the least of which is that we cannot always have what we want. What is it that you think you want?"

"I don't know," I said. But I did know. The fear of it made me unable to speak it aloud.

"Perhaps I should speak to him."

Again that hot jealousy arrowed through me, and I recognized it as an appendage to the fear. I didn't want Corvino to speak to Iris, she of the blonde hair and purple eyes, she who'd seem to him not unlike the enchantress he'd known as a mortal man. "He said that only I can see him," I said defensively.

Iris laughed. "Demons lie, my friend. He can manifest himself to whomever he chooses." Then she looked at me in surprise. "He's your demon. I don't aim to take him from you, Rae."

I remembered again what he'd said, that no mortal witch had charms that could enslave him. But still I felt jealous. Iris was so much prettier than me . . . but it was ridiculous. I'd never in my life been jealous of another woman. I'd never doubted my own ability to keep my man, had never felt that any man that would be so easily led away by someone else was worth keeping. But Corvino was not a man . . .

"What would you say? How would you . . . summon him?"

"I wouldn't summon him, Rae." Iris raised one delicate eyebrow. "To summon him would indicate that I wished to . . . *partake*. He's the sum of your desires, not mine. From your description, he's—"

"Not your type. I know. Like gentlemen, you prefer blondes."

"But still, I'd relish the opportunity to see such a being, to speak to him. He's stayed by you for some time now . . . there must be a reason for that. Perhaps he'd just show himself to me, too, because there's no doubt that he can. Ask him."

Some time now. It had been no time at all, not in the great scheme of things, not in the span of a lifetime, not in the span of eternity. *Some time now.* Again that fear coursed through me like ice water, like poison. How eternal would time seem to me, once Corvino was gone?

THIRTY-ONE

For a fortnight, I forgot about losing Corvino and concentrated on having him. He was never waiting around for me to entertain him when I got home from work – in that, as much as in any other aspect, he was so much more blissfully better than a husband. If he was always there, I'd never get anything done. I had to clean the house, do the laundry, pay the bills, speak to my sister, text Darlene, visit Iris. But after all the social obligations are met and all the chores finished, it's time for sleep, *the death of each day's life*. And before sleep, there would be Corvino.

After the first several days, I noticed a subtle detachment about him, no doubt born of the fact that he'd known so many women: there was nothing about any of us that was going to surprise him, me least of all. He went about the technical aspects of the thing with eagerness and relish, but he was neither surprised nor complimented by my gushing appreciation. It was what he did; he was there to accomplish my pleasure, and neither needed nor expected my praise. I should sooner praise the joy wrought by a spring day, and then expect its acknowledgement of my enjoyment.

I came to understand that he wouldn't even say, "Ah, gee, thanks, Rae," when I'd abandon myself completely, when I'd scream his name and clutch him to me in paroxysms of ecstasy. Sometimes he might smile slyly at me, smugly, as if he was again underlining the fact that I was incapable of telling him no. But he wasn't affectionate: like a whore, any kiss or caress was to the purpose.

I'd noticed it from the first, this lack of warmth. But so enrapt was I in his physical perfection and the physically sublime things he could do with it, that I ignored it. But after a while, after we giggled and talked and made merry outside of the somewhat single-minded confines of coupling, after I experienced more of his wit and intelligence and charm, over and above just sex; his lack of demonstrative affection became almost glaring. I wouldn't dare to think I could teach him anything else, but I was determined to teach him *this*.

It was on a Thursday evening, the day before I was supposed to go to my sister's dinner party. I'd just climbed into bed beside him, and when he reached for me, I put my hands firmly on his smooth chest and said, "No, Chauncey. Tonight it's gonna be my turn. Let *me* love *you* for a change."

That insufferably smug grin quirked the corners of his flawless mouth, and he leaned back on the bed, put his hands behind his head. It was one of his more breathtaking poses; he had the most exquisite arms of any man I'd ever seen. "So you would be as Lilith, would you? Be careful, Rae. Not unlike myself, Lilith was damned for her conceit. The old Jews feared that they couldn't satisfy a woman who would so seek to satisfy herself. They called her demon, succubus. I, on the other hand, have no doubts about my ability to—"

"Shut *up*, Chauncey!" I cried, annoyed and delighted as always with his limitless ego. "I didn't mean . . ." But now that he'd brought it up, the thought of the further ecstasies that such a simple change of position would engender almost blunted my purpose. But no. There would be time enough for that later. "I said, *let me love you.*"

He tilted his head and looked at me with that maddening curiosity, as if I spoke of something beyond his ability to comprehend. I smiled back fondly at him, and kissed his brow, his nose. I ran my fingers through his hair, lightly caressed his cheek, his shoulder.

I buried my face in his neck and whispered, "I love you, Corvino. For all that you are . . . for all that you *were*. I love you for so much more than just what you *do.*"

He laid his hand softly on my cheek, then caressed my hair, and my shoulder, as I had done to him. His eyes still regarded me oddly, but at last he kissed me with tenderness, with affection – almost with innocence. But he didn't speak, didn't say he loved me. I hadn't really expected him to – hadn't he told me that he would not be kept?

At last his ardor bloomed again – affection is, after all, simply a lovely precursor to the main event. And afterward, he held me gently and kissed me delicately on the nose, on the forehead. But he didn't say anything, and I was left to wonder: had I at last touched something in him? Or was he – as the golden sorceress had initially found him to be – just an apt pupil in this arena? Was he merely *mimicking* the loving gestures that I'd shown him?

THIRTY-TWO

When I got home from work the next day, before I got ready to go to my sister's dinner party, I again stood in the middle of my sacred circle, now faded, smudged. It was no longer necessary. I stood with eyes closed, arms outstretched. As always, I felt him before I could see him. When I opened my eyes, he was there in my arms. He kissed me tenderly, as he had so recently been taught, and it was incredible as always – but again I felt that fear. How long would he stay? What would I do when he was gone? Would my confession of love for him the night before hasten his departure?

He looked at me inquisitively, and I wondered suddenly if he knew of my unspoken wish. "There's a disturbance in the Force, Luke," he said and grinned. An earthbound spirit for four centuries, he was not unaware of popular culture. He'd seen movies. He could use a cellphone. "What troubles you, Rae?"

So he could sense it, but he didn't know what it was. The fact that I'd admitted that I loved him was no doubt not unexpected, and he thought nothing of it. But I did love him, and I couldn't bear to see the derision in his eyes, couldn't bear to hear the melodious voice tell me that I was just like all the others, wanting to keep him. *What do you think you could possibly have that you would seek to enslave me with it?* he'd ask. Then he'd laugh, secure in that beauty that had damned him, and now might be damning me. I didn't seek to enslave him, but it was beginning to seem that he'd enslaved me. He'd laugh at my grasping love, and then he'd be gone.

"I'm not really looking forward to seeing my sister," I replied.

"Do not shirk familial responsibilities," he admonished. "Some of us have not seen our families for many lifetimes. Some of us are damned."

"Sometimes I feel damned that I have these responsibilities," I said flippantly. "My sister is . . ."

"Your sister is what God has given you," he said. "Make the most of it."

I released him and began to pick out something to wear. I'd talked to Iris earlier in the day, and she'd reminded me again that she wanted to *meet the incubus.* I said, "My teacher would like to see you."

Corvino lounged on the bed, again dressed like Romeo. "Indeed? Would that be all three of us together, or would she prefer a more private visitation? Just the two of us, perhaps?"

I looked at him mildly, immediately abandoning my outrage at his suggestion. He was a sex demon, after all. It would only seem natural to him that I'd be proposing such a thing. "She doesn't want to . . . *summon you*, Chauncey. She told me that some women go their whole lives begging to even *see* an incubus. Since I have been so fortunate . . ." *Or infinitely unfortunate*, I thought helplessly. "She's my friend. She'd like to meet you. To talk to you."

"Indeed?" he repeated. "And you are amenable to this . . . meeting?"

"You're not her type, Corvino. She's just curious to speak to you." Here was dangerous ground. I couldn't say, *I trust my friend*, and I certainly couldn't say, *I trust you*. He was a spirit, a demon, my desires made flesh. But he would not be commanded. He'd do as he willed.

But I did trust Iris, and I thought it was the least I could do for her, to let her see him. If it wasn't for her influence, no incubus would have manifested himself to me. No flawless demon lover would I have known, no release incomparable . . . no dark, nagging fear would I encompass.

"As you wish, then," he said. He tossed my cellphone to me. "Arrange it."

I called Iris, then looked at him for direction. "Tell her to light her candles and say her prayers, and invoke me by my Christian names. I will appear. We'll . . . talk."

I told Iris and she giggled. "I can't wait," she said, and hung up.

THIRTY-THREE

Corrine's dinner party was interminable. The eligible bachelor she'd lined up couldn't have been less eligible, even if I hadn't recently been holding truck with demons. He was fat but not jolly, intelligent but not witty, educated but not poetic. And he liked me even less than I liked him.

The minutes crawled by; Corrine had gone all out, constructing an appetizer course and an entrée course and a dessert course. After what seemed like a lifetime, I helped Darlene to clear away the last of the dishes. Once in the kitchen, she consulted an imaginary watch on her wrist and said, "Rolling Blackout comes on in about forty minutes. Are you down?"

I nodded gratefully. How nice it would be to escape from this disaster. How nice it would be to see Wes Thomerville again, listen to him sing. How nice it would be to forget my intimacies with his infinitely more attractive spiritual counterfeit for a few hours, to put away the inescapable knowledge that one day I'd go home and stand with my arms outstretched and they would remain empty.

"I told Mom that you promised to go with me this week, because you haven't been for a while," Darlene was saying. "I knew the minute I saw this guy that he wasn't your type. She bitched about us leaving early, but a promise is a promise, is it not?"

I nodded. Thank God for Darlene. If it wasn't for her, I would've been stuck there making mindless small talk all night. I smiled winningly at my sister and brother-in-law, and told their guest how *unspeakably* nice it had been to meet him. He said the same, but didn't go so far as to say that he hoped he'd see me again soon. Darlene and I tried not to run out the door.

The fan club was all present at *The Beachcomber*, all except for Amy, who still kept company with her young Wes Thomerville knock-off. I wondered how long I'd keep company with mine, but I pushed the thought away in favor of watching the man himself. He was still just as cute as he wanted to be, and the fact that he was the basis for the incomparable demon I'd summoned was not lost on me. Wes was mere flesh and blood, shorter and younger, but his voice was almost as melodic, and his eyes just as blue. I wondered what his wife would give up to keep him.

I laughed and giggled and had a few drinks with the girls. Just before the band's set ended, I walked up to where they stood before the tiny stage and told them thanks again for having me. It had been a nice evening, but I wasn't in the mood to stand around and wait while they cornered their favorite singer and asked for autographs. I told Darlene that the tediousness of her mother's dinner party had worn me out and then told them all goodbye.

On the way out to the car, my phone rang. "What a prideful demon he is!" Iris said with a laugh.

"He wasn't . . . he didn't . . . you didn't . . ." I couldn't help myself.

"He was modestly clothed. He told me the highlights of his story again; we spoke at length about the nature of sin. He praised my craft. He thanked me for instructing you."

"He thanked you?"

"Indeed," Iris replied. "He's quite taken with you, Rae."

But he didn't love me. "What exactly does that mean, Iris?"

"I think we've chosen the right path, asking him to tell his story. That seemed quite unusual to him. He says he's never known anyone like you, not in four hundred years. Good job, Rae."

"Does that mean he'll . . ." I felt some ridiculous stirring of hope, but still I couldn't speak it out loud. *Does that mean he'll stay?* He didn't have to love me, and long as he stuck around and allowed me to continue to love him. But I couldn't say it. I couldn't bear to hear Iris laugh at me, too.

"I don't know what it means, Rae. I found him to be a haughty and self-congratulatory creature, unrepentant in his vanity. If all the girls loved him, how was it his fault? He was as God and his doting mother had made him. He was astounded that I only wanted to talk to him, couldn't believe that I wasn't powerless before his beauty. But after I assured him that he was indeed beautiful, just not to my tastes, we had a nice little chat."

"I don't quite know what to say, Iris. Sometimes I think I'm losing my mind. You had a nice little chat with an incubus."

"With *your* incubus," she said. "If we're insane, it's a shared delusion." Again Iris laughed. "Although all I did was converse with him, while you've been . . . well, you know what you've been doing with him. Keep it up, Rae. Enjoy yourself. It's a once in a lifetime thing."

"How long . . ." I finally summoned the courage. "How long is this gonna last, Iris? How long will I be able to . . . keep him?"

"Why, that's entirely up to you, Rae!" Iris said in surprise, and laughed again. "Come by and see me again soon."

"I will, Iris. And . . . thanks. Thanks for everything."

"You owe me no gratitude, my friend," she said seriously. "We all live in the world of our own choosing, eventually. You might not always be thanking me. Talk to you soon!"

I told Iris goodbye and hung up.

THIRTY-FOUR

Corvino didn't immediately appear when I closed my eyes and imagined him. After a few moments, I began to feel silly, standing there all alone. I wondered where the panic was – was he gone already? But I didn't believe that he was gone just yet, so there was no reason to panic. He'd told me that he wouldn't always manifest at my command, and I believed that he was too theatrical to just disappear. I felt as though there'd be a scene first, something that would buff up his ego. He wouldn't just leave without first telling me how bored he'd become with me and my tiresome proclamations of love.

So I poured myself a glass of wine to keep the bar buzz going, and took a hot bath. I thought about the lonely sterile life that would lie ahead, after he *was* gone – after experiencing him, what paltry, solitary fantasy would ever again suffice, even potion-enhanced? Perhaps that was the danger in holding truck with demons. Perhaps my soul wouldn't be damned for eternity, as his was, but the rest of my life would surely be cursed.

I crawled into bed and again thought of him, relishing every detail. Still he didn't show himself. Eventually I drifted off to sleep – Corrine's dinner party *had* been tiresome, and I was more than a tiny bit drunk. Sometime before dawn, I snapped awake, aware that I was not alone. I sat up in bed. My demon lover was standing in a shaft of moonlight, admiring himself in the mirror.

He turned and smiled at me. "What think you of my raiment?" he asked. He was wearing an excellently-cut, modern black suit, complete with Italian shoes, a white shirt, and a dark blue tie. I thought him rather a one trick pony in his choice of colors, but black with a touch of blue certainly complimented him. He looked impeccable, as usual. "I thought it suitable attire for my conversation with your teacher. What say you?"

"Where have you been?" My own words so shocked me that I covered my mouth with my hand. Who was I to be asking a demon where he'd been?

"Where have *you* been?" he returned immediately.

"I went to my sister's for dinner. I told you that." I was as shocked with his question as I was with my own. What possible difference could it make to him where I'd been? "Then I had a few drinks with my niece."

Corvino turned back to admiring himself in the mirror. "What was the purpose of your sister's dinner party?" he asked.

"Purpose?"

Still he primped, tugging a little at his sleeves, adjusting his cufflinks. "I spoke at length with your teacher. I found her to be a skilled and beauteous witch. We talked about you – she mentioned that your sister had invited some suitor for you, that there was a possibility that you would make match with this man."

"Make match?" How ridiculous his phrasing was sometimes. "Yes. I guess you could put it that way. My sister wanted to fix me up with some friend of her husband's from work."

"And did you find him . . . suitable?" The demon looked at me expressionlessly in the mirror, over his shoulder.

I laughed at the *as if* of that. "I did not. He was old and fat and boring, just like I expected him to be."

"And yet still you attended." He turned around again and looked at me blankly. "You seek a husband."

"Are you insane?" I asked him, dumbstruck. "My sister was just being nice. She thinks I'm lonely. Why would I seek a husband when I have . . ." But I didn't *have*, now did I? "I don't seek a husband, Corvino."

"What do you seek, then, if not a husband? You are of an age, nay, nearly past it. I daresay, your time is running out. If not a husband, some lover then?"

I gawped at him. *If it be now, 'tis not to come; if it be not to come, it will be now; if it be not now, yet it will come: the readiness is all.* His unkind remark about my age steeled me a little bit. I was ready; it might as well happen now. I might as well get it over with. Time to pay the piper. Cop to my weakness. "I want no lovers. I want what I cannot have."

He shrugged, noncommittal. "You live, you breathe. You have free will. You are fair enough, have riches enough. Pray tell me what it is to which you would aspire, that you cannot attain?"

I looked up into his dark blue eyes, guileless. He had no idea what I was talking about. "I wish to have you, Corvino. I love you."

He smiled crookedly at me. "What makes you think you cannot have me?" There was that muffled thunderclap noise again, and the black suit was gone. He stood before me, naked, glorious, winged. I noticed for the first time that Iris had not been incorrect: the incubus had webbed toes.

"Haven't you told me all along, how you warned all the girls that they could have you, but they couldn't keep you? Wasn't that the core of your story? Didn't you tell me that you are a crow, intrigued for a season by shiny things?" I gestured at his wings. "But then you take to the air and are gone?"

"Did you not summon me out of the ether with the power of your desire?" he answered my question with a question. "Didn't I tell you that I was yours to command?"

I swung my legs over the side of the bed and sat on its edge. "Didn't you say that you wouldn't always answer my call?"

"Have I not always answered it? Yet still you seek—"

"I seek nothing, Corvino. No other but you."

"Why have you never said this before? As the poet said, you *are but in moment's sunlight, fading in the grass*. I am doomed forever. And yet . . . consider carefully what you would ask, Rae."

"Why?" I asked angrily, helplessly. "Do I again barter with my immortal soul, if I say that I want no other but you?"

He disappeared his wings and sat beside me on the bed. "I can be yours, Rae. You have only to ask it. You haven't done so, and since you sent me to visit your teacher, since you attend dinners with other men, I've been under the impression that you seek company of a more earthly sort. It's the way of things.

"I'll remain by your side until the day you die, if you so desire. If you wish it, why haven't you said so before?" He looked at me solemnly. "Yet consider for a moment longer, before you speak this simplest of requests. There is a catch. If you would so bid me, you can have no other. If I would be yours, you would be mine – I am unmovable in my possession, in my jealousy. If you say you want me exclusively, then would change your mind and invite any other, he'll die by my hand."

Relief flooded me. I put my arms around his neck. "Oh, Chauncey! You're so ridiculous! You're perfection to me! I love you! How could I ever want any other?"

"It is done then," he said and kissed me.

THIRTY-FIVE

If my life was a movie, what followed would be the montage segment. Like parts of a Quentin Tarantino feature, our *romance* would've been shown like a cartoon, like comics, like a graphic novel, lest its intensity sear the eyes of the audience. Only static drawings could be shown: a smile, a glance, a kiss, a modestly draped embrace. He was now tender when the mood called for it, but in passion, no mortal man could equal my demon lover: he was an incorporeal spirit, tireless, damned to his purpose. And he had four hundred years of experience.

The rest of the montage would be like home movies: Corvino and I talking, cooking, watching television, playing board games, playing chess. There would be a scene of me pouting when he beat me at *Scrabble;* he had four hundred years' experience with languages, too – my own and scores of others. There would be a clip of him manifesting his wings in annoyance and frowning petulantly when I trounced him at *Risk.* There would be scenes of us playing cards with Iris, and having further discussion on the nature of sin. There was laughter and joy. There was fun and camaraderie.

He was so much more enjoyable than any real man could've ever been. He was ageless physically, of course. But he also had a zest for the modern world, almost child-like. How quickly would the psychiatrist have thrown away the key had I described my black-haired, black-winged demon lover to him, perched upon a chair, positively riveted to what he was perusing on the internet? Corvino knew no depression, no ennui. The availability of four hundred years of art and philosophy and literature enthralled him, and he loved to excitedly discuss it with me. The humor and perversity of modern culture tickled him, and he sought to tickle me with it. The discovery that the political motivations and methods of the rich and powerful had not changed since his time amused him, and he never failed to warn me about it.

There was love, at least on my part. I'd felt love for Corvino from the instant I'd seen him. How could I not love my own vision? I felt more for him than just a physical desire – he'd been a man once, and I loved that part of him that was still a man, as much as the parts of him that were so deliciously demonic. It was this love that had made me fear losing him, had made me quail at the thought of what I might undertake to keep him. And it only grew as the days passed.

I told him frequently that I loved him, and when he would just smile back at me blankly, I'd hasten to add that it didn't matter if he loved me back, and then, feeling stupid, I'd just as quickly change the subject. I suspected that perhaps he was, as doomed Leonor had said, incapable of love, or at the very least, incapable of expressing it. He never even brought up the concept for consideration. The closest we ever came was in a discussion about the afterlife.

"Don't you fear what will become of you after you die, Rae?" he asked me bluntly.

I shrugged. "I'll be dead, I suppose," I said.

"There is no death," he said. "There's only damnation and redemption. Damnation is continued existence, after all you have known has passed away. Damnation is never seeing your family again. How I miss my mother's smile sometimes . . . but she's on another plane. With my father and sisters. With that son I never knew. I must remain here, until that repentance which I cannot see is revealed to me. After all this time, I lose faith that such a thing will ever overtake me. Yet I am content." He smiled blankly at me.

"Whom will you seek when you pass on to the next plane, Rae? You've chosen to spend your life with a damned soul. You've chosen a demon for a bedmate. There'll be no beloved to meet you on the other side."

"No mortal man would suffice, once I beheld you, Chauncey." I smiled at him, this unearthly being that had manifested through all my earthly desires. I was unable to think ahead to the other side, some place I'd never really thought about anyway, some place of clouds and harps and angels. A place in which I'd never really believed. "The only beloved I'll ever again seek is you."

He shook his head. "Yet in the end, you'll be alone, Rae. Were you'll go, I cannot follow. You've foresworn that which in this life can lead to bliss eternal: the company of a kindred soul with whom you can eventually spend eternity. You'll pay for the folly of choosing me. You'll be alone. Bereft of the one thing you've lived for. Though no longer earthbound as I am, that'll be your damnation."

"Repent, for the end is near!" I cried playfully, perhaps blasphemously.

"I cannot. I will not. Nor, apparently, can you."

"*We can't always get what we want*, Corvino, as the poets say. I'm healthy, not yet ancient. So I don't think I need to contemplate my afterlife just yet."

He shrugged, frowned. "Don't say I didn't warn you."

THIRTY-SIX

The precursor to my afterlife would overtake me far sooner than anticipated, however. Out of the corner of my eye, I saw the big white truck run the light, and barely had time to brace for the impact. There was a muffled *wumf* sound of metal rapidly folding, a shower of glass – painless. Then blackness.

Next was another movie-like scene, derivative of every hospital drama ever filmed: I seemed to be a simple bystander, a spectator, as emergency room doors flew open. There were doctors and nurses scrambling, working on the limp form on the bed, even as the gurney was rushed down the bright hall. The bleeding body on the wheeled cot was me.

Then I found myself seated on a white plastic chair, in the first row of innumerable white plastic chairs in a completely white room. It seemed like nothing more than an ordinary waiting room, except for the blinding whiteness of everything. There were other people sitting in the chairs around me, some my own age, some older. The occasional teenager, the odd child. Sometimes their lips moved, but I could hear no words. No one looked at me. Everything was silence.

There was a window in the wall to my left and one in the wall to my right. Behind me were the innumerable white chairs, and in front of me, after what seemed like some distance, there was another blank white wall. The windows were of thick glass, the kind with the wires embedded in it, and there was a white door beside each window. The glass to my left was usually whited-out, like there was a fog bank behind it. But every now and then, one of the people in the room with me would go over to the left and speak to smiling others behind it. They could always hear and understand each other, but they had only brief conversations. After speaking at the window to my left, those from the waiting room would either go through the door beside it, or they'd cross in front of me and go out the other door. They never sat back down.

There were shadows and colors behind the window to my right, sometimes frightened, worried faces. My companions would try to talk to these people, but the ones peering through the window with fear and concern, pity and sorrow etched on their faces seemed to be able to neither see nor hear the people on my side of the glass. My people seemed to be able to hear them sometimes, however. Sometimes they would listen for a while, then sit back down. Sometimes they would disregard what was being said, and cross over to the left-hand window and converse with the smiling faces there. I noticed that once they talked to the smiling people, they too, never sat back down. They always chose one or the other of the doors and walked through it.

I seemed to sit in the silent whiteness for quite some time, without a thought, just watching the people around me talking soundlessly, or conversing at the windows, sitting back down, going through the doors. Once they left the room, they never came back. But still the room didn't empty. The chairs were always more or less occupied.

Once, I caught a glimpse of Corrine and Warren looking in through the window on my right. Corrine's face was tear-stained but stoic, the same visage she'd displayed at the funerals of our parents. This expression gave me pause – why was my sister sad? I went over to the glass and peered through it at her, but she didn't see me. She looked right past me; she didn't speak. Warren was also silent, also looking sad. What did they have to be so sad about? Had something happened to Darlene? It didn't occur to me to try the door. After a while, they faded from view; others stood before the window, strangers to me, and people from my room went over and looked at them, tried to speak to them. Since I could hear nothing that was said, I sat back down.

Some indeterminate time later, I seemed to come to, as if from sleep. I could hear Wes Thomerville's muted voice, singing *My Disgrace*. I looked at the right-hand window and there was Darlene, gazing right past me, holding up her phone. That was where the music was coming from. Iris was standing beside her, looking solemn. I went up to the window.

Through the glass, I clearly heard Darlene say, "The doctor said it couldn't hurt if we talk to her, or she hears familiar music."

I glanced over my shoulder to where Darlene was looking, but there was nothing there but whiteness. No one was standing in front of the window but me.

Iris seemed to be looking right at me, but still missed making eye contact, like she was looking at my cheek or the top of my head. "I feel like I can almost touch her," she said and reached out toward the glass. "As if she's right there, waiting."

"I am right here, Iris!" I cried. There was no reaction from either of them; they could neither see nor hear me.

Iris leaned a little closer to the glass. "You have to come back to us, Rae. You have to come back to *him.*"

"To *him?*" Darlene asked. "To who?"

Iris smiled blankly at my niece, nodded at the phone in her hand. "Why, to your blue-eyed singer, of course. Who else does she know?

It's a good idea for you to play his music for her, I think. I'm sure she can hear it. I'm sure she knows we're here."

"Yes! I can hear you, Iris!" I yelled, but maddeningly, she kept looking past me.

Then she leaned forward until she was close enough to the window for her breath to almost fog it. She said softly, "He can't come to you there, in the middle realm, neither sleeping nor waking, neither alive nor dead. Though incorporeal, he's still tied to this plane, Rae. I can touch you . . ." Iris pressed her hand to the window, and I put my hand up to hers; I could feel the warmth of it through the glass. "I can speak to you and I know that you can hear me through this veil between us. But he can neither speak to you, nor touch you, nor even manifest before you while you lie dreaming in this state. You have to wake up from the dream, my friend. You have to come back from that place between life and death. You have to come back to us," she repeated. "You have to come back to Corvino."

"Covina?" Darlene said in confusion.

Iris glanced over at her apologetically. "I'm sorry. You must pardon my mumbo-jumbo, Darlene. I'm worried about your aunt, just like you are, and I'm afraid the superstitions of my background are just tumbling out. In my belief, it's possible to lure a person back from the brink of . . ." Darlene's eyes grew wide with fear, and Iris continued quickly. "We believe we can entice a person back to consciousness with promises of . . . good things. Happy remembrances. Could you play that song again? I think I saw her eyelids flutter." While Darlene pushed buttons on her phone, Iris again whispered for me to return to Corvino.

Corrine and Warren appeared behind them. "Turn that noise off," she snapped at her daughter. "This is a hospital, for God's sake."

Iris's warmth pressed through the glass to my hand for another second, then she said, "I'll leave you alone with your loved one. I have prayers to speak. I'll be back to see you soon, Rae." And then she faded from view.

"Who the hell was that, Darlene?" Corrine asked irritably.

"That was Rae's friend. Her name is Iris. She introduced herself to me in the hall."

"Your aunt always did prefer weirdos for friends." My sister's use of the past tense was not lost on me.

THIRTY-SEVEN

From Iris's diary, dated April 30 — *As soon as the last candle was burning, the demon appeared. He was winged, web-footed — but he was also modestly covered, seeming for all of creation like a fallen angel instead of a demon, a soul damned. He looked at me somberly.* "What say you, Witch?"

I shrugged, and continued lighting incense for the Ritual of Healing. "The doctors are cagey. They speak in platitudes. They say that her injuries are not that serious, but on the other hand, there might be complications. They make no promises."

"They make no promises to hide their ignorance. Perhaps a priest—"

"She knows no priests, William." *I called him by his Christian name, as I'd been instructed to do.* "It's an irreligious era."

"Yet you pray."

"I'm not irreligious. But I say my own prayers. I'm confident that I need no priest's intercession for them to reach their mark."

He threw himself listlessly onto my bed, and traced the pattern on the duvet with a long, graceful finger. I was amazed to see a tear drop onto the back of his hand. "What say you, Demon?"

He looked up defiantly at the appellation, but then his eyes misted again. "Since I can't see her or touch her, I'm overcome with a disbelief more paralyzing, more stupefying than I've ever known, at her absence. The suddenness, the unexpectedness of her loss has unmanned me, Iris. I am amazed. I'm unable to prevent these tears, nor staunch them once they begin. I cannot stop the meaningless, ridiculous phrases, repeated over and over in my mind:* This can't be true! This can't have happened! *I sink beneath this utter agony of helplessness, because it* has *happened. It is true. My woman is gone.*

"Every thought comes in short sentences. How could this happen? I was with her but yesterday!" *He emphasized the word like a curse.* "And now she's lost to me. The phrases and conjunctions of high-flown philosophy fail me, just as they have for my entire existence. Three words, or four. The entire sphere of the universe, of life, of history, of damnation eternal, are narrowed now to three and four-word thoughts, like rats on a wheel.

"She may never awaken from this twilight land between life and death. She's lost to me forever. For all eternity. I cannot reach her there. Never am I to gaze upon her, hold her in my arms, hear her laughter. Never again will we talk. Never. Again. And there was no farewell, just a cutting off, like a candle extinguished. A guillotine.

"The ache overwhelms me. I died once, and it was as a drifting off to sleep. There was no pain. Though it cannot happen, I feel that I must die again from this *agony of loss. Never again will I look upon her. Every cell cries out for her, as it never did when she was beside me. And still the rats run in endless circles, the words loop round my brain:* This can't be true! This can't have happened!

"I've never felt such all-encompassing pain in the sum of my existence, Iris. There is no soothing balm or soporific palliative to cure this."

"God will relieve your suffering. Confess your fault."

"My fault? What is my fault?" He flapped his black, leathery wings in irritation. "I ask your aid to relieve the unrelenting suffering at the loss of my woman, and you prate about my fault."

"Your woman is only flesh, Demon. She is but a moment in time. How many women have you known?"

"None like her," he said and looked down again.

"Did you tell her that?"

He shook his head with infinite sadness. "I never realized just how unique she was — not till she was gone."

"Perhaps she knew," I said. It was the sum — all the comfort I could offer to him. Then another thought occurred to me. "It's not for her loss that you grieve. You know that if she loses her battle, she'll go to a better place. It's not for herself that you mourn. It's for the loss of the love you share. You love this puny being that must return to dust, that goes where you cannot follow. You grieve for the loss of what you shared — she will go on there, while you, because of your unwillingness to repent, must remain here. There will be other women, Demon, just like there have been legions before. But none like her. You love her."

"And what if I do?" he asked in annoyance. "You talk of love as if it's physic. My love cannot overcome her injuries. I must rely on quacks and machines."

"Her injuries may not prove fatal. Only time will tell. Her fate, like you say, is out of your hands. Get thee to church, Demon. Confess thy fault."

"What is this fault that I must confess?" *he roared.*

"You still can't see it? You pule and whine and cry over the loss of your woman. I tell you, it's the loss of your love for which you weep, not herself, her smile, her laugh. It's the loss of your love for these things for which you grieve. How many scores of women wept for the loss of your *love? Upon how many did you inflict the kind of pain that you now encompass?"*

A look of realization crossed his elegant face, an expression of infinite shame. "I caused others to feel this agony?"

"At the loss of your favor, William. At the loss of your love, the withdrawing of your affection. Some women love utterly — you say that you could see their desire plainly enough, that no words could disguise it from you. No words from you could prevent them from loving you, no warnings beforehand of your own unflagging inconstancy. You love Rae utterly, and this pain you feel — it's what you brought to others. Those that you wouldn't love in return, after allowing them to love you — they felt what you feel now. Love should be a two-way street, William — had they not

160

two-way streets, even in Efisga? You did harm by never loving them back, when you saw how completely they loved you."

"I never meant—"

"You never meant," I scoffed. "You saw their devotion, but you dismissed it. What did it matter to you if they loved you? It was not your fault. You were as God created you – beautiful. But you used your beauty like a weapon, never caring about whom you destroyed with it. Now you're destroyed by the loss of your own love. When you consider all the multitudes of broken hearts and twisted minds your disdain engendered, now that you feel within yourself the kind of destruction you wrought, do you feel regret?"

"I do, Iris." The tears fell freely now. "I would never wish this kind of pain on another living creature."

"Then get you to church, Demon. Repent."

With a sound like a muffled thunderclap, he vanished.

I finished the Healing Ritual for my friend, and sat down to record all that has occurred. I think Rae will enjoy hearing about it when she wakes up.

THIRTY-EIGHT

After a period of time – just how long it was, I can't gauge – a feeling of restlessness came upon me. I grew weary of just sitting in the plastic chair. I felt a need for action. I glanced over at the window to my right, but someone was already standing in front of it, trying to communicate with his unseeing, unhearing family through the wired glass. So I arose and went over to the left-hand window. As I approached, the fog behind it cleared and I was amazed to see my mother standing there, as young and lovely as she'd been when I was a child. I gawped at her in amazement, unable to speak, and was then further amazed when my father, also young again, joined her. He put his arm around her shoulders and they smiled at me.

"So I'm dead, then?" I asked at last. "We're all dead?" I gestured at the other people. We were all there together, but we were all separate. No one even made eye contact with anyone else; they spoke – to themselves, it seemed, or to the people they recognized at the windows – but I couldn't hear them.

"You're not dead, Rae," my father said. "You're just hurt. You have to decide if you want to go back and deal with the pain of your injuries, or if you want to give up and die."

"How badly am I hurt?" I asked.

My mother shrugged. "What difference does it make? When were you ever a quitter?"

And then Corvino was there, unwinged, standing beside my parents, dressed in white as they were. He placed his hand against the window, and I put mine up also, but I couldn't feel any warmth through it like I had from Iris. I couldn't feel anything but the coldness of the glass.

His face was more beautiful than it had ever before seemed to me: his blue eyes glowed with love and hope. I thought that I'd caught that look of affection once or twice recently – sometimes when I'd wake up to find him gazing down at me – I'd told myself that I'd seen love in his expression. I hadn't attached much to it – it would never matter to me if he loved me back. He'd said that he'd stay with me forever – that was love enough for me, coming from one such as him.

But never had I seen on his face any expression of hope. He'd long centuries ago accepted that he was damned, hopeless. But he'd said he was content.

I immediately put my hand on the doorknob. Whatever he'd told me about his being unable to follow me where I would go when I died – obviously, that had all been bullshit. Demons lie. There he was, just on the other side of the door, waiting for me. I turned the knob.

Corvino shook his head. "Don't open that door, Rae." He smiled, chuckled. "Wait for the cliché: it's not yet your time. You have to go back, through the other door. You're still needed over there, in the lives of others. You have to still be around to make your sister reluctantly smile sometimes. You're going to have to be there to help Darlene change diapers. So many diapers! You must go back and continue to amuse the clever, golden witch."

"Your sister's going to need you," my mother said. "She won't take well to being a grandmother alone."

I shook my head, unable to digest all this talk of Darlene changing diapers and my sister being a grandmother. Instead I spoke to the wingless incubus. "What about you, Corvino? What are you doing here? My dad says I'm hurt. Will you be there to help me overcome the pain? Maybe I don't want to face all that. Maybe I *should* just open this door. So I can be with you."

"Is this your man, Rae?" my mother asked. "I must say he's an improvement over that idiot you married, and quite the step up from that deadbeat boy you took up with." My mother smiled at Corvino and he smiled back.

Apparently the dead do see all, I thought.

"Too bad he's dead," she said.

"He's been dead for four hundred years, Mom."

"Yet still, through the grace of God, you were able to find each other. Across the generations. Your souls were destined for each other. But we don't have time for all this metaphysical horseshit right now, Rae. Your man's right. You have to go back."

This being that I was talking to could be no one else but my mother. She was the only person that I'd ever know that could mention *the grace of God* and *horseshit* in the same sentence and not seem sacrilegious. But while it had been many years since I'd spoken to my mom, it was my demon lover that concerned me the most right then. His presence. His absence. "Will you be there with me, Corvino?" I asked again. "If I go back?"

He shook his head, but not sadly. "By your love have I been redeemed."

"By my –? What?"

"Time grows short, Rae," he said and frowned. "You must go back through the other door."

163

I looked across the room. Corrine and Warren, Darlene and Iris were standing at the window. But they still looked past me.

"I don't want to go back, Corvino." I added petulantly, "I want to be with you."

He frowned. "What if I said that I didn't want to be with you anymore, Rae? I'm at last freed from damnation, freed from my whorish earthbound curse. If I tell you that we're on different paths now, will you go back?" He chuckled hollowly. "All my redemption is for nothing if there's yet still another woman that would die for me."

I blinked in shock at the brutality of his words. I thought that I saw the Corvino that Leonor had seen: careless, cruel, inhuman. No wonder he was damned. I was beginning to see the justice in it, beginning to believe he'd deserved it, after all.

"To say to thee that I shall die, is true; but for thy love, by the Lord, no. Why would I die for you, Corvino, if you say you don't want me?"

Although, like Prince Hal, my blood had lately begun to flatter me that perhaps he *could* love me someday. The gentle looks, the soft kisses, the tender embraces . . . But apparently, I had been mistaken. Apparently, I'd only been lying to myself, had only wished that he could ever show me his heart. Why he was there with my dead parents, I couldn't say. But it wasn't to tell me that he loved me.

"Do you think I'm weak, like Leonor?"

I still couldn't believe that he was foreswearing me now. I'd been so sure that I'd seen love in his eyes lately. All I saw there now was pain, although he was trying to disguise it with this sudden disdain. He wouldn't answer me.

"Is that the way it is then? You no longer want me? What happened to *I'll stay beside you till the day you die?* So much for the promises of demons. But then you never were much for promises, were you?"

"How ridiculous you are, Rae!" my dad marveled. "Only you would stand here and argue with a ghost."

"You have to go back, Rae," my mother said. "This man will tell you anything to get you to go. He'll even lie to you. Why would he waste one second of his eternity, telling you to go back, if he didn't love you?" Again she smiled at Corvino, patted him on the shoulder. "It's quite obvious to me that he loves you."

"Do you love me, Corvino?" I cried.

"Will you go back if I say I do?"

"I'll go back if you tell me the truth."

164

He smiled at me then. "Yes, I love you, Rae. It's just as your mother says. I love you, and that's why I'm telling you that you must go back.

"I love thee to the depth and breadth and height
My soul can reach, when feeling out of sight
For the ends of being and ideal grace.
I love thee to the level of every day's
Most quiet need, by sun and candle-light.
I love thee freely, as men strive for right.
I love thee purely, as they turn from praise.
I love thee with the passion put to use
In my old griefs, and with my childhood's faith.
I love thee with a love I seemed to lose
With my lost saints. I love thee with the breath,
Smiles, tears, of all my life; and, if God choose,
I shall but love thee better after death."

THIRTY-NINE

I opened my eyes. His name was on my lips, but I didn't speak it. Relief washed concern from my family's drawn faces like a sudden spring downpour. I tried to sit up, but there was a knifing pain in my leg, so I gave that idea up.

"Go get the doctor, Warren!" Corrine commanded. "She's awake!" My brother-in-law scuttled quickly out of the room.

I said to Darlene, "Where's Darryl?"

She looked at me, nonplussed. "Darryl?" She glanced at her mother in confusion.

"They say people say odd things when they come out of a coma," Corrine opined sagely. "Tell your aunt where Darryl is, Darlene."

"I broke up with Darryl, Rae. He said he was sick and tired of me mooning over Wes Thomerville. I've been seeing someone new. His name is Bo. He's a musician."

"Do you love him?" I asked. My voice sounded scratchy and thick and I cleared my throat.

Again Darlene looked at her mother in confusion. "I could love him, Rae. I don't know if I love him yet."

"I predict a bright future," I said, thinking that if Corrine wanted to hear odd things, I'd be prophetic. "Where's Iris?" I asked.

"I'll call her," Darlene said. "She told me yesterday that she thought you might wake up soon." Darlene went out into the hall to electronically summon my witchy friend.

"How long have I been out?" I asked my sister.

"Three days," she told me, just as Warren, breathless, came back in with the doctor.

He said his name was Hawkins, and asked me how I was feeling. I told him that I had some pain in my leg, that I wasn't sure I could sit up.

"That's because it's broken in two places," he told me, with a totally unwarranted cheerfulness. "And you have a concussion, and you're going to have quite the attractive scar on the side of your head." I reached up and touched my head, found it bandaged. The doctor smiled. "Don't worry. Your hair'll cover it. We're so glad you decided to rejoin us, Rae."

I wasn't sure that I was so glad. I was beginning to feel little aches and sharp pains that hadn't been present in the white-white waiting room. My head hurt. My leg howled.

"Now that I'm back," I said, "would it be possible to get a little something for this pain? Doctor?"

FORTY

Iris showed up precisely on cue, just as my sister and her family were leaving. I couldn't help but think that she'd planned it that way. When they were gone, I told her all that I had experienced while in the white waiting room, sitting in a white plastic chair between life and death.

"He said he loved me, Iris. I can't wait to get out of this hospital so I can see him."

Iris's smile faltered. "Your incubus is gone, Rae. You won't be seeing him again, at least not on this—"

"Gone?" I felt tears well up in my eyes, hot, burning. What had I come back for, if not for him? "He said he loved me, Iris! Haven't you, hasn't he, told me all along that he's a demon damned? How can he be gone?" I closed my eyes and tried to picture him, begged desperately in my mind for him to manifest.

"Didn't you say that he told you that your love had redeemed him? What do you think that means, Rae?"

I opened my eyes. Iris was there alone. The tears spilled down my cheeks. "Apparently, it means he's forsaken me. Changed his mind. He said he'd be with me forever, until I die." I swiped at my eyes, trying without success not to feel sorry for myself. "Apparently, it's just like you said, Iris. Demons lie." I didn't think of his humble eloquence in reciting Browning's timeless paean of love to me. It was all a lie. He didn't love me. He just wanted to be rid of me. He was gone.

Iris shook her head. "I've said it before: sometimes I think you just don't pay attention, my friend." She tapped the side of her head. "Or maybe this concussion, the drugs they're feeding you, have scrambled your brains. It's a story as old as time. A self-absorbed reprobate is unfettered from his empty prison by true love. Your demon is redeemed – a demon no longer. He *will* be with you forever. You've been inordinately blessed, Rae, and still you can't see it."

Iris went on to tell me about Corvino's revelation, that the pain he was feeling at my apparent loss was the same as that pain he'd inflicted on all the women he'd so arrogantly abjured, all those women that had loved him.

"Why me?" I asked. "What's so special about me that I should be his deliverer?"

Iris shrugged. "I don't know what's so special about you. You're a trifle thick-headed for my tastes." She grinned. "But you touched him somehow. He loves you, and this accident caused him to feel all the pain of the loss of love, something he'd never before experienced. It showed him at last the nature of his sin, Rae. It wasn't adultery that damned him. His adultery hurt no one in and of itself, just as he'd always maintained. His sin was his studied indifference. His taking that which was offered and giving not one part of himself in return. When he at last realized his crime, he was sincerely contrite; remorseful. He begged forgiveness and was forgiven. As we all will be."

I sighed. "I don't see why that means he won't come to me anymore."

"He's dead, Rae! He's redeemed; no longer on this plane!"

"So when I die—"

"You'll *meet 'im later on, at the place where 'e is gone*—"

"But in the meantime—"

"I must take your blasphemy as ignorance, Rae," Iris said darkly. "The Christian prayer for burial goes, *Earth to earth, ashes to ashes, dust to dust; in sure and certain hope of the Resurrection unto eternal life*. After all you've seen and experienced — dancing with the dead, the manifestation of demons — why can't you believe this one universal truth? Corvino is waiting for you. You will be reunited with him."

"Apparently, I have to believe it, don't I?" I said angrily, selfish myself. "The doctor tells me I may have a limp from this," I gestured at my shattered leg, "but if I do what the physical therapist says, I might even avoid that. He says I am quite healthy overall, and should have no lasting effects from the accident. I should live to a ripe old age." I shook my head. "Alone."

Iris reached into her bag on a chair beside the bed and brought out a small sketch book, and handed it to me. In it, in charcoal, she'd rendered a startlingly accurate portrayal of Corvino — she'd caught the sly smile, the fall of shiny black curls.

I looked up from the sketch in amazement. "I didn't know you could draw, Iris."

She shrugged. "But I can't sing. Sometimes a picture can be of enormous comfort, a precious aid to the mind's eye. Keep that as my gift to you. It's the least I can give you — I feel that you wouldn't be where you are today had it not been for my influence. But if you'll allow me to influence you yet a little further — be content, Rae. Don't waste the rest of your life in resentment of your loss, at sadness over what you can no longer touch. More than most of us, you've been given a glimpse of what comes next. Be content, Rae, live every day to its limit. Because you will see him again. He's waiting for you."

Just like a great shrink or a good bartender, just like a persuasive infomercial pitchman, the fact of Iris's belief was convincing, compelling. Just like I'd danced and done God-knew-what with Troy in a Chinese restaurant that no longer existed, I *had* been in that white waiting room. I'd seen my mother and father, years dead. I'd seen Corvino, there where he'd said he could never go. He'd told me that he loved me. And I'd never had much of a capacity for resentment, anyway. As for sadness? *There is nothing either good or bad, but thinking makes it so,* and why should I make the rest of my life a prison by being sad?

I'd had a near death experience – how could I be ungrateful when I'd had the rest of my life given back to me? Even if it was to be without my demon lover? We had met across time, space, centuries, damnation and bliss – how could I not believe we would meet again?

FORTY-ONE

The physical therapy was not as grueling as I'd been led to believe, and I was up and around again in a very short time. There was a hefty insurance settlement, and with that in the bank, the decision to take early retirement was effortless. I spent my days at *Mohini's House of Dreams* with Iris; I spent my nights alone.

To my surprise, I found that *the hey-day in the blood* had at last grown tame; there was no mortal man that could equal Corvino's touch, and I sought not even the merest masculine companionship. It was utterly unnecessary – after I'd realized the truth to his confession of love, even the fear of dying alone that had once gnawed at me evaporated. It was as Orson Welles had noted – we all die alone, in voiceless, noiseless silence. But I knew that after death, after but a brief walk across that white-white waiting room, my Raven, my Corvino, would be waiting for me.

Iris had beseeched me to be content, and I was – I had not one single thing to be discontented about, and I was really too busy to be manufacture anything. The year after my accident, Darlene married Bo. He bore no resemblance to Wes Thomerville and was a much better guitar player. She was a glowing bride – she'd found her match, and never darkened the doorway of *The Beachcomber* again. She'd once said that she and her friends would always go to see their favorite band. They'd never imagined that anything in life could intervene to take time away from their favorite pastime. But life always intervenes, and always is a long time.

And then the babies came, just as had been foretold. First, there was a little boy, then not six months after he was born, Darlene gleefully announced that she was pregnant again. Motherhood became her – she loved her baby and her husband and everything was right with the world.

Sadness descended right before Darlene's second child was born: her dad had a heart attack and died suddenly, then there were complications after her delivery, and Darlene was confined to bed for several weeks. At the same time, Corrine was paralyzed with grief at Warren's loss. Just like my mother had predicted, my sister needed my help with her grandmotherly duties.

Corrine's sadness passed in its season. She and I and Iris are all old now, taking our chief joys from watching Darlene's four kids as they thrive and grow like weeds.

I am content. Sometimes I talk to Corvino's picture, confident that he can hear me. Though there are no signs, no manifestations, no spiritualist-type table-rappings in response – he's on another plane – I know he hears me. And he smiles.

****

Also by LM Foster

A Passing Resemblance
Contrariwise – A Tale of Twins
Crypsis
Duck Feet
Peter's Sisters

Two Green Keys:
Two Green Keys
Adapted for the Screen

One Wilde Ride Trilogy:
Part One: It Might Have Been
Part Two: An Exceptional Boy
Part Three: What Should Never Be

Stars and Guitars:
Talk To a Movie Star
Where The Guitars Play

Tom and Wiley:
This Carnival of Strange
Wiley Royce
Generally Recognized as Safe
Wiley Royce Versus The Martians